HEROES

SAVING CHARLIE

HEROES

SAVING CHARLIE

A Novel

Written by Aury Wallington

Story by Jeph Loeb

Based on the series *Heroes* created by Tim Kring,
including without limitation the following episodes
"Seven Minutes to Midnight" Written by Tim Kring
"Homecoming" Written by Adam Armus & Kay Foster
"Six Months Ago" Written by Aron Eli Coleite

DEL
REY   BALLANTINE BOOKS • NEW YORK

Copyright © 2008 by NBC Universal, Inc. & ® or ™ where indicated.

All Rights Reserved. Used Under Authorization.

Published in the United States by Del Rey Books, an imprint of The Random House Publishing Group, a division of Random House, Inc., New York.

DEL REY is a registered trademark and the Del Rey colophon is a trademark of Random House, Inc.

Library of Congress Cataloging-in-Publication Data

Wallington, Aury.
Heroes : saving Charlie : a novel / written by Aury Wallington; story by Jeph Loeb; based on the series Heroes created by Tim Kring.
p. cm.
ISBN-13: 978-0-345-50322-0 (hardcover : alk. paper)
I. Loeb, Jeph. II. Kring, Tim. III. Heroes (Television program) IV. Title.
PS3623.A3643H37 2008
813'.6—dc22
2007043845

Printed in the United States of America
on acid-free paper

www.delreybooks.com
www.nbc.com/Heroes

1 3 5 7 9 8 6 4 2

First Edition

Book design by Katie Shaw

For my sister, Sylvanie Wallington

Acknowledgments

A million thanks to everyone who helped me with the writing of this book, especially Keith Clayton, Cindy Chang, Lisa Grubka, Debra Drucker, Ollie Grigsby, and Emily Lewis. Extra-special thanks to Tim Kring, Jeph Loeb, Michael Green, Aron Eli Coleite, Mark Warshaw, and the amazing writers, producers, cast, and crew of *Heroes*.

NBC Universal would like to thank the following people for helping make this book a reality: Jesse Alexander, Charlie Andrews, Steve Berkowitz, Cindy Chang, Keith Clayton, Aron Eli Coleite, Pierluigi Cothran, Bruce Evans, Kay Foster, Matt Frank, Neysa Gordon, Marc Graboff, Michael Green, Dennis Hammer, Safronia Johnson, Julie Kenner, Tim Kring, Jeph Loeb, Daniel McPeek, John Miller, Betsy Mitchell, Richard Nathan, Kim Niemi, Rick Olshansky, Jerry Petry, Katherine Pope, Scott Shannon, Ben Silverman, Jennifer Sprague, David Stevenson, Mark Warshaw, Erin Gough Wehrenberg, and Beth Whelpley.

HEROES

SAVING CHARLIE

1

HIRO NAKAMURA WAS IN LOVE.

Full-on, head-over-heels in love.

Charlie was *perfect*. Smart, funny, *gorgeous*—God, was she gorgeous, with that red hair and those small soft hands and that smile . . .

He had waited his entire life to have a girl smile at him like that. And it had finally happened, lightning had finally struck. Six thousand miles from home, at a tiny greasy spoon smack in the middle of Texas, he'd finally met the girl of his dreams.

Charlie. Mmmmm.

Hiro peacocked in front of the men's room mirror, bringing sexy back. He felt like slaying a dragon or saving a village or pounding his chest with mighty fists—something masculine and rugged and virile, to announce to the world that Hiro Nakamura was in love with Charlie . . . um . . .

Charlie Something-or-other.

Huh. He didn't know her last name.

Hiro's shoulders slumped for a second, then he shook it off.

Well, so what? Who cared what her last name was? If he played his cards right, she might just end up as Charlie *Nakamura*!

He gave his reflection a goofy smile.

Okay, maybe he was going overboard. Maybe *love* was too strong a word for what he felt, given that he'd known her for less than an hour, and they spoke different languages, and she was probably only talking to him at all because he'd happened to sit down in her section in the diner.

All right, then, he'd admit it: maybe he wasn't actually *in love* with Charlie.

But he was definitely smitten. *No one* could argue with that.

2

"N<small>O WONDER EVERYONE IN</small> A<small>MERICA IS SO FAT!</small>"

Hiro surreptitiously glanced around the diner, checking out the other customers to see if Ando was talking about anyone in particular.

A group of chattering women in tennis whites took up three tables in the back; a sketchy-looking trucker with a baseball cap pulled low over his eyes, shielding his face, nursed a solitary cup of coffee at a table by the door; a pair of businessmen were anchored down the counter; and two men in police department uniforms lingered over the newspaper a couple of tables away.

The younger of the two, whose bushy sideburns threatened to take over his face, scowled down at the crossword puzzle, erasing an answer so vigorously that he tore a hole in the paper. But the older—and fatter— cop looked up, meeting Hiro's gaze with a friendly nod.

Hiro smiled back, trying not to look alarmed at the way the sheriff's chair creaked ominously anytime he shifted his considerable bulk. Then he returned his attention to Ando, who was scowling down at the laminated menu in consternation.

"All there is to eat is waffles and french fries," Ando complained.

Hiro leaned back in the comfortable padded booth and grinned. "You *like* french fries."

"I've gained four kilos from french fries!"

Hiro opened his mouth to respond, then thought better of it. Half a dozen replies sprang to mind, each one more hilarious than the last, but he knew that his friend wouldn't find any of them funny, at least not until he'd had some coffee.

So Hiro simply shrugged and picked up his own menu, happy just to be out of the car.

Hiro and Ando had been on the road since dawn, steadily ticking off the miles on the endless monotonous ribbon of I-20 East from El Paso. Ando was lucky enough to be doing the driving, but for Hiro, it was the most boring morning of his life.

There had been nothing interesting to look at, scenery-wise—just scrubby brown earth, divided by barbed-wire fences that seemed utterly pointless to him—what were they trying to fence in? There was nothing there!

At one point they'd passed a squashed armadillo by the side of the road, and after that Hiro hadn't been able to look out the window at all. Yet there was nothing else to do—he'd read all the manga he'd brought along a million times already. His *9th Wonders!* was in tatters, he'd memorized every word of *Tengu Ninfuuden Shinobu,* and he'd flipped through *Robogirl* so often that the pages were all coming loose.

He'd tried to buy the latest issues when they'd stopped for gas the day before in Las Cruces, but the woman running the little newsstand had no idea what he was talking about, even with Ando translating for him. She kept trying to press a copy of something called *Fish & Stream* on him, which as far as Hiro was concerned was worse than having no reading material at all. She was so insistent that he'd finally shelled out the $3.95 and taken it, just to get her off his back, but the second he was out of her eyesight he tossed it into a trash bin.

And even though Ando had turned out to be a far better traveling companion than Hiro had expected—really, a better *friend* than he ever would have dreamed—he was grouchy in the mornings and never wanted to talk until the caffeine from his coffee had fully kicked in.

He didn't want to listen to Hiro talk, either, and had even snapped at him to stop humming, "because it's interfering with my driving."

Hiro wasn't sure how his *practically inaudible* humming could affect Ando's ability to steer the car—in a perfectly straight line, no less—but *whatever*. He wasn't going to fight about it. So he agreeably folded his lips inside, then stared silently up at the cloudless, unremittingly blue sky. It had been that way for hours and hours, until finally, on the outskirts of a small town, they'd spotted the faded red sign of the Burnt Toast Diner.

Ando flicked on the turn signal and pulled into the parking lot. *Hallelujah.*

Hiro bolted out of the car before it had even come to a full stop.

"Breakfast!" he crowed, and hurried to the diner's front door, stopping to hold it open for Ando.

Hiro loved diners. He loved the food, loved the retro chrome-and-vinyl décor, loved the little individual jukeboxes sitting on each table. He always flipped through the playlist, even though he had yet to recognize a single song. What he loved best, though, were the menus, which frequently had pictures of the food printed next to their descriptions, so you knew exactly what you were going to get.

It was just like Tokyo, where every noodle joint in Shinjuku had plastic models of each dish displayed in the window. It made ordering a lot easier, and it was one of the few things he'd encountered so far on this trip that made Hiro feel at home.

It was especially helpful in a place like this, where the dishes were given colorful, incomprehensible names and descriptions. Hiro wavered back and forth between the Oil Rigger breakfast sandwich—scrambled eggs, cheese, and Canadian bacon, pressed between two waffles, dipped in batter, and deep-fried to golden gooey perfection—and the Strike It Rich special, with pork-and-apple sausage patties piled on a fresh homemade biscuit and smothered in country gravy.

He was so absorbed in the menu—did he feel more like the fried square thing or the white creamy thing?—that he didn't even notice the waitress bustling up to their table until she spoke.

"Anything looking good, guys?"

Hiro glanced up and froze, thunderstruck.

Standing in front of him was the most beautiful girl he had ever seen.

Eyes like a baby koala's, strawberry-blond hair that swooped fetchingly down her shoulders, a body you could toast marshmallows over. She looked—*holy moly,* she looked just like Robogirl, the main character in Hiro's all-time number one favorite manga, brought to life.

And Hiro *worshipped* Robogirl. Since he was twelve years old he'd devoured every issue about the sexy female robot with weapons for hands and sadness in her heart. And now here she was, standing right in front of him.

But instead of having lethally sharp stilettos or spiked clubs at the end of her arms, this girl had two coffeepots clutched in her hands, one of which had an orange spout. She held them up invitingly.

"Yes, please!" Ando begged, righting the upside-down cups that were preset on saucers on the table, and quickly pushing his in her direction.

The waitress poured, then turned her smile onto Hiro. "Would you like some coffee?"

Hiro just stared at her, a foolish grin planted on his face. Even if he knew the English words he needed to answer her, he didn't think he could speak.

She lifted a shoulder in a little half shrug and reached across the table to pour him a cup anyway. As she bent toward him, Hiro saw that she had a name tag pinned to the left pocket of her pink blouse.

CHARLIE.

He studied the name, deciphering the unfamiliar combination of letters, attempting—*why didn't I pay more attention in English class*—to sound it out, when—*ouch!*—Ando kicked him under the table.

Hiro scowled at him, indignant. "What did you do that for?"

Ando answered in a low voice, in Japanese. "Stop leering at her!"

What? "I wasn't," Hiro protested, but then a second glance at Charlie made him realize that, yeah, he kinda had been.

Oops. But he stole another glance anyway, noticing the necklace Charlie was wearing, a filigreed heart-shaped silver locket nestled in the hollow of her pale, slender throat.

"Tell her I like her necklace."

"I will not."

"Why not?"

"Because it's a completely transparent excuse for having been ogling her."

"I wasn't—"

"Hey, I don't blame you. But I'm not going to help you hit on some poor defenseless girl—"

"Ando!"

Charlie, who was looking back and forth between them as they argued in Japanese, raised an eyebrow.

"Wow, you two are a long way from home," she said, interrupting their discussion. "We don't get a lot of tourists out here."

"How you know we tourist?" Hiro garbled, then kicked himself. *Duh.*

"Just a guess," she answered, managing not to sound too sarcastic. "What's that on your shirt?"

Her eyes moved to the white kanji lettering on the pocket of Hiro's dark blue jacket.

"Bachigai," she read, carefully sounding out the unfamiliar symbols. "That means 'I don't belong here,' right?"

Hiro's jaw dropped, and he straightened up in his seat, delighted.

"You know Japanese!" he exclaimed—then stopped dead and spent an excruciating moment wondering if that meant she had understood them talking about her.

But no, she was smiling, so it was probably okay.

"I got a Japanese phrase book for my birthday six months ago," Charlie explained. "I started poking through it last week." She cleared her throat, then carefully recited in Japanese, *"One bento box with shrimp, please."*

Hiro clapped. "Very good! High grades."

She smiled and lifted one shoulder in a modest little shrug. "I'm still learning."

"You learned that from a book in just one week?" Ando asked, looking amazed.

"I remember lots and lots. Just something my brain started doing lately." She paused, then added, almost to herself, "Whether I want it to or not."

Her smile faltered, just for an instant, but then she gave her head a little shake and the cheerful look returned. "So, what'll it be?"

"You pick," Hiro told her in English. "Something delicious for me." He glanced at Ando out of the corner of his eye, adding, "And for my friend, he need food for *fato fato.*"

Ando's mouth dropped open in protest.

But Charlie piped up before he could say anything. "Got just the thing," she said. "One chilaquiles . . . and one cottage cheese plate coming up."

She gave Hiro a flirtatious little wink and twirled away. He watched her go, a dreamy smile appearing on his face.

"Who says no one in America is nice?"

"Oh, quit staring at her," Ando snapped, then he buried his face in his coffee cup.

"The dance floor lights are cool," Charlie said, covering the phrase book with her hand and reciting the sentence from memory.

"Perfect! You ready for disco!" Hiro cheered. He threw one arm into the air in a haphazard John Travolta move.

"I got it right?"

"Yes. Almost."

After twenty minutes of picking dispiritedly at his cottage cheese platter, Ando had demanded a waffle after all. Hiro happily took advantage of the delay by joining Charlie at the counter, quizzing her on her Japanese.

"Don't let me off easy now," she said, so Hiro repeated it slowly, correcting her pronunciation.

She tried again, and nailed it. Then the next one.

"I don't like this song. Let's get a drink."

Hiro's eyes widened. "You learn very fast."

"I sort of remember everything I read. At least lately I do." She self-consciously dropped her eyes, flipping to the next page in the phrase book with studied casualness. "It's kind of a skill, I guess."

Hiro knew *exactly* how she was feeling, better than she ever could have imagined, he thought. But a crowded diner in the middle of the breakfast rush wasn't the right time or place to go into it. So—

"My own skill much more complicated," he said lightly.

"Oh yeah? What can you do?"

"I can teach Japanese to anyone."

Charlie laughed. *"You're sweet,"* she said, her Japanese flawless.

Hiro ducked his head shyly, looking for the phrase on the new page in the book. But it wasn't there.

"Sweet," she repeated, this time in English. "It means nice. Cute."

Hiro looked confused. "That not in book."

"No," she said, turning a light shade of purple as she met his eyes. "It's just true."

They grinned at each other, looking like two little kids sharing a secret, he guessed. Hiro's heart gave such a loud *ker-thunk,* he was surprised everyone in the diner didn't look over to see what had made such a ruckus.

The order bell dinged, interrupting the moment.

"Sorry, someone's Denver omelet's up." She slid off her stool and touched his shoulder with her hand, gesturing for him to stay put.

Ker-thunk! Ker-thunk! Ker-thunk!

"Be right back."

Charlie disappeared into the kitchen, and Hiro swiveled around on his stool to face Ando, who was sprawled in their booth, reading a newspaper.

"I'm sweet!" he shouted in Japanese, and threw his arms joyfully up in the air.

Ando rolled his eyes and went back to his paper. But Hiro spun his stool around in a circle, beaming.

Sweet. How awesome was that?

Hiro had rarely been lucky—not in games, not in timing, and especially not in love.

His attempts to flirt with girls were generally met with some combination of laughter, pity, and blank stares. And on the few occasions when he did manage to ask a girl for her phone number, by the time he'd summoned up the courage to call her she'd either forgotten who he was, disconnected her phone, or just met her future husband.

In his entire life he'd gone on only a handful of dates, each more humiliating than the last. He'd never had sex, never said *I love you* out loud.

At twenty-four years old, Hiro wasn't just a virgin—he was an embarrassment.

But this time? This time, it looked as if his luck was changing.

To be sure, it was lucky that, out of all the coffee shops and truck stops and fast-food joints they could have driven past that morning, they had stopped at the Burnt Toast Diner.

It was even luckier that someone had happened to give Charlie a Japanese phrase book, as opposed to a Spanish or Polish or Greek one.

And the fact that Charlie actually seemed to like Hiro back? That was the most amazing, hands-down *luckiest* thing of all.

Although, really, what wasn't to like? Hiro asked himself. Nice eyes, spiky black hair, hip clothes—okay, so maybe he was a little more Bambi than badass, but all in all?

Not bad.

He should ask her out. He bet if he did, she'd say yes. Why wouldn't she?

After all, it was his lucky day.

"Hiro, no!" Ando groaned, letting his head loll around on his neck.

"Why not?" Hiro said, wounded. "You don't think she'd say yes?"

"It doesn't matter *what* she'd say! We don't have time for you to go out on a date—we have to get back on the road."

"We've got *plenty* of time. Besides, the car needs to rest."

Ando shot him an incredulous look. "What—"

"It's not good for the motor to drive for hours and hours on end, without giving the car a break." Hiro was becoming desperate.

Ando shook his head in disbelief. "How would *you* know what the car needs? You don't even drive!"

"*Everyone* knows that," Hiro said, trying very much to sound as if the subject was closed. Then he leaned across the table and gave his friend a happy little grin. "She called me sweet."

"So what? I'll call you sweetie-baby-honey-pie if it'll get you into the car."

Hiro shook his head, his grin growing wider. "I think she likes me."

"*So what?*" Ando said again. "We didn't come all the way from Tokyo just to meet pretty girls. We need to get to New York!"

"We've got plenty of time," Hiro said with a nod of finality. "I'm asking her out."

Ando stared at Hiro for a second, and the expression on his face said that he was debating putting him in a headlock and physically dragging him out to the car. But then he shrugged.

"Okay."

Hiro blinked with surprise. "Really?"

"Sure. Ask her out. You can do it right now." He raised a hand and, before Hiro could stop him, waved at Charlie, motioning her over.

Damn it.

Hiro shot Ando the blackest look in the history of the world as Charlie strolled up to their table carrying a coffeepot.

"How are you guys doing?" she asked.

Ando grinned at Hiro, waiting for him to chicken out.

Which he did.

"Ando need more coffee," Hiro muttered.

"Sure thing," Charlie said, pouring it into his cup. The order bell dinged again, and with a quick smile for Hiro she was off.

Ando leaned back in his seat, smirking. "What happened? Why didn't you ask her out?"

"Well, I wasn't going to do it with you there."

"Face it, Hiro. You're never going to ask her out. You're too scared."

It's true.

Hiro scowled at him. "I am not."

He took a deep breath. *Screw it. Were the samurais scared when they rode into battle? Were the Bushido warriors scared when they had to face the unknown?*

Well—*yeah,* actually. They probably were. But the point was, they faced their fear.

And so would he.

Hiro stood up. "I'm going to do it."

Ando stared at him, both surprised and impressed. "Really?"

No.

"Yes."

He looked over to where Charlie was pouring coffee for the two police officers, laughing at something the one with sideburns was saying.

"Just as soon as I get back from the men's room," Hiro added hastily.

Then he turned and, with as much dignity as he could muster, hurried past Charlie into the restroom, Ando's mocking laughter chasing after him.

She's not going to say no, Hiro reassured himself. She already liked him. All he had to do was ask.

"Wanna get out of here?" he murmured to his reflection. He tossed himself a little wink-and-smile combo that made him look—if he did say so himself—pretty irresistible.

"C'mon. You and me, baby."

He'd spent the last ten minutes staring at the mirror, psyching himself up to ask out Charlie, and he was finally ready.

Sort of.

At least if she said no, he'd never have to see her again, he rationalized. He and Ando could just get into their car and drive away, and never think about her again. It wouldn't be like the time he asked Miyoki Akayawa to the amusement park.

She had stared at him, speechless with disbelief and horror that he dared to think someone like her—pixie haircut, star gymnast, gaggle of friends—would ever in a million years go out with someone like him—glasses, zero friends, picking at a scab while he asked her.

For years, literally *years* after that, every time they walked into the same classroom or passed each other in the hall, he had to endure all her friends going, "Look, Miyoki, there's your *boyfriend*," and Miyoki screaming and laughing and pretending to vomit.

But—that wouldn't happen this time. Especially because Charlie was going to say yes.

Yes.

All he had to do was ask.

He turned and strolled back out into the dining room, rubbing his hands together in anticipation, a hundred—well, *ninety-nine*—percent ready and confident.

But the instant he stepped through the doorway he knew that everything in the diner had changed. That something was terribly wrong.

There was a weird, hollow hush hanging over the room, an uncomfortable silence punctured by an occasional wail or moan, like in the aftermath of some great catastrophe, some ruinous natural disaster.

None of the customers were at their tables any longer; the creepy dude with the baseball cap had disappeared, the tennis players were huddled in little groups, clinging to one another, and everyone else was gathered in a shaking uncertain formation around the open metal door that led to the diner's storeroom.

Ando walked up behind him, and Hiro turned to him, puzzled. Even Ando had a stunned look on his face.

"It's Charlie," Ando said, his voice heavy with sympathy. He put his hand on Hiro's shoulder and kept it there, firm and steady, offering comfort and support, although Hiro still didn't understand why.

"What?" he asked, already dreading the answer.

"Charlie—in there . . ." Ando tilted his chin toward the storeroom, where the people were clustered.

Sideburns Cop was giving orders, speaking into a walkie-talkie, his voice a cross between a bark and a sob, while tears trickled down his face into his mustache.

An older waitress had fallen to her knees, and she was weeping. Other people were crying, whispering, eyes wide and scared.

And beyond them, on the floor of the storeroom, Hiro could just make out a sliver of the pink fabric of Charlie's blouse. A pale hand, still and cold, and a steady, widening pool of blood.

Hiro felt his whole body sag as his knees began to buckle.

That was Charlie, lying on the floor in there. That was her blood, her motionless hand.

Charlie was dead.

Only Ando's hand, strong on his shoulder, kept Hiro on his feet as the terrible truth hit him: it wasn't good luck or bad luck that had brought him to this diner and allowed him to meet Charlie.

It was destiny.

3

IN HIS FINAL YEAR OF HIGH SCHOOL HIRO WAS SUMMONED TO THE office of his guidance counselor, Reiko Asakawa, for the obligatory career assessment all graduating students had to go through. Even though he knew it was pointless.

Hiro's entire future was already laid out for him, at his father's decree, like endless lines of type in a long, dull textbook.

He would spend the next four years attending a university picked out by his father—or rather, where his father had managed to beg, bribe, or cajole the administration into granting him admittance, despite his lousy grades, abominable class ranking, and complete dearth of extracurricular activities.

Upon graduation, he would go to work at his father's company, Yamagato Industries, where he would start at the absolute bottom and spend the next quarter of a century working his way up through the ranks. He would master all facets of the business by attending deathly departmental meetings and moving pieces of paper from one stack to another and following, silently and watchfully, in his father's footsteps.

Hiro would then take the reins of control from his father and spend the next thirty-odd years running the company himself, until finally, ultimately, he passed the legacy along to his own similarly doomed son.

At which point he would quickly succumb to the ravages of age and stress, making a hasty exit to the ancestral mausoleum in Kyoto, where he would lie in his father's shadow for all eternity.

Done and done.

There was no wiggle room in this plan. Hiro's own interests and desires and talents had no bearing on his future. Yamagato Industries was his destiny, and he had learned a long time ago not to hope for anything better.

Still, he showed up in Reiko's office when summoned, if for no other reason than the fact that his counselor was the best-looking teacher in the school, and the youngest by about forty years.

"*Everyone* has choices," Reiko said, her expression growing more and more perplexed as she listened to Hiro elaborate upon the path that had been laid out for him.

Yeah, he had a choice: do what his father wanted, or commit seppuku for the dishonor he'd brought down upon his family.

Reiko glanced down at his file, which lay open in a manila folder on her desk, and smiled up at him.

"Well then, what do you want to do with your life?"

Didn't they just go through this?

"Work at my dad's company, I guess," he said with a shrug.

"No, what do *you* want?"

She leaned forward, propping her elbows on the desk and resting her chin in her cupped palms, giving Hiro a perfect view down the front of her shirt. She had on a red silk bra, and Hiro could see a small brown mole peeking through the lace.

Damn.

"What are you interested in?" she continued. "What sorts of things do you like?"

With Herculean effort, Hiro lifted his eyes up to meet hers.

Comic books. Video games. Kung fu movies.

Somehow he didn't think those things would impress her, so he shrugged again, and Reiko made an impatient gesture.

"Look. Forget what your father wants. Just tell me what *you* want. And I promise I'll do everything I can to help you achieve it."

Hiro hesitated, and Reiko gave him an encouraging smile.

"Well, I've been reading a lot about the Bushido lately."

"Bushido?"

"Seventeenth-century samurai warriors."

She looked puzzled again, so he leaned forward to explain.

"They were so cool—completely fierce and fearless, and they lived by this code of chivalry and honor."

The smile was quickly vanishing. "I don't understand."

"It's called the Bushido code," Hiro said. "The Way of the Warrior. Its seven principles were what the Samurai lived by: bravery, equanimity, compassion, hon—"

"Yes, I understand what the Bushido code is," Reiko said, cutting him off. "What I don't understand is—what does it have to do with your future?"

Um.

"Well, you asked what I wanted to be. And if I could choose anything in the world? It would be that."

"A *samurai*?"

Hiro nodded. "A Bushido."

"That's what you want to do with your life? Become a seventeenth-century warrior?"

Well, if she put it like *that*, but—Hiro nodded again.

"Yeah."

The counselor looked at him for a long minute, the expression on her face identical to the one he saw on his father's face whenever he brought home another failing report card, or accidentally kicked the ball into his own team's goal in soccer, or that time he'd tried to go an entire evening speaking Klingon instead of Japanese. A combination of bafflement and disgust, sort of the way you'd look at a two-headed calf or the bearded lady at the circus.

Reiko sighed. Then she flipped his folder shut and leaned back in her chair, folding her arms across her chest, the red lace bra disappearing from sight. After a few more moments of uncomfortable silence, she finally spoke.

"Have fun working for your father."

Eight years later Hiro was sitting in his cubicle at Yamagato Industries, just as expected, when something happened that was completely *unexpected.*

He stopped time.

One instant he was staring at the bland white face of the clock on his desk, watching the second hand chunk past the two, the three, the four . . . marking off the hours and days and years he was forced to endure in this unwanted life.

He wished he could just stop everything. Wished that if he concentrated hard enough, focused every molecule of his body and brain and being, he could still the unending, monotonous, *constant* sweep of the hands advancing around the clock.

So he screwed his eyes shut, as tightly as he could, and—

And in the next instant, the hand stuttered and stuck, moving back a tick and then . . .

Staying there.

The world fell silent, immobile; frozen as easily as if Hiro had flipped a switch. People turned to stone, the wind stopped blowing, the earth ground to a halt on its axis.

Hiro slowly opened his eyes, scarcely daring to breathe, afraid to look around him, in case what he was seeing, what he was hearing, wasn't real.

But it was.

Hiro Nakamura had stopped time.

The Aborigines in Australia bend time and space when they enter the Dreamtime. The Yogis in India have been doing it for thousands of years. And now Hiro had done it, too.

"I did it!" he shouted, breaking his focus.

And just like that the world clicked back on, in all its noise and movement and chaos. The hands resumed their journey around the clock face. And Hiro went racing through the hubbub of the sixteenth floor of Yamagato Industries to where his best friend Ando was sitting, in his impeccable cubicle, surfing the Internet for porn.

"I did it!" Hiro exclaimed.

Ando glanced at him, then returned his attention to the naked woman on his computer screen. A slim, busty woman, pale, with long blond hair, peering seductively into the webcam.

"What now?" he said distractedly.

"I've broken the space-time continuum!"

"Good for you," Ando mumbled, clearly not paying attention to a word that was being said to him.

Hiro waved his hands, frustrated by his unflappable friend.

"My clock. I made it go back one second, using only my mind, my thoughts."

"Too bad you're not paid by the hour. You'd be on to something."

"Ando!" Hiro exclaimed with a stamp of his foot. "I'm *serious*."

Ando sighed and closed down the window on his monitor, then swiveled his chair so that he faced Hiro.

"I have discovered powers beyond any mere mortal," Hiro continued proudly.

"Right. You and Spock."

Finally!

"Yes. Like Spock. Exactly."

Ando just rolled his eyes. "Fine. Let's say you really do have this power . . . What do you do with it? Join the circus? Go on TV? I mean, no one ever got laid by stopping the second hand of a clock."

Hiro shook his head emphatically. "That's just the beginning. As I develop my powers, I'll learn to bend space, too. Then I can teleport myself anywhere on the planet."

"Like *Star Trek*," Ando said.

"Yeah, like *Star Trek*."

"And then what?"

Good question. "Then I'll fulfill my destiny."

Ando started laughing.

Hiro scowled at him. "In every superhero myth, the hero must learn his purpose," he said defensively. "When he does, he will be tested and called to greatness."

"Okay, 'Super-Hiro,'" Ando said, still laughing. "You go ahead and boldly go where no man has gone before. Me? I'm going to get back to work."

Hiro turned his back on his friend and stalked away. He was livid. Let Ando make fun of him. *Fine.* He'd see.

Hiro had a power—a *superpower*—and that meant he was destined for something greater than life in his father's footsteps. When the call to greatness came, he'd be ready.

He wouldn't have long to wait. He was sure of it.

. . .

On the subway home that night, Hiro was clutching the handrail above his head, staring at a monitor across from him that was playing an advertisement for "Vacations in New York City," but he wasn't really seeing it.

His mind was replaying the conversation with Ando, over and over.

I do have powers.

They're real.

The images on the monitor flickered—the Chrysler Building, the Statue of Liberty, the Empire State Building, Times Square.

Hiro's eyes drooped shut, lulled by the rocking of the train. Even so, he felt overwhelmed with emotion: the frustration of trying to make Ando believe, the longing for his destiny to be fulfilled. His whole being was consumed by the desire to make a difference, to be special, to be a hero.

I can bend time and space. My powers are real! Emotion surged within him.

The train lurched to a stop, and somehow everything felt *different*. Slowly he opened his eyes, and—

Hiro found himself in New York City. *Times Square!* Just like on the screen.

Holy cow!

He had done it—he had bent the laws of physics and traveled through space. It was real; it was all really happening!

Walking down 42nd Street, Hiro stopped at a newsstand, scanned the newspapers, and realized—with some effort, since his grasp of English was limited—that he had bent *time*, as well. He had traveled a month into the future.

Holy moley!

Before this could sink in entirely, his attention was grabbed by a comic book in the rack that stood to the side of the newsstand. There in front, prominently displayed, was a comic called *9th Wonders!*

And there, on the cover of the comic book, stood Hiro Nakamura, in the middle of Times Square.

Hiro had gone to look for the one person in New York he hoped could give him some help, and some answers: a comic-book artist named Isaac Mendez.

Mr. Mendez was the writer *and* artist for *9th Wonders!*, and when Hiro arrived at his apartment he found that it was filled with paintings of a terrifying future.

A nuclear bomb going off in New York City.

The city in flames.

Millions of people being killed.

Paintings of Hiro himself, in America with Ando, on a mission to stop the bomb from exploding. Isaac had painted Hiro's destiny.

He wandered through the apartment, terrified and amazed by what he saw.

Hiro had already stopped the world. Now all he had to do was save it. That much was clear.

But he was too late to save Mr. Mendez himself.

The artist's body lay on the floor, in a chunky pool of half-congealed blood. His head—Hiro stumbled, choking back a mouthful of bile—his head had been riven in two, the top three inches sliced clean off, and his brain had been removed.

Mr. Mendez had been murdered.

4

A ND NOW CHARLIE HAD BEEN MURDERED, TOO.
 In exactly the same way as Mr. Isaac.

"Did she say anything? Sound like she was scared?"

The sheriff, the fat one who had smiled at Hiro earlier, studied his and Ando's faces, looking for any clues that might be hidden there.

They were back at their table, sitting quietly, just—waiting. After the initial chaos, the atmosphere in the diner had become unnaturally subdued, all the warmth and spark of the morning snuffed out. Turned to ash.

Hiro looked past the sheriff to where a couple of young paramedics, looking barely old enough to have graduated from high school, were coming out of the storeroom wrestling with a gurney that had a body— Charlie's body—lying on it, covered in a pale blue sheet.

Hiro couldn't bear to watch.

He tried to look away, but at the last second some terrible defeatist instinct made him turn his head, and he caught a glimpse of a lock of red hair, matted with blood, spilling out from underneath the blue sheet and over the side of the stretcher.

Without thinking he stopped time, freezing everything around him.

He tried to get up, to smooth that lock of hair back on Charlie's forehead, to take her hand and murmur comforting things. To smile and flirt with Charlie over chilaquiles and coffee, to do something, *anything*, but he was frozen, too. As if, in stopping time, he had ended up stopping himself instead.

It was impossible to breathe, impossible to move. He was sure his heart had stopped beating, that his blood sat stagnant in his veins. His ears were filled with the droning of bees, everything went inky-purple around the edges, and the only thing Hiro could see was that strand of fiery red hair, too vibrant to be in any way connected with death.

He stared hard at the body on the stretcher, really kind of expecting Charlie to pull the sheet off her face and sit up, combing her hair out with her fingers. But she didn't move, so he started time again.

Maybe *now*, now she would sit up and explain it had all been a misunderstanding, a joke that had gone too far.

But she still didn't move.

And then the paramedics were wheeling the gurney away, out the door, into the waiting ambulance, and Ando was touching him very gently on the arm, and Hiro knew that all this was real, and Charlie was gone.

It was the mission to save the world that had brought them to Texas and to the Burnt Toast Diner in the first place. Hiro knew—he was positive—that Charlie's death was in some way connected with everything that had happened.

And if that was the case, then there had to be something he could do.

He took a deep breath, then let it out, feeling his taut muscles start to relax as the idea took shape and grew. There *was* something he could do.

He could bend time.

He could go back.

I could go back! Of course! He'd go back in time and save Charlie's life, then return to today, to the mission that lay ahead of him.

Excitement buoyed up inside him. He would save the woman he loved from the evil villain. What could be more heroic than that?

He turned his face back toward the sheriff, who asked again, "Did she say anything?"

Ando shook his head. "No. She seemed very nice."

"She was," the sheriff answered, his voice hoarse and oddly muffled. "Too nice to die like that. Head ripped open and . . . I ain't never seen anything like it."

Don't worry, Hiro thought. *You* won't *ever see anything like it, not if I have anything to say about it.*

"We're very sorry," Ando told the sheriff, who nodded and labored sluggishly to his feet.

"Y'all stick around," he said gruffly. "We need to take your statements."

The sheriff moved away, and Ando turned to Hiro, his face dark with compassion.

But Hiro shook his head, eager to share his plan with his friend so he could hurry up and set things right.

"I'm going back," he announced.

Ando's expression changed, a mixture of pity, hope, and disbelief. "It's too late," he said. "She's already dead."

"It's *not* too late," Hiro insisted. "It's *never* too late." ,

"There's nothing you can do."

"I can go back."

Ando sighed, exasperation replacing all the other emotions that were playing across his face.

"You're seriously going to jeopardize our entire mission, just for a cute girl?"

Yes.

"No!" Hiro said. "But—"

"But what?"

"Charlie is more than just a cute girl."

"Was," Ando said firmly, but not unsympathetically. "Charlie *was* a cute girl."

Hiro narrowed his eyes at his friend, his expression hardening. Yet Ando didn't stop.

"I'm sorry, Hiro, but you have a job to do—a job you were *destined* to do, and Charlie isn't a part of it."

"But her memory. Her power—"

"—is just a coincidence! That's all. It has nothing to do with you, with the mission. Even if you don't want to believe it."

"She was killed the same way as the painter, Isaac Mendez, when I saw him in the future." He gestured toward his forehead, jerkily indicating the result of an encounter with the Brain Man, as Hiro thought of the killer. Then he quickly dropped his hand back to his lap. "*That* can't be a coincidence."

"Then we should be extra-careful," Ando said.

Hiro shook his head. "Why else did I get these powers if I'm not supposed to help?"

"We're already on one mission. You don't need another."

"But she's already part of it!" Hiro insisted.

Ando let out an exasperated *pffft*.

Hiro kept talking. "It's destiny that brought me to her. Why else would we have stopped in this particular diner? Why else would she happen to have been reading a Japanese phrase book? Why else would we be here when the Brain Man came? These things are connected, they have to be!"

He shut his eyes for a second, trying to think of a way to make his friend understand why this was so important to him, why he *had* to do this.

"I don't know what this all means, but I know that it means *something*. I have the power to save her, so I have to try. I can't just sit back and do nothing—"

"Sure you can! It's easy!" Ando said, his worried frown belying the glibness of his words.

Hiro shook his head firmly, his mind made up. "I'll just go back to yesterday. I'll stop her from coming to work. If she's not here, she can't be killed."

"But *you* can be!" Ando exclaimed. "You don't have control of your powers yet. The last time you teleported, you ended up in the future! In another country!"

"If I'm too scared to use my powers, then I don't deserve them," Hiro said quietly. "I have to try."

"You're supposed to save the world!" Ando said, in one last desperate attempt to change his friend's mind. "What's going to happen to the world if you aren't here to save it?"

"I can do both. I'll go save Charlie, then I'll be back to save the world. You'll see."

Hiro reached across the table and laid a light hand on Ando's arm.

"I won't be late. Just count to five and I'll be back. We'll celebrate my victory."

Hiro shut his eyes, screwing up his face in concentration.

Take me back to Charlie, he thought, not sure whom he was addressing. He condensed all his emotions into a single clear thread: *Take me to Charlie, take me back so I can save her, oh please please please let me go back and save Charlie . . .*

"Hiro, please! Don't do this!" Ando begged. But he was too late.

Please. Take me back . . .

And just like that, Hiro was gone.

5

F OR AS LONG AS HIRO COULD RECALL, HIS FATHER HAD KEPT A SMALL
golden plaque on the wall of his office at Yamagato Industries. It
hung right next to his desk, always close at hand.

Etched across the front, in thin curvy hiragana lettering, were the
words, THIS IS NOT A FAIRY TALE.

Hiro remembered once, when he was about four years old, climbing
sleepily into his dad's lap and asking him about the meaning behind
those words. This was before Hiro had started disappointing his dad in
a measurable way, so he was still, briefly, willing to ask direct questions
and initiate physical contact and, really, spend any more time with his
father than he absolutely had to.

Kaito Nakamura lifted the plaque from the wall and held it out so
Hiro could run his fingers over it, feeling the bas-relief of the letters.

"This is not a fairy tale," Kaito read aloud. "I keep this here to remind
me that *life* isn't a fairy tale. Things don't happen by magic, or by wish-
ing on a star. It takes hard work, discipline, control."

He took the plaque back from Hiro and peered at it for a minute.

"There are no happy endings," he continued. "There is only what we
achieve, and what legacy we leave behind."

He hung it back on the wall and lifted his son gently off his lap.

"Now run along, Hiro. Your father has to get back to work."

Hiro wandered out of his father's office, thinking about what he had just been told.

There are no happy endings.

Well, of course not, he told himself, *because in the end everybody dies. But you can be happy right up until the end, can't you?*

Even at age four, Hiro thought his father's saying was one of the stupidest things he had ever heard.

Who cared how the story ended? It was the happiness in the middle that made a story a good one.

6

H IRO SAT UP STRAIGHT IN HIS CHAIR, HIS EYES SHUT TIGHT, SCARED
to open them.

What if it hadn't worked?

His only hope of saving Charlie was to teleport back. He *had to* succeed—he had no other options. And he couldn't face the possibility that, for all his powers, she might still be dead.

But as long as he kept his eyes closed, he could keep his hope alive.

Of course, he couldn't spend the rest of his life sitting in a diner with his eyes shut. Still—

"You okay there?"

He was interrupted from his reverie by a voice, a gorgeous musical voice with just a trace of Texas drawl . . .

Hiro snapped his eyes open, so excited, so relieved he nearly burst into tears.

There was Charlie, standing in front of him: revenant, whole, perfect. *Alive.*

"Oh thank God!" He leapt up from his chair and gave her an impromptu hug, knocking her slightly off balance.

"Careful," she said, smiling but serious as she struggled not to spill the hot coffee she was holding.

Oops.

He let go of her and sat back down, but he couldn't keep a wide grin from taking over the better part of his face.

"Sorry, but I'm just so glad to see you—you have no idea!" he said in a rush of Japanese. "Listen, Charlie, I have something important to tell you—"

"I'm sorry," she interrupted, speaking in English and tossing him a confused smile, "but I don't understand a word you're saying."

Oh, of course. She hadn't started really studying her Japanese phrase book until she'd met him.

Hiro rolled his eyes up in a little *my bad!* and Charlie laughed. Okay, so he'd warn her in English.

No problem.

"My name is Hiro Nakamura," he said, and then he paused.

Hmmm. What was the English word for "urgent"? No idea. He also didn't know how to say "crucial," "dire," or "impending disaster."

Damn it! He should have gotten Ando to write it out for him in English before he came. Well, too late for that. So—

Okay, what *did* he know how to say?

"My name is Hiro," he repeated, looking Charlie straight in the eye. "I'm here to save your life."

That ought to do it.

But instead of being so overcome with gratitude that she leapt into his arms and kissed him passionately right there on the tabletop—which, honestly, was kind of what he was hoping would happen—Charlie didn't so much as crack a smile. She just stared at him, her expression way more *who-is-this-lunatic-and-why-is-he-talking-to-me?* than *oh-kind-sir-let-me-thank-you-with-my-body-and-soul.*

Huh.

Was he saying it wrong? Did she not hear him? Should he say it again?

But before he could, a short, perfectly round woman in a vast ruffled apron waddled over and plucked at Charlie's sleeve. "Hey, Charlie, come blow out the candles!"

Hiro blinked, and for the first time he noticed all the other stuff going on around the diner. The place was bustling with activity.

Three tables had been pushed together, and the surface was crowded with brightly wrapped presents, along with a couple of dozen plastic champagne glasses full of something red and fizzy, and a big sheet cake covered in blazing candles.

A banner over the tables spelled out HAPPY BIRTHDAY, CHARLIE, in big glittery letters.

A group of people—Hiro recognized the two policemen and one of the cooks—stood eagerly close by, party hats perched ridiculously on their heads.

When Charlie saw them, her face lit up. She glanced at Hiro and grinned. "Hold that thought," she said cheerily. "I gotta go make a wish."

Hiro's face fell, but she rolled up her eyes, imitating his *my-bad!* look to make him smile again. It worked.

"Come on!" she said, crooking a finger at him, then skipped over to where her friends were waiting.

Hiro got up and headed after her. *Are you kidding?* he thought. He would follow her anywhere.

But he was starting to feel a little worried, too. What if he couldn't make her understand the gravity of her situation? Of how important it would be to skip work the next day? She seemed more focused on the party than on the fact that he was trying to save her life.

The round waitress poked Hiro on the arm with a chubby finger. "Would you mind taking our picture, hon?" she asked. She handed him a camera, and everybody crowded in next to Charlie.

Hiro obliged, snapping the photo.

Charlie smiled at him.

"Now let me get one with you."

Hiro moved in so he was standing next to her. Her arm pressed against his, soft-but-firm, radiating heat.

Oh my God—his mind leapt and his pulse raced, but he yanked his thoughts back to the present. He'd have plenty of time to think about that later, after he'd delivered his message. But for now . . .

"Please listen! Very important—" he started when the huge waitress interrupted him again.

"Say *cheese!*"

Hiro smiled obediently.

Flash!

His smile vanished.

"I teleport from future," he said. "Do not go to work tomorrow!"

But Charlie wasn't listening. She shut her eyes, and her lips moved in a silent wish. Then she bent over the candles and blew them all out.

Hiro made his own wish—*please let this work*—sending it up to the universe on the curl of smoke from the extinguished candles.

Charlie's friends cheered, jostling to get close to her, and Hiro was pushed aside.

Okay.

He took a deep breath, forcing himself to relax. There was still plenty of time to warn Charlie. As soon as the party calmed down, he'd talk to her. So he moved over to a table a little off to the side of the celebration, and sat down to wait.

He was still sitting there, forgotten and ignored, an hour later.

Charlie had opened her presents—a world map, a leather passport cover, a travel diary—and *oohed* and *aahed* over each one. She hugged all her friends, cut into the cake with great fanfare, and finally slipped away to the ladies' room. She emerged moments later, like something out of a dream, in a jade-green dress, decorated at the collar and hem with gold embroidery and dozens of tiny mirrors.

Her eyes fell on poor dejected little Hiro, slumped all alone at his table, and she flashed a smile at him, raising more than just his spirits.

He straightened up in his seat, returning the smile.

Charlie spangled over to him.

"Having fun?" she asked, setting a piece of birthday cake down in front of him.

Hiro looked at it. Chocolate cake, vanilla frosting, a big pink rose made of icing. Hiro *never* got the piece with the rose.

"Thank you," he said breathlessly.

"Of course," she said, in an *it's-your-lucky-day* tone, and handed him a fork. "I'm sorry we didn't get to talk earlier."

"It is okay," he said, "but I need you to listen! Very important you not come to work tomorrow."

"Yeah, that's what you said. Why not?"

"Very bad man—" he started when the policeman with the sideburns barged over.

"You ready to go, babe?" he asked Charlie, cutting Hiro off mid-sentence.

For crying out loud! What was wrong with these people?

"Lloyd, I'm talking to my new friend Hiro," Charlie said pointedly.

Lloyd dug a pinkie into his ear and rooted around, either unaware or unconcerned that he was interrupting them.

"How ya doin'," he said to Hiro, then turned back to Charlie without waiting to hear if he was doin' fine or lousy.

"We should get going—I made us lunch reservations at La Pendule in Odessa!" He said the restaurant's name with a little *ta-da* flourish.

Charlie looked suitably impressed. "Really? But that's such a fancy place."

"Nothing's too good for you," Lloyd said, clearly smitten.

Hiro glared at him. What a *tool.*

Lloyd tucked the umbrella he was holding under his arm, then put his hand on the small of Charlie's back to usher her out. But Charlie skirted his touch and looked at Hiro.

"Hang on, Lloyd—Hiro was just telling me something. Why shouldn't I come to work tomorrow?"

"Because . . . because . . ." He trailed off, looking from the umbrella under Lloyd's arm to the front window of the diner, which was streaked with rain.

Wait a minute. This wasn't—

He wrinkled his forehead, perplexed.

"Hiro?"

"It not raining yesterday," he said.

"Yes, it was," Charlie said, and Lloyd nodded. "April showers. Been storming all week."

"April?" Hiro said, shocked and confused. *No way.* He had only teleported back one day—so there was no way in hell it could be April.

"No. No, October."

"No, it's April," Charlie insisted. "April twenty-fourth. My birthday."

She pointed at the calendar hanging behind the register, a calendar hanging open to a date six months earlier than Hiro had thought. Then she turned back, and the expression on her face showed genuine concern. "Are you okay?"

He nodded, quickly shoving a bite of cake in his mouth to keep himself from bawling.

Ando was right—he didn't have control of his powers yet. He had overshot by half a year.

"Happy birthday," he mumbled.

Then Lloyd intervened again, and a moment later he was escorting Charlie out the door into the rain-soaked April afternoon. Hiro sank back in his seat, walloped by the realization that he might just have made the biggest mistake of his life.

W*HAT AM I GOING TO DO?* HIRO ASKED HIMSELF FOR THE EIGHT
millionth time, squirming in agony from the toxic combination of
too much cake and too much anxiety. *What in the world am I going to do?*

He had been lying there for hours, on top of the greasy flowered
bedspread in his room at the Midland Motor Lodge, incapacitated by
uncertainty and dread.

Six months.

He was six months off from where he had tried to go, where he
needed to be. How could he have let this happen?

Hiro would be the first to admit that he had made a lot of miscalcu-
lations in his life. In fact, if you asked certain teachers or, say, *his father,*
they would probably share the opinion that pretty much everything he
had ever attempted had been a mistake. But *this*—God, Hiro writhed in
agony at the mere thought of it—this was his most colossal, cata-
clysmic, downright apocalyptic screwup yet.

He had put the mission at risk, abandoned Ando, jeopardized the
very existence of life on earth—and for what? Just because some girl had
said he was sweet?

God.

He was pathetic.

Worse than pathetic—he was downright *dangerous.*

Just by being here, he was messing with the space-time continuum. Who knew what could happen as a result? He may have already unwittingly caused some huge, irrevocable devastation to Life As We Knew It. But since he clearly had zero control over his powers, he couldn't risk teleporting back to where Ando was waiting for him. He might end up anywhere.

Lunch for a T-Rex.

Deckhand on the *Titanic.*

Sparring partner for a gladiator.

Thinking about it, Hiro let out a little bleat of distress. No, teleporting again was out of the question. Besides, even if he survived, there was no telling what havoc he might create from traveling willy-nilly through time.

He had to face it—he was stuck.

But what was he supposed to do—stay in this motel for the next six months? He gazed miserably around the dingy little room, with its cigarette burns on the rug, wood-paneled TV bolted to the table, and ugly paint-by-the-numbers lighthouse hanging on the wall. He could barely stand to stay in here for one night.

Hiro turned onto his side, curling his body up into a little ball and hugging the lumpy foam pillow for comfort.

Some superhero I turned out to be.

He pressed the heels of his hands into his eyes, hard, and let out a long shuddering breath. Then he steadied himself.

This was no time to start doubting his powers. No way. Out of everything that had happened to him since he had started this journey, he had never once questioned the fundamental fact that he was fulfilling his destiny. So if his mission had brought him to this place, at this point in time, then there must be a reason for it.

He sat up a bit, starting to feel better. A hero didn't *wallow;* a hero took the hand he was dealt and moved forward.

So that's what he would do.

Hiro sat the rest of the way up, absently snapping his fingers a few times while he tried to figure out where to start. He needed to take stock of everything he had, and make a plan.

Good!

Okay.

Now, what did he have?

Um. He looked around the room again, his shoulders starting to sag.

Nothing. He had nothing.

No, that was ridiculous. *Think positive!* Look, he had this *really super* motel room, for starters. And true, it wasn't exactly the luxury suite at the Hotel Okura, but at least it was a roof over his head. And it was private, too—the way his luck usually ran, he could've ended up in a capsule hotel like the ones in Roppongi, stuffed into a three-by-ten-foot coffin and stacked up with half a dozen drunken businessmen.

No, compared with that, this room was great. And it was within easy walking distance of the diner.

All right. That was one thing. What else did he have?

He had his powers. Maybe he couldn't risk teleporting, but he could still freeze time; that one he could control pretty well.

Just to prove it to himself, Hiro scrunched up his face and concentrated. He opened his eyes and looked around the empty hotel room. Nothing was moving, but then again, nothing had been before, so . . .

He heaved himself up off the bed and peeked out through the heavy, scratchy shades onto the concrete corridor outside his room. A statue of a man was getting ice from the machine, and a dozen cubes had frozen in an immobile waterfall.

Hiro blinked again, the ice clattered down into the bucket, and the man clumped away.

Nice. That was two. *What else?*

He had Charlie. Well, he didn't actually *have* her, but—silver lining—he now had six months to get to know her better. And she was worth it—*love* was worth it. Even though she appeared to be dating that barbarian Lloyd, which might be a problem when it came to having her fall in love with him.

Could that be part of my mission, too? Hiro wondered, grasping wildly at any straw that might make him feel better. To win her away from Lloyd?

No, that was stupid. How could he win her when he couldn't even understand her? Six-months-from-now-Charlie had only just started learning Japanese. Current-Charlie didn't speak a word of it.

For that matter, how was he supposed to save her from getting, uh, de-brained if he couldn't communicate with her?

Shoot.

Hiro wilted back down onto the bed and wished he could talk to Ando—*he'd* know what to do. But that was impossible. Ando was stuck six months in the future, so Hiro would just have to . . .

Wait a minute!

Hiro stood up very slowly and began pacing, trying not to let this train of thought get away from him before he followed it all the way to the end.

He and Ando had left for their big trip to America in September. If Hiro, standing right here right now in this hotel room, was six months in the past, it meant that they hadn't come to the States yet, or at least that Ando hadn't, right?

Last April, Ando had been working on a spending report for the mergers and acquisitions department—Hiro remembered it clearly, because Ando had complained nonstop about having to work late during cherry blossom season when the universities were on vacation and the bars were full of drunken college girls.

Which meant that at this exact moment, Ando was sitting in his cubicle at Yamagato Industries, and if Hiro wanted to talk to him . . . all he had to do was pick up the phone.

Hiro clapped his hands together in glee. Six o'clock here meant that it was eight in the morning in Tokyo, and Ando should already be at his computer, halfway through his second cup of coffee.

He grabbed the phone on the nightstand and dialed.

"Yamagato Industries" came the polite, clipped greeting of the receptionist.

"Ando Masahashi, please."

"One moment, please."

Oh my God, it's going to work!

A tinned Muzak version of Cyndi Lauper's "Time After Time" floated through the receiver as Hiro was put on hold. Hiro hummed along, trying to figure out what he would say to Ando. It had been hard enough to convince him of his powers when they were face-to-face; he wasn't sure how he was going to do it over the phone.

Well, he'd figure something out—all that mattered was that he had this lifeline.

"*Moshi moshi!*"

Hiro's face split in a grin at the sound of his friend's voice. He clutched the phone tighter, words bubbling out of him.

"Ando! I need your help! I—"

"Sorry, Ando is sick," the voice on the other end of the line said. "This is Hiro Nakamura."

"Great Scott!"

Hiro dropped the receiver with a clatter. Holy moly! He had just talked to himself! A *definite* violation of the space-time continuum. This wasn't good.

This wasn't good at all.

Hiro stared at the phone, wondering what horrific events were happening to himself in Tokyo as a result of that phone call. Although— there was a tiny ray of hope—maybe past-Hiro, as he thought of himself for lack of anything better, hadn't recognized his voice. That might mean that the space-time continuum hadn't actually been breached.

Because if it had, he would feel it, right? Like, he would remember it now if he'd ever gotten a phone call from the future, wouldn't he?

This was the problem with time travel. There were so many theories about wormholes and parallel chronologies and paradoxical incongruities that you didn't know which one to believe. And it was all conjecture anyway—there wasn't a definitive set of rules written down anywhere, a Bushido code for mucking around with history.

He remembered the first time he'd tried to explain to Ando, right after he'd discovered his power. They were sitting at a back table in a bar in Shinjuku, nearing the bottom of their bottle of *shochu*.

"Most people perceive time as a straight line, always going forward," Hiro had said, shouting to be heard over the pink-haired girl who was singing onstage, mangling a karaoke version of "Groove Is in the Heart" at top volume. "Like this," he continued.

He'd dipped a chopstick into the small dish of soy sauce on the table, left over from the order of *shabu shabu* they had inhaled, and used it to draw a narrow straight line on his paper place mat.

"But time is actually more like this—"

Using his finger, he smeared the soy sauce into a circle.

Ando raised his eyebrows, either impressed by Hiro's knowledge or considering whether to order another plate of *shabu shabu*. "Where did you learn all this?" he asked skeptically.

Hiro shrugged, a little deflated. "Comic books, mostly," he admitted.

"Awesome," Ando had said, his voice flatly ironic. Then he lifted a hand and motioned for the waiter.

But actually? He had learned a lot from comic books. Everything he knew—really, everything *anybody* knew—about time travel came from comic books, sci-fi movies, or old Ray Bradbury and Isaac Asimov stories.

His entire life, Hiro had devoured every bit of science fiction he could get his hands on, and it was lucky for him that he had. Even if he couldn't predict for certain the final result of bending time and space, at least he had a good idea of where he needed to tread lightly.

And chatting on the phone with his past self? Unanimously considered a bad idea. So Hiro couldn't risk trying to call Ando again, even though this time there seemed to have been no harm done.

Except to his bank account—Hiro picked up the little card that sat next to the phone, listing the rates, and his jaw dropped. *Holy cow!* Apparently that ninety-second call had cost him close to thirty bucks.

What a ripoff.

Well, he could afford to pay it, he thought, adding another tick to his list of positives.

His paycheck at Yamagato Industries may have been as puny as his position, but Hiro himself was loaded. Mostly because his grandmother was exceedingly generous with her only male progeny when it came to birthdays and holidays. And with no girlfriend to take out to fancy restaurants, or buy jewelry for, or whisk away on romantic weekend trips, Hiro had nothing to spend his money on.

His parents had bought him his apartment as a bonus for managing to get through four years of college. So other than comic books, video games, and the occasional evening out at a karaoke box with friends, Hiro saved every yen he received. As a result, could easily pay for anything he needed on this trip, even if it was going to last six months longer than he had originally expected. Plus, there was always his Yamagato Industries corporate card, in case of emergencies.

Too bad he couldn't just write out a check to save Charlie, he thought ruefully. Or pay to make her fall in love with him. Or buy her the ability to speak Japanese.

Oh my God.

Lightning struck twice, as he realized he *could* buy her the ability to speak Japanese!

Future-Charlie was learning from a phrase book—*one that she received on her birthday.*

It all made sense!

Hiro would give her that phrase book—once again, it was destiny. He wasn't altering the space-time continuum by being here at all, because when he met Charlie in the future, he had already given it to her.

Hiro let out a shout—trying for "boo-yah!" like they said in America, but ending up with something closer to a gargle. He jumped up and down, doing a little booty-wiggle dance of joy.

Saving Charlie was part of his mission—that phrase book was proof.

"Boo-yah!" he burbled again, then grabbed his jacket and headed for the door. All heroes need a place to start, and Hiro had just found his.

He was going to the mall.

8

HIRO STOOD INSIDE THE FRONT DOORS OF THE MUSIC CITY MALL, squinting in the bright fluorescent lighting, his good mood completely evaporated.

He had had such a hard time finding his way here, it was nothing short of a miracle that he hadn't just tried teleporting, even if it did mean risking running into a *T. rex*.

Midland-Odessa's public transportation system rivaled Tokyo's sprawling, tangled subways for confusion and complications. Hiro had checked and double-checked his phrase book to make sure he was saying it correctly.

"Please take me to the shopping center."

But either the phrase book's author didn't speak a word of English or the bus-riding citizens of Midland weren't the brightest folks in town, because everyone he asked pointed him in a different direction.

Three transfers and forty-five minutes later, he had somehow ended up at the main bus terminal in Odessa and was *this close* to bursting into tears of rage and frustration. How was he ever going to tackle the Brain

Man if even the vapid, dough-faced ticket booth attendant could get the best of him?

He was attempting and failing for the millionth time to make himself understood by the reviled ticket agent when an elderly woman sitting on a nearby bench crooked a gnarled rhinestone-covered fingernail at him, gesturing him over to her seat.

She rummaged in her enormous denim pocketbook for a pen, then scrawled "Music City Mall" on the back of a Starbucks receipt. Without a word, she pinned it onto the front of Hiro's jacket, like he was a little kid on the first day of school.

It was supremely humiliating, but . . . it worked.

The attendant pointed him to the correct bus, and the next thing Hiro knew he was walking through the spotless glass doors of the mall.

Hiro's big sister, Kimiko, was a big believer in retail therapy.

Whenever she was upset, she'd go buy something to cheer herself up. Hiro had always thought this was the dumbest thing he'd ever heard. A new pair of shoes wasn't going to erase the worry about a failing grade or being berated by your boss—it just didn't make sense.

But after an hour of strolling around the mall, Hiro had to admit his sister may have been on to something, because he was feeling a thousand times better. The Music City Mall was *awesome*—he could happily spend the next six months wandering its halls.

He had figured that, while he was there, he might as well buy a change of clothes and a toothbrush, since it looked like he was going to be stuck here-and-now for quite a while. But since he couldn't make heads or tails out of the giant plastic shop directory that stood by the front entrance, and he wasn't in the mood to try to ask anyone else for directions, he decided just to walk around until he stumbled across the stores he needed to visit.

After all, it wasn't like he was in a hurry—he couldn't see Charlie again until the next day, and if the mall closed before he found everything he needed, he could just freeze time and shop as long as he liked.

He ate dinner at a restaurant called the Chik-Fil-A in the food court, spent an amusing ten minutes at the indoor ice rink watching the skaters fall on their behinds, and found a surprisingly large selection of phrase books for Charlie at the B. Dalton bookstore. He'd also gone a little overboard shopping for himself.

He'd meant to just pick up one or two things, but by the time he'd finished he was loaded down with two pairs of blue jeans, some black track pants, two white buttondown shirts, a blue western-style shirt, a green DON'T MESS WITH TEXAS T-shirt, a navy T-shirt with a silhouette of a skateboarder on it, a red hoodie, two three-packs of underwear, a white trucker's cap that said HOT SLICE across the front, some black-and-silver Puma sneakers, and—he wasn't sure *why* he wanted them, he just knew that he had to have them—a pair of red ostrich cowboy boots.

Well, he was going to be here for six months, he rationalized, adding a belt, some black plastic sunglasses, and a six-pack of socks to the pile at the last minute.

Already wrestling with his purchases, he stopped by the big Phar-Mor drugstore and got the basics—toothbrush, comb, shampoo that smelled like raspberries. He also, feeling a little guilty, bought himself a handheld electronic basketball game. He knew he wasn't here—in the past, in Texas—to have fun, but he also saw a lot of empty, lonely hours stretching out in front of him, and he just couldn't face going back to the hotel with nothing to do and no one to talk to.

He headed toward where he thought the exit was, then realized he'd gotten completely turned around. Foot Locker, Orange Julius, Forever 21 . . . wait—Foot Locker again? Would a mall have two Foot Lockers?

He shut his eyes for a second and took a deep, calming breath, making a silent vow to be more diligent in studying his English.

Then he opened his eyes and picked a new direction to walk in.

Okay, this wasn't right, either—but it was okay, he hurried to tell himself, he was calm, he was Zen, lots of people got lost in malls, he'd find his exit eventually.

And when he turned to try a different way out, he saw something that would have made him throw his arms up into the air in happiness if they weren't weighed down by close to six hundred dollars' worth of new clothes.

A comic-book store.

And not just *any* comic-book store, but a big one, a superior one, a *heroic* one, he thought delightedly. Because it carried manga.

Hiro stepped inside and moved through the aisle, running a reverent finger lightly over the spines of the chunky graphic novels he loved. A bunch of the titles were in English, series he had never heard of. But— aha! He pounced on an issue of *Fushigi Yuughi,* which technically was for girls, but he didn't care—he'd be happy with a battered copy of *Sailor Moon,* just to have something familiar.

He kept rummaging through the stacks. A *Hagane no Renkinjutsushi* he'd already read, but—*who cares*—he was getting it. *Gōsuto Suīpā Mikami Gokuraku Daisakusen,* which he'd never heard of, but it was in Japanese, so—*definitely getting it.*

He was juggling half a dozen comic books and still looking for more when the gangly sales kid working the cash register moseyed over. He had a handwritten name tag on his shirt that said PJ, and he dangled an empty shopping basket from one finger.

"Need a hand?" PJ took the books Hiro was holding and examined the titles as he put them in the basket. "You like the Japanese ones, huh?"

He had a pimple like a third eye taking up most of his forehead. Its ripe yellow yolk glared down at Hiro.

"Yes, thank you."

"Then get a load of *this*—"

PJ pulled open the storage drawer underneath the comics display and pulled out three plastic-covered books, handing them to Hiro with a grin.

Hiro gasped.

Robogirl!

Three perfect, pristine issues of *Rachel Red: Robogirl.*

He suddenly found it hard to breathe.

Robogirl was an android, a bounty hunter whose robotic hands could morph into any weapon in the world. She was built and programmed to be a gun for hire, a ruthless assassin who would track down and kill her targets quickly, tirelessly, and dispassionately.

But someone, somewhere along the way had reprogrammed her. A couple of wires crossed, circuits rerouted, and just like that Robogirl had developed emotions. She could *feel*—compassion, love, regret.

It was at once an act of misguided mercy and one of astounding cruelty. Because it didn't alter her fundamental purpose: she was still a killing machine. Only now, with each new assignment, she ended up killing a little piece of herself in the process.

She was more than just a comic-book character to Hiro, and not just because she had fueled every fantasy, every dream that he had experienced since he was twelve. Robogirl was constantly searching for connection, a way to feel like she was part of things, like she belonged.

Hiro knew exactly how she felt.

And to find her here, in this too-big, too-noisy shopping mall? Hiro clutched the comic books to his chest, something heavy pressing behind his eyes, feeling like he was going to cry or faint or start hooting like an owl or something. He hadn't found just his favorite manga in this utterly foreign place. He had found a *friend.* A sense of Home.

Robogirl wouldn't give up on a mission just because she was scared and alone and far from home. *Hell no!* She'd use that as an excuse to kick even more ass. She'd push through it and get the job done.

So that's what Hiro would do, too.

"These books are *sick,*" PJ said, snapping his fingers in Hiro's face to wake him up. The pimple was throbbing like it had a heartbeat of its own. "She's supposed to be a robot, but—*check out her rack!*"

Hiro looked at him, his face serene. Perhaps he wasn't the only one with an active fantasy life.

"I'll take them," Hiro said, dropping the *Robogirl* issues into his shopping basket and digging out his cash one more time.

He knew he could handle finding the right bus back to the motel now. He could handle anything.

Because now, he wasn't alone.

9

H<small>IRO'S NEW AND IMPROVED CONFIDENCE STUCK WITH HIM FOR THE</small> rest of the evening, but the second he turned out the light to try to get some sleep, all his insecurities came rushing back.

He lay on the gummy motel sheets in a cold sweat, eyes wide open in the dark room, terrified about his plan—about the fact that he *had* no plan, aside from giving Charlie the phrase book.

How was he supposed to convince her that, six months from now, she needed to stay home from work so she wouldn't get the top three inches of her head lopped off? He couldn't just tell her that and leave. She'd think he was nuts.

Actually, she'd probably think he was nuts anyway, or some kind of stalker, if he just hung out in the diner all day, every day until October. He needed an in, a way to get close to Charlie without seeming creepy or crazy, and he had no idea how to go about it.

He tossed and turned for hours, churning up the blankets in a froth of panic and self-doubt, until he couldn't take it anymore. He turned on the light, sat up, and his eyes settled on—*salvation!*—the giant bag of Cheetos he had bought at the mall.

He crouched in front of the minibar, selecting a three-dollar can of

Coke. Then he stuck his head out the door, checking both ways to make sure no one was around, and scurried across the ten feet to the ice machine, clad only in his underwear.

He scooped up ice in a plastic cup and dashed back to his room. There, he poured the Coke over it.

Half of it was gone in one gulp, so he topped it off with a second soda, then carried the Cheetos and the cup back to bed. He settled back against the headboard, opened the bag, took a sip of his drink, and propped open one of the new mangas he had bought, resting it on his knees.

He just needed to read for a few minutes and take his mind off the Charlie problem, he thought. Then he could get a good night's sleep and start fresh the next day.

He opened the comic book.

Probably his brain would come up with a plan while he was asleep, he decided. Let his subconscious figure it out.

Hiro finally managed to drift off to sleep as the glowing red numbers on the beside clock-radio blinked from 5:16 to 5:17, and when the alarm went off an hour later, he slapped it silent with a groggy hand and fell back onto the pillow.

He only woke up for real when the sun had risen so high that it slanted through the venetian blinds and hit him straight in the eyes.

He struggled upright and was dismayed to discover that it was already after ten.

Son of a—

Great start to his big, heroic rescue, he mused bitterly.

He raced through a shower, ripped the tags off his new jeans and skateboarder shirt and threw them on, then trotted the short distance from the motel to the diner, his brain working like sixty. He still didn't have any idea how he could get close to Charlie.

He glanced around wildly, hoping to be inspired. He needed a sign, something to tell him what to do. And as he drew near to the diner, he got one.

Literally.

Taped up in the front window of the diner was a small piece of paper, with HELP WANTED written on it in Charlie's curvy cursive script.

Bingo!

Hiro slowed his pace, catching his breath and mopping the nervous sheen of sweat off his brow before he approached the door. He'd never had to apply for a job before . . . but how tough could it be?

He checked out his reflection in the glass of the diner window, nodding in approval. Then he took a deep breath and sauntered inside.

The diner was nearly empty—the breakfast crowd had already paid up and hurried off to work, but it was too early for the lunch rush to have begun.

Maybe oversleeping hadn't been such a bad thing after all.

Charlie looked up from the counter, where she was rapidly filling in all the blank spaces in a newspaper crossword puzzle.

"You're back!" she said, and she treated Hiro to such an irresistible smile that any lingering doubts he'd had about the mission vanished for good.

God, she was cute.

Hiro nodded. "Yes, I decide to stay in Midland. Six months," he said as casually as he could manage. He settled onto a stool at the counter across from where she was standing, and carefully placed the plastic bag containing the Japanese phrase book on the seat next to him.

Charlie coffee-and-doughnuted him. Then, after a quick glance around the diner to make sure no one needed anything, she poured herself a cup, as well. She rested her elbows on the counter and smiled at Hiro.

"I thought about what you said, about not coming in to work today," she said, sounding a little guilty, "but I couldn't afford to miss a day's pay. So."

Oh yeah.

"That's okay," he said. He dipped his cruller into his coffee, the same way Charlie was doing, then popped it into his mouth.

Heaven.

She passed him a napkin. "You never told me why you thought I shouldn't come in, though."

Hiro chewed carefully, buying time while he figured out how to answer.

He probably shouldn't just blurt out that he had seen her murdered, off in the future. After all, he had six months to convince her to stay away from work—no need to scare her off in the first five minutes. And he needed to earn her trust. He needed to take things slow, reveal his powers when the time was right.

"Old tradition in Japan," he finally said awkwardly, "Skip work day after birthday." Hiro Nakamura, Master of Improvisation.

But Charlie seemed to buy it. "Someday I'm going to go to Japan," she said wistfully. "I'm going to go everywhere. And Tokyo is going to be the third stop on my trip around the world."

Perfect—nice and easy, straight down the middle.

"This help when you get there—" Hiro reached for his bag and pulled out the phrase book, which he'd clumsily wrapped in paper covered with cartoon penguins wearing party hats. "I bring you gift."

"Really?" Charlie took the present, looking surprised and pleased. "Well, thank you."

He shrugged one shoulder, looking down at the counter modestly.

"Happy birthday," he said.

She tore off the wrappings, and her eyes lit up when she saw the book.

"Oh—I love it! Now we'll be able to understand each other."

"Exactly."

Charlie opened the book, flipping through the pages until she found what she was looking for.

"*You are a kind and generous man,*" she read, her Texas accent flattening out the Japanese vowels.

"You read very well."

"Thanks, I just—" Charlie's cheeks turned a little pink. "Lately I can do all sorts of new things that I never could before. It's weird." She absentmindedly reached behind her back to grab the steaming coffeepot, refilling both their cups.

Hiro wrinkled his nose. "Weird for you. Great for me. Now I have someone to talk to while I here. Teach me good English."

Charlie laughed, still thumbing through the book, her eyes racing over the text, photographing it.

"Are you staying in Midland for vacation?"

"No—I look for job," Hiro said, and flapped a hand toward the sign in the window.

"Oh!" Charlie sat up straight, clapping her hands together excitedly. "Our busboy is moving to Austin—I don't suppose you'd be interested—"

"Yes! That be perfect."

Charlie grabbed Hiro's hand and pulled him around behind the counter into a tiny employee break area crammed between the short line and the giant silver dishwashers.

A row of cubbies lined the cramped hallway that led into the break room. Hiro could tell at a glance which one was Charlie's. Stickers of silver and gold stars were pressed around the edges, and inside was a stack of books—Hiro couldn't read the titles, but they looked serious and intelligent. They fought for space with a well-worn pair of running shoes, a jumbled pile of work aprons, a toy hula dancer, and the bottom half of a small toy globe, which held an assortment of hair ties, earrings, and bottles of nail polish.

The little collection perfectly reflected Charlie's personality: fun, smart, girly . . . a dreamer.

Hiro touched a finger to the hula dancer, making her bobble and sway.

Charlie, still holding Hiro's other hand, gave a tug, pulling him the rest of the way into the break area.

A sphere-shaped woman was seated at a card table piled high with newspapers, empty mugs, and half a dozen cases of Tabasco sauce, her feet up on the mismatched chair across from her. Hiro recognized her as the waitress who had snapped the photo of him with Charlie the day before.

She was eating a piece of something she called apple pandowdy, and crumbs kept dropping down and landing on the shelf formed by her massive breasts.

"Good news, Lynette!" Charlie announced, "I've found us a new busboy."

Lynette rolled to her feet, smiling broadly.

"I'd like you to meet Hiro Nakamura, from Tokyo, Japan," Charlie said, giving Hiro a little encouraging push forward.

Even though Lynette barely came up to his chin, Hiro felt like she was looming over him. She seized his hand, shaking it so vigorously that the crumbs on her chest were all knocked to the floor.

"How do you do?" Hiro said, in English, and he gave her a polite little bow.

Lynette beamed at Charlie.

"How do you like that!" she said, sounding impressed. "I thought they only did that bowing in the movies."

Hiro just shrugged and, without thinking about it, bowed again. Charlie and Lynette both laughed, and Hiro straightened up, embarrassed.

"Hiro's going to be visiting Midland for a few months," she told Lynette, "and I told him that it worked out perfectly for us, what with Daniel leaving for Austin and us needing a busboy so desperately."

"Well, bless his heart." Lynette turned her gaze back on Hiro. "Are you looking for a job, sweetie?"

"A job, yes."

"Well, then, let me find the paperwork."

She started rummaging through the mess on the table, and Hiro shot Charlie a worried glance.

"Papers—" he said in English, then stopped. *Uh-oh,* he thought. You probably needed some sort of visa or stamp on your passport to work in America. Which he, of course, didn't have.

Damn it!

Maybe he could counterfeit the papers somehow? He was pretty good at Photoshop. If he could get onto a computer, he could probably whip something up. Only—he didn't know what they were supposed to look like.

Okay, no problem—he could freeze time, break into whichever government office handled this sort of thing, and find a sample work visa that he could use as a template. Then—

No, that was too complicated.

It would be easier just to pretend he was a US citizen. Hiro Smith. That gangly kid at the comic-book store looked like the type of guy who would know where to get fake IDs. He could go back to the mall and slip the guy a few bucks. As long as no one else took the busboy job in the meantime, it could work out.

Simple, right?

"I don't have my work papers with me right now—" he started to explain in Japanese, but Lynette caught his expression and gave him a reassuring thump on his back.

"We just need to get your contact info." Her voice dropped to a whisper. "We pay in cash, y'know, so—no harm, no foul."

She shifted her eyes around the room, as though she expected to see INS agents lurking behind the industrial-sized vats of Crisco.

Caught up in the moment, Hiro also scanned the shadows.

Huh.

Well, cool by him.

Lynette finally unearthed a crinkled, xeroxed form from under a stack of ancient *Newsweek*s. She pulled a pen out of her apron pocket, uncapped it with her teeth, then looked at Hiro expectantly. "What's your address?"

Hiro glanced from her to Charlie before he replied. "Midland Motor Lodge, room sixteen."

Charlie raised an eyebrow.

"You're going to stay in that grody motel for six months?" Hiro opened his mouth to answer, but she cut him off. "No. You need to find an apartment."

"I guess so," Hiro said uncertainly.

Charlie wasn't finished. "There are four places available within walking distance of here. Six Twenty-four Westland Drive, Ninety-three East Seventh Street, Seventy-one Twenty-three Grubb Road, and Forty Progress Street." She stopped and let out a little embarrassed snort. "I saw the classified ads in this morning's paper and, well—that's just how my brain works."

Ah. In that case—

"Can you tell me how to go these places?" he managed in English.

"If you don't mind holding off until after the lunch shift, I'll take you there myself."

Awesome!

"Okay. I wait for you."

Charlie gave his arm a friendly squeeze. "Wait for me, nothing—it's time for you to get to work!"

She turned to Lynette, who was still waiting patiently with her pen poised over the form.

"He's apartment hunting," Charlie told her in a matter-of-fact voice.

Lynette shrugged, dropped the paper back into the chaos on the table, then waddled over to an empty cubby and pulled out a laundered white apron, which she handed over to Hiro.

"Welcome to the Burnt Toast family!"

10

ONCE A YEAR, THE MANAGERS AT YAMAGATO INDUSTRIES ADMIN-
istered a mandatory survey—similar to the Stanford-Binet test—
to all their employees.

The Hasaii Personality Index contained nearly five hundred questions, ranging from "If there are no towels in the restroom, and no one
else is around, would you wash your hands anyway?" to "How many
times have you cried in the past year?" It was designed to assess employees' emotional health, measure workplace satisfaction, and red-flag any
problems that might affect worker efficiency and productivity.

It was also yet another way Kaito Nakamura could keep tabs on his
son.

He had been giving Hiro the test ever since he was a little boy, and
Hiro had never once failed to disappoint his father with the results.

It wasn't that the tests indicated that Hiro was stupid or mean. They
just showed an overall lack of ambition that both angered and baffled
his father.

"What's the matter with you?" he'd asked Hiro every year since he
was five and had first started at the *yochien*.

Kaito would lean forward, sitting in the straight-backed wooden chair in his study, and shake the test results at Hiro, making the paper snap in the air.

"How are you ever going to be a success if you don't apply yourself? What on earth could have possessed y—

Then he would pause and shout, *"Put down that comic book and look at me when I'm speaking to you!"*

Hiro would dutifully drop the manga and fasten his eyes onto his father's face, but his mind would still drift away. He'd heard this speech a million times before, and it always ended the same way: "If you don't straighten up and get busy, you're going to end up washing dishes for a living!"

When it was over Hiro would always stand and bow, rolling his eyes while his face was down and his father couldn't see them. Then he would say "Yes, Father, I'll try harder," and he'd go back to behaving the exact same way he always had.

Never once in all those years did he ever imagine that his father might be right.

11

Hiro spent a surprisingly pleasant afternoon at the diner, wiping down tables and carrying trays of dirty plates back to the dishwasher. Even though he couldn't always understand everything that was said to him, he was so cheerful and greeted all the customers so enthusiastically that an hour into his shift, he had already made a dozen new friends.

Charlie had absorbed a large portion of the phrase book during her breaks, and although he had to correct her on her accent here and there, by the time they left work and headed off to check out apartments she was speaking in excellent Japanese.

Does she have any idea how great her superpower is? Hiro wondered. Did she even realize that it *was* a superpower and not just a fluke, some random *Ginkgo biloba*–fueled synapses waking up and getting busy?

No one at the diner seemed the least bit surprised by the rapidity with which she was able to memorize this utterly foreign language. But maybe she had always been this way, always remembered lunch orders for a dozen people without writing them down. Never forgot anyone's birthday, and rattled off the phone numbers of everyone she knew without batting an eye. Maybe her friends thought these new abilities were just a part of that, part of how she'd always been. Charlie-with-the-good-memory, like Bill-who-can-wiggle-his-ears, or Suzy-with-the-squeaky-laugh.

Hiro was dying to ask her about it, if for no other reason than to help put his own powers into context. He'd talked to Ando about how extraordinary it felt to wake up one morning and suddenly have this unbelievable ability to bend time, but since Ando didn't have a superpower of his own, it wasn't the same. Ando didn't know what it felt like.

Nobody did . . . except maybe Charlie.

But: *maybe.* He kept getting stuck on that word.

Because if Charlie didn't recognize that what was happening to her memory was nothing short of miraculous, or if she suspected it but didn't want to face those suspicions, squashed them down into some dark corner of her brain where she wouldn't have to think about them, then Hiro might ruin everything by bringing it up too soon.

They reached the first apartment building on the list, and he followed Charlie to the front door, feeling slightly guilty about checking out her sway, poured into a perfectly faded pair of jeans, as she skipped up the steps in front of him.

Six months, Hiro reminded himself. He had six months to get past that *maybe. But would it be enough?*

Charlie rang the doorbell, then turned to smile at him, and he blushed, jerking his eyes up from her body to her face a split second before she caught him staring.

He could do it. Look at how far he'd come in just one day.

"It's a little small," Mr. Roiz said, "but like I always tell the wife, it's not the size that matters—it's how much you pay in rent!" He elbowed Hiro in the ribs and chuckled, revealing two gleaming rows of tiny, Chiclet-shaped teeth.

Hiro shot a questioning glance at Charlie, but she just rolled her eyes: *Don't ask.*

The landlord squatted down, knees protesting creakily, to fish the door key out from under the worn sisal welcome mat. His shorts drooped, revealing a good three inches of the deep cleft dividing his plump pink buttocks.

Hiro winced, managing to wrestle his expression back to neutral as Mr. Roiz heaved himself upright and unlocked the door.

"Behold!" he said, standing back to let Hiro and Charlie enter ahead of him.

Hiro took one step inside and practically bumped into Charlie, barking his shin on the coffee table that occupied most of the available floor space.

Small? No, the apartment at 40 Progress Street wasn't small—it would have had to double in size just to become small. It was tiny, minuscule, barely the size of Hiro's cubicle at Yamagato Industries. You couldn't even describe it as a closet—it was a *cupboard.*

A bed took up fully half the room, stacked with lumpy throw pillows to form a makeshift couch, with less than six inches of wiggle room between it and the coffee table, which was a groovy chrome-and-glass 1970s throwback. A microwave oven, precariously perched on top of a dorm fridge, made up the kitchen. Plywood shelving ran floor-to-ceiling up the side wall.

Mr. Roiz gestured expansively around the room, pointing out the highlights.

"That mattress is practically brand new, and the wife crocheted the afghan herself."

Charlie translated, and Hiro made appreciative *aah!* sounds. Mr. Roiz beamed.

"You got your color TV here," he said, crossing to the shelves and brushing a thick layer of dust off an ancient set. "You wanna change the channel, you just use these pliers, keep 'em right here on top of the set."

"Very smart," Hiro agreed.

"Whaddaya think?" Mr. Roiz crossed his arms over his chest and nodded, like he was agreeing that *Yes, this place is spectacular!*

"Where's the bathroom?" Charlie asked.

"Down the hall, first door on your left."

She raised a skeptical eyebrow, and the landlord's face took on a wounded expression, as if she'd just said his baby was ugly.

"Utilities are included," he informed her, then shifted his weight Hiro-ward, turning his back on Charlie, as much as he could in the small space.

"What do *you* think?" he asked Hiro pointedly. "You like? You take?"

Hiro took another look around the room. Despite its obvious flaws, Hiro had a good feeling about the place. Progress Street—Charlie translated the word for him—he liked that. It felt hopeful, prescient. How could he *not* succeed at his mission living on Progress Street?

"Yes, I take it," he told the landlord, who clapped him on the back, then shuffled off double-time to get the lease.

"Are you sure about this?" Charlie asked him, her nose wrinkling slightly. "We could probably find something nicer if we kept looking."

"No, it'll be great. You'd be surprised at what a difference a little hot water and elbow grease will make," Hiro reassured her, then cringed. *Elbow grease?* What was he, ninety?

But Charlie smiled. "Well, as soon as it's fixed up you'll have to have me over for a housewarming."

Hiro jumped. "How about Friday?"

"You'll have time to get this place into shape by Friday?"

Hiro nodded—he had all the time he needed.

"Okay then," Charlie said, "Friday it is."

12

WHEN THE DOORBELL RANG, HIRO TOOK A DEEP BREATH, QUICKLY squeezing his eyes shut and freezing time, then tornadoed around the apartment, making sure all the finishing touches were in place.

For the last couple of days he had spent virtually every minute, both natural and frozen, getting the apartment—and himself—ready for his date with Charlie, and he wanted every detail to be perfect.

Although—*was* it a date?

It was time spent alone in the evening with the woman he adored, but that didn't necessarily make it a date.

You could have a crush on, oh, say, for example, the woman who ran the math enrichment program at the *juku* where you were cramming for your university entrance exams. But just because she offered to come to your house and tutor you in calculus, which you were failing, it didn't mean that was a date.

And if you acted like it was and, again, just hypothetically, tried to put your arm around her shoulders and touch her boob using the yawn-and-stretch method you'd seen in practically every American movie they showed at the Shinjuku Bunka Cinema, you were going to find out pretty fast that it *wasn't*. And you'd better have some ice on hand for your fat lip, and a plausible excuse at the ready for your father, who *"can't believe the phone call I just received,"* and *"are you trying to send me to an early grave?"*

No, Hiro wasn't sure if tonight was a date or not. But he *hoped* it was. And he'd certainly prepared for it as if Charlie were expecting to be whisked directly from the door to the bed to . . . paradise.

The most important thing, he had decided, was to make sure everything was clean. Hiro might not have had much luck or experience with women, not personally, but he knew enough from listening to his sister's stories about the dates she went on. He knew that the one unforgivable sin in any man's apartment was dirt. Filthy bathtubs, food-specked dishes, rumpled piles of clothes—basically everything he'd had in his apartment in Tokyo was a surefire way to repulse women.

But in Tokyo he'd never bothered to pay attention to the state of his home. Here, though?

Here cleanliness mattered.

Hiro had polished the place until his reflection bounced back at him from every surface, sterilizing and scrubbing from floor to ceiling. Then, dizzy from the fumes, he'd reeled out onto the front lawn, where he lay woozily until Mr. Roiz came over and revived him with a can of Red Bull.

But in the end, all his hard work paid off. After a quick visit to the hardware store and a few hours of solid effort, Hiro had managed to transform the dank little room into a cross between a ninja's lair and an opium den, with a little FAO Schwarz thrown in for good measure.

He painted the shelves a lacquered candy-apple color and found a couple of sleek, enameled chairs and a midget-sized table to match. He returned the musty homemade afghan to the landlady, with much bowing and *domo sumimasen*–ing to show that there was no disrespect intended, and replaced it with a soft black jersey bedspread.

White walls and a pale bamboo floor covering made the room seem bigger and more serene. And after struggling to connect a DVD player to the ancient TV, he'd finally replaced it with a new and bigger one.

He debated for a long time about whether or not to light candles when Charlie came over. Would that seem romantic? Perhaps too romantic? Too creepy?

In the end he decided to have a candle displayed—a big fat pillar with three separate wicks—but not to light it. Not unless he was encouraged.

With his growing collection of manga splayed across the coffee table and his clothes neatly stowed on the shelves, the apartment was good to go.

Getting himself ready had taken even longer. He spent an hour in the shower, another in front of the mirror.

Choosing the perfect outfit had required four additional trips to the mall, getting lost only twice—*See? progress already!*—as he assessed and revised every single item of clothing he had planned to wear, from his sexy-yet-modest underpants (black briefs with alternating shiny and matte stripes) to his shoes—oh, how he wanted to wear those red cowboy boots, but in the end he chickened out, going with his new black Pumas instead—to his T-shirt, which he actually *ironed,* just in case Charlie didn't equate rumpledness with masterful virility.

He was set and ready to go a good forty-five minutes early, so he used the remaining time to stare tensely in the mirror, his mood cycling wildly through every emotion from excited to nervous to vaguely nauseated.

Did he need a haircut? His bangs would look better if they were a little spikier. Maybe he could borrow some scissors from Mr. Roiz and—no! Cutting his own hair was a terrible idea.

He needed to *calm down*!

He took a deep relaxing yoga breath, then spent the rest of the time before Charlie arrived tugging at his bangs, trying to manhandle them into spikiness.

But finally, finally the doorbell rang, and he froze then unfroze time and opened the door for his date.

13

"OH MY GOD, I CAN'T BELIEVE IT!"

Charlie clapped her hands, looking around the apartment in wide-eyed amazement.

"It's so different—it's like magic!"

Hiro shrugged modestly. "I didn't do much."

"Well, I'm very impressed." She grinned at him, then held out the white paper shopping bag she was holding. "Happy housewarming."

Charlie looked like a present herself, in a pale green top that turned her hair carroty, he thought as he eagerly took the bag. He opened it and pulled out a waffle iron.

Awesome.

"In case you don't get enough waffles at work."

"Are you kidding? I *never* get enough waffles. Thank you."

He carried the waffle iron into the "kitchen" and balanced it carefully on top of the microwave, while Charlie made herself at home.

She plonked down on his bed.

"What's this?" she asked, reaching for one of his mangas. "*Robogirl?*"

"It's a Japanese comic book," Hiro said, his voice going high and squeaky at the sight of Charlie sitting on his bed. It felt strangely intimate, like she was rifling through his underwear drawer or something. "You read back-to-front."

Charlie flipped to the last page while Hiro reached into the fridge for the wine he had chilling.

He poured two glasses and carried them into the "living room." Then he sat down next to her, completely unnerved. This was the closest he'd ever gotten to being in bed with a girl. How pathetic was that?

Charlie kicked off her shoes and waggled her feet as she read the manga.

Hiro stared at them, transfixed. Each tiny toenail was painted a different shimmery pastel. They looked like candy. Hiro wanted to swoop down and tickle them. But that probably wouldn't be proper hosting etiquette. So he took a sip of his wine instead.

"Maybe next time she'd get lucky," Charlie read out loud. *"She had to hold on to her hope—it was all she had left."* She closed the book and looked up.

"That's so sad."

"Robogirl is always sad. Her adventures always end with her alone. But it's also awesome. She's my favorite." He took another sip of his wine and said without thinking, "You remind me of her."

"So, you think I'm going to end up alone?" Charlie looked at him with mock-sadness, then smiled and nudged him with her shoulder. He could feel the heat from her arm through their shirts. She felt . . . nuclear. "Or do you mean because I'm your favorite, too?"

Hiro blushed. "I mean, I think you look like her."

She glanced down at herself, at her pink denim skirt demurely covering her knees, her thin green shirt clinging loosely to her small but—Hiro thought—perfect figure, and wrinkled her nose.

"Really?"

She had a point—Robogirl was over-the-top sexy, all boobs and legs and lips. And even though Charlie was about the sexiest girl Hiro had ever seen, the sexiest girl he could *imagine,* it was a different kind of sexy. Not as—aggressive—as Robogirl.

But Hiro hadn't just been talking about looks. There was something about Charlie, some kind of spark or chemistry, that Hiro couldn't quite describe. She *glittered.* He'd never met another girl like her, had never imagined he could feel such an attraction, a physical tug, as if she were a magnet drawing him to her.

He had dreamed about feeling that way, with Robogirl always playing the starring role in those dreams. But since he had met Charlie, Robogirl was banished to the chorus line.

Charlie was watching Hiro, a teasing smile on her face, and Hiro blushed harder.

"I just mean 'cause you have red hair," he mumbled.

"I don't know," she said, flipping through the comic book to a picture of Robogirl, in spike-heeled leather boots and a bustier that barely covered her nipples, straddling a guy, clutching him between her thighs as she Ginsu-ed his carotid arteries with razored hands. "I kind of see what you mean."

Hiro gaped at her for a second, stunned, then burst out laughing.

Charlie shut the book and swatted him on the arm with it, laughing, too. "I still think it'd be nice if Robogirl ended up happy."

"Oh, but in Japan, it's not about finding happiness," Hiro said, his thoughts flickering to the plaque in his father's office: THIS IS NOT A FAIRY TALE. "It's about finding *gi*."

"*Gi?*"

"The courage to face life with equanimity."

"That's very Zen."

"Actually? It's one of the principles of the Bushido code," Hiro said, excited to be sharing something so important with her. "There were seven principles the samurai lived by. *Gi, yu, jin, rei, makoto, melyo*, and *chugo*," he recited. "Those mean—"

"Wait, don't tell me—"

Charlie drew her feet up so she was sitting cross-legged on the bed, facing him.

"Equanimity, bravery, compassion—" She bit her lip, searching for the translations somewhere in her brain. "—courtesy, honesty, honor, and . . . um. *Chugo?*" She frowned. "I don't think I know *chugo*."

"Devotion," Hiro told her in English before switching back to Japanese. "It's listed last, but it's the most important. At least, that's what Takezo Kensei thought."

"Who's he?"

"The greatest Bushido warrior of all time!" Hiro settled himself more comfortably against the cushions on the wall. Then he started to tell her the story he used to beg his father to repeat every night at bedtime when he was a little boy.

"Takezo Kensei had been a wild savage with great power. All Japan feared him. Until one day he found a sacred sword, frozen in the snow."

Charlie leaned forward, already caught up in the tale.

"From the moment Kensei held it, it focused all his strength. He said the sword let him control his power. And so he became a great leader. A hero."

As he spoke, Hiro could see the scene laid out before him: the frozen ground, the breath of the horses billowing white as they were ridden into battle, the crashing bedlam of sword against sword.

He let out a sigh and smiled at Charlie.

"I have a book at home of the Kensei Tapestries, which are hanging in the Meiji Museum. They show all the legends of Kensei. I wish I had it here to show you."

"Someday I'll go to Japan and see the real ones myself."

"On your trip around the world?"

Charlie nodded, then tilted a sip of wine into her mouth. A few drops lingered on her lips, and Hiro stared at them, fighting the urge to lean over and brush them off. In the nick of time she pulled herself up from the bed.

"Is there more wine?"

She reached out and took Hiro's half-empty glass. Her fingers brushed against his, electricity sparking between them, and—

Uh-oh.

Hiro found himself instantly, and, um, *profoundly* affected by her touch. Jeez—how completely mortifying.

"Yes," he managed to wheeze, and Charlie headed off to the kitchen.

He grabbed the pillow he had been leaning against, covering up his lap before Charlie could see it.

Mr. Roiz in the shower! he thought, frantically trying to come up with the most deflating image possible. *Grandmother in a bikini! Ando popping a zit on his butt!*

Nothing.

Damn it! What was the matter with him? Wasn't he supposed to be able to control this sort of thing by now? Maybe if he went into the bathroom and splashed some cold water on it? But that was all the way down the hall, and—*oh God*—Charlie was coming back with the wine.

"I bet you've traveled all over the place," she said, handing him his glass and settling back down beside him.

Hiro, still balancing the pillow over his crotch, clinked his glass against hers, then—painfully—crossed his legs.

"When I was younger, my dad used to take me along on business trips." The mere mention of Kaito Nakamura started to do the trick. Hiro breathed a little easier, but kept the pillow on his lap just in case.

"It wasn't very fun, though," he told her.

"Why not?"

"My father and I do not see eye-to-eye on things." *Like, everything.* "I do not think he likes me very much."

"I never knew my parents," Charlie said. "They died in a car accident when I was just a baby."

God, could he be a *bigger* jerk? "I am so sorry—"

"It's okay," Charlie said, touching his knee. "I was so little, I didn't even know them."

He shook his head. "Here I am, complaining about my own father when—"

"Seriously, Hiro, it's okay," she said again. She took her hand off his leg and leaned back against the wall. "I grew up with my aunt Erika. She worked at the diner, so everyone there became my family."

That explained a lot. No wonder everyone loved Charlie so much.

"Where is your aunt now?"

"She got married last year and moved to Phoenix with her husband. I went to stay with them at Christmas." Charlie let out a rueful little laugh. "That's about as far out of Midland as I've gotten—not exactly a banner start to seeing the world."

She gazed off past Hiro, perhaps seeing snowdrifts and battlefields of her own. "Someday, though . . ."

Watching her, Hiro felt a sudden splash of sorrow, a fierce ache of regret for the girl who was going to be murdered in the storeroom of the Burnt Toast Diner before she ever had a chance to go anywhere at all.

But *that* girl didn't have Hiro to save her. That girl wasn't Charlie—not anymore.

So, really? There was nothing to feel sad about. Charlie was still going to get to see the world; he was here to make sure of that.

Even with that hope and certainty, though, he couldn't stop himself from wondering how Kensei had ever managed to find *gi*. Because if equanimity was the sign of a true Bushido warrior, then Hiro guessed he'd never be a samurai after all.

14

"ITALY. THAT'S DEFINITELY GOING TO BE THE SECOND STOP ON MY trip," Charlie said, using her fingers to break the long string of melted cheese that stretched from her mouth to the slice of pizza on her plate. "Can you imagine if we were eating this in the Piazza San Marco?"

It was an hour later. Hiro and Charlie had moved from the bed to the table and ordered in a large pizza with sausage, mushrooms, and onions.

Hiro had hesitated when Charlie was placing the order, weighing the probability that the pizza toppings might interfere with the likelihood of them kissing each other good night. But before he had come to a firm conclusion, Charlie was already hanging up the phone, so Hiro decided that since both of them would have onion breath, it wouldn't make much difference either way.

"If Venice is second, where do you want to go first?"

"Munich. Definitely Munich. To see the Joos van Cleve at the Alte Pinakothek."

"The who at what now?" Hiro asked.

"The Alte Pinakothek is a museum," she explained. "It's got the Joos van Cleve painting *Death of the Virgin* in its collection—it contains a picture of the martyrdom of Saint Nicasius."

"Oh, of course," Hiro said, nodding.

Charlie grinned at his confused expression. "I went to Saint Nicasius's when I was growing up—that's a parochial school in Midland. And in the auditorium where we had assembly every morning, they had a giant reproduction of that painting hanging over the dais."

"Every day for twelve years, I stared at that painting and thought about what it would be like to be standing in front of the real one, in a place where I didn't know anybody and no one knew me, with people speaking German all around me . . ."

She smiled at the memory and took a sip of her wine.

"I think that's what gave me the travel bug in the first place. Instead of paying attention to what the nuns were saying, I'd just look at that painting and plan the itinerary for my trip."

"So first stop: Munich and the alto pink disco-tech," Hiro finished.

"Alte Pinakothek," Charlie said, laughing, "but yes." She smiled at Hiro, then finished her wine and set down her empty glass. "Well . . ."

"I can get you a refill," Hiro said.

Charlie shook her head. "It's getting late—I should probably get going."

Oh God, it was time—he had to kiss her good night.

"Will you be okay getting home?" Hiro asked. "I can walk you—"

"My car's right out front," she said, standing up. "I don't live too far from here." She grabbed their plates and the pizza box and carried them into the kitchen area.

Okay, just grab her by the shoulders—no, around the waist!—and plant one on her.

Be tender, yet masterful.

He followed Charlie to the front door, flapping his hands anxiously by his sides.

"Thanks for the waffle iron. You must come back for breakfast sometime." Wait—did that sound dirty? God, he *sucked* at this!

"Sometime soon," Charlie agreed. "This was fun."

"I had fun, too." *Kiss her! Kiss her now!*

She put her hand on his arm, and his knees buckled, just a little bit. "Whoops!"

"Are you okay?"

"Yeah, I just—too much to drink."

Oh yeah, he was a smooth operator all right. A real sex machine.

"Good night, Hiro," Charlie said. She leaned close and brushed his cheek with her lips.

Then she disappeared through the door.

Hiro didn't move for a few minutes. Partly because, for the second time that night, walking would be—um, *difficult* in his condition.

But mostly because as long as he stayed by the door, at least in a little way, the evening wouldn't end.

15

THE NEXT FEW WEEKS CAME CLOSE TO BEING THE HAPPIEST IN Hiro's life, as he and Charlie grew closer and closer. The one thing marring his pleasure was the knowledge, always hanging over him, that the clock was running, and he still hadn't figured out a plan to save her.

With each passing day, his fear and determination grew in equal measure. He couldn't let himself fail; he *had* to succeed, not just for himself, but for everybody around her.

The more he got to know the people at the diner and in the town of Midland, the more he realized just how important Charlie was to them—they cherished her, she was the glittering, beating heart of the place. And because she treated Hiro with such clear affection, the rest of the folks at the diner, employees and customers alike, welcomed him into their midst with open arms.

Hiro, who had never managed to fit in anywhere, was amazed at how well he fit in here. Within days everybody was greeting Hiro—and one another—with a friendly *"ohayo!"*—Japanese for "good morning!" Bob, the good-natured but alarmingly toothless chef, put a "meatball Hiro sandwich" on the board as a weekly special. Hiro wasn't crazy about the dish itself, a meatball sub doused in teriyaki sauce, but he was honored to have a sandwich named for him, so he ordered it after his shift every time it appeared.

The only person who didn't seem happy about Hiro's continued presence at the diner was Lloyd, the muttonchopped policeman.

Frankly, Hiro wasn't too crazy about Lloyd, either, because he knew the policeman was, at least occasionally, dating Charlie.

Though what she saw in such a big hairy doofus was beyond him.

Adding to his confusion was the fact that, while it was obvious that Lloyd had a big drooling Neanderthal crush on Charlie—Hiro was half expecting him to club her over the head and drag her by the hair back to his cave—Hiro couldn't figure out how Charlie felt about the policeman in return.

She never talked about him, or lit up when he walked into a room, or anything like that, which was definitely a good sign as far as Hiro was concerned. Then again, she wasn't exactly rubbing herself up against the milk shake machine at the sight of Hiro with his busboy tray, either.

And every now and then Hiro would see Charlie rest a light hand on Lloyd's shoulder while she was taking his order, and the sight made Hiro want to run over and let the cop know to keep his stupid shoulder—and every other part of him—far, far away from Hiro's—*ahem!*—girlfriend.

"Hey Charlie," Lloyd said, clumping after her into the storeroom, his spit-shined boots making little squeaks each time he set his foot down. "You want to come out with me on Saturday?"

"You know you're not supposed to be back here, Lloyd," Charlie reminded him, with a smile to show she didn't really mean it. She sidestepped both him and his question and reached up to the high shelf where the giant bins of sugar packets were stored.

Hiro looked up from the table where he was marrying ketchups—not to eavesdrop, just to double-check that she was all right.

The Sun-Maid calendar hung open to June to reassure Hiro that it would be months until the Brain Man came, but every time the storeroom door swung open, it still made his mouth go dry, a gut reaction. The image of Charlie's murdered body splayed on the floor seemed etched on the back of his eyelids.

But there was no avoiding it—all the prep work for the diner happened in this room, so short of bricking the door shut Hiro had to accept the fact that Charlie would be going in and out of the storeroom a hundred times before That Day.

And that was the only day that mattered.

In the meantime, at least he was here to keep an eye on her, just in case.

He watched as she shifted up on her toes, not quite balancing the heavy box of sugar packets on her fingertips, her shirt rising up at the waist an inch as she stretched, exposing a strip of smooth pale skin. Hiro stared at it, captivated—then realized Lloyd was watching him watch her.

Their eyes met for an instant, Lloyd's expression somewhere between *Caught you looking, you pervert!* and *I know, right? She's so freakin' hot . . .*

Hiro felt his face turn red and quickly dropped his gaze, returning to his work. He carefully balanced a nearly empty bottle of ketchup upside down on a half-full one, so the ketchup would drip down and combine into one full bottle. Technically, marrying the ketchup was part of the waitresses' duties, but Hiro always pitched in. Charlie, Lynette, and Shelby, who only came in on Sundays, all tipped out ten percent of whatever they'd made to him for keeping their tables immaculate, so he helped them out with their shift work in exchange.

Lloyd, who had a good eight inches on Charlie, lightly took the box of sugar from her and set it down on the counter.

"Come on," he wheedled. "The RockHounds are playing on Saturday and I got tickets to the game. Say you'll come."

Hiro looked up, accidentally knocking over half the bottles he'd managed to balance.

"RockHounds?" he echoed in a hopeful voice.

The RockHounds were the local farm team, and Hiro was dying to go see them play. He *loved* baseball. At home Yamagato Industries had a box at the Meiji Jingu Stadium, and Hiro and his father went to all the Swallows' home games together. It was the only activity they ever did together that didn't involve shouting, tears, and Kaito informing Hiro that he had brought shame on the family.

"I want to go see the RockHounds," he told Charlie in Japanese, earning an annoyed look from Lloyd.

Hiro's English had improved by leaps and bounds in the weeks he'd been working at the diner, enough so that he could carry on conversations with most of the customers he met, as long as they didn't speak too fast or have too much drawl in their West Texas accents.

But he usually stuck to Japanese when he was with Charlie, because it was easier and she liked to practice. To Hiro, it felt like an intimacy they shared. An unexpected bonus was the fact that it drove Lloyd batshit crazy that he couldn't understand them.

"It's not that I care what they're saying," Lloyd had complained a few days earlier. He was talking to Herbie, a retired oilman who was a permanent fixture at the diner counter, third stool from the end. "It just makes me feel like an ignorant hick—and I'm a *cop*, man."

Lloyd's voice rose in indignation and Hiro, who was quizzing Charlie on her transitive verbs while she brewed a new pot of decaf, hesitated.

But Charlie didn't appear to hear a word Lloyd was saying.

"I mean, I spent twenty-eight weeks at the academy in Odessa, and scored better than a seventy on every test they gave us. Plus I had tear gas shot right in my eyes, and didn't even flinch!"

Herbie let out a wheezing laugh that turned into a cough. "Sounds like somebody's jealous," he said, following Lloyd's gaze directly to Charlie.

"Jealous of *him*? Hell, no!" Lloyd grabbed a toothpick from the little porcupine canister on the counter and jammed it into the corner of his mouth.

"Not that I got anything against the little guy," he added, contemplatively stroking his sideburns. "But I mean, *come on*. He can barely grow a mustache." Lloyd snickered. "He probably doesn't even have hair on his yin-yang yet."

What the—? Hiro's jaw tightened, and his hands clenched into fists. Lloyd was lucky Hiro didn't go Yakuza on his ass. Only—Hiro wasn't sure what happened in America if you hit a policeman, though judging from some of the scary-ass shit he'd seen on CNN, it wasn't good. To say nothing of the fact that this particular policeman could flatten him with a single punch.

Still, he couldn't let the guy get away with saying something like that!

But Charlie caught Hiro's eye and gave a barely perceptible shake of her head, then picked up the fresh pot of coffee and headed over to the counter.

"Can I warm you up, boys?" she asked sweetly.

"Sure, Charlie, thanks," Lloyd said, and slid his cup toward her for a refill.

Charlie started to pour, then deliberately tilted the pot too far, sloshing hot coffee over the counter into Lloyd's lap.

"*Son-of-a-!*" Lloyd yelped, jumping to his feet and brushing the damp stained fabric at his crotch.

Charlie's eyes widened in dismay. "Oh my gosh, Lloyd!" she cried. "*Sumimasen!*"

She paused, just for an instant.

"That means 'I'm sorry' in Japanese."

Then she turned on her heel and walked back to Hiro, giving him a smile so triumphant, so satisfied, that he fell in love with her all over and over and over again.

Thinking of that now, Hiro could barely suppress a grin. "I didn't think the RockHounds were playing this weekend," he said in Japanese, scissoring his eyes from Charlie to the beefy policeman, who scowled at him.

Charlie smiled down at her sugar packets.

"It's an exposition game," she told him. "They're playing the Frisco RoughRiders on Saturday. Then the Wranglers on the eighth, the Hooks on the fourteenth, and the Threshers the day after. But those are all away games—they won't be at home again until the twenty-first, when they play the Tulsa Drillers."

Charlie rolled her eyes at her perfect retention of the Texas League schedule, then shrugged. "The Drillers are 14–0 this season, so it's not looking good for our boys."

"Do you think Lloyd could get an extra ticket for me?"

"Probably—the stadium's never more than half full anyway."

Lloyd tennis-balled back and forth between them, his expression growing stormier, until finally he couldn't take it anymore. "So, whaddaya think?" he burst in. "About Saturday?"

"I'd love to go," Charlie said. Then, as Lloyd's face broke into a grin, she hurried to add, "—and so would Hiro."

Lloyd gawped, his mouth still hanging open while his brain wheeled through possible responses. But just when the lights snapped on—

"Go where?" Lynette asked, backing into the storeroom, struggling under the weight of a full tray of silverware.

"Damn it!" Lloyd blew out his breath in frustration, then took the tray from her and set it on the counter.

"Lloyd's getting tickets to the ball game this weekend," Charlie told Lynette, flashing a mischievous look at Hiro.

"I'm in!"

Lloyd gave up. "How many tickets do we need?" he asked, his sideburns dropping glumly.

"I bet Greg and Sammy would want to come, too. We should make a day of it," Lynette said. She plopped down heavily at the table next to Hiro and began shredding a napkin into a million tiny pieces. Lynette had given up smoking—again—three days earlier. Now everywhere she went, she left behind little piles of ripped-up paper and magazine covers and labels from bottles.

"So—six. Or maybe eight, just to be on the safe side."

Lloyd sighed. "I'll make the call."

Hiro threw his arms up into the air. "Let's happy big sports fun!" he cheered in English, even though he knew better, just to mess with the cop.

Charlie snickered, quickly turning away so Lloyd wouldn't see, then stretched the sugar bin back up on its shelf.

Hiro watched her, grinning, no longer caring at all if Lloyd saw him or not.

16

HIRO LOOKED UP, STARTLED, AS HIS FATHER CAME THROUGH THE door of his bedroom without knocking, surprised by both the unexpected intrusion and the fact that it had been months since his father had ventured into his room.

Kaito Nakamura glanced briefly around, frowning in distaste at the *Star Trek* posters on the walls, the piles of laundry draped over the desk and bureau and chair, the tsunami of comic books, sneakers, homework, video games, half-eaten slices of pizza, baseball cards, and action figures strewn across the floor.

Then he perched himself gingerly on the edge of the bed, upsetting the jumble of metal gears and wires and motors Hiro was in the process of assembling into—fingers crossed—an actual working robot dog.

Hiro was turning thirteen the next day, and he felt a brief flash of hope that his father had come in to ask him for last-minute gift ideas— *robot parts!*—or to discuss the details of his birthday party. He hoped for all-day passes for himself and three friends to the Korakuen amusement park next to the Tokyo Dome.

But his hopes quickly turned to abject mortification when his father leaned forward, clasping his hands in front of him, and informed Hiro they needed to have a discussion about the facts of life.

Only not the *hard-work-is-a-part-of-life-and-that's-a-fact* sort of discussion Hiro was used to having with his father. Also, it wasn't so much a *discussion* as a *lecture,* a carefully prepared and rehearsed lecture on the birds and the bees. Or, as Kaito called it, the physical implications of becoming a man.

He kept the lecture short, dignified, and thorough, using lots of words like *tumescence* and *priapic* and *zygogenesis.* When he was finished, he asked Hiro if he had any questions.

Honestly? *Yeah.* Tons.

Not about the deed itself—while he wasn't acquainted with the vocabulary his father used, he was familiar with the process he described. No, Hiro's questions were less about the technicality of the act and more about everything you needed to do to lead up to it. Like, how did you get a girl to go from ignoring you in homeroom to being in a position where zygogenesis might actually occur?

He didn't have sex questions, he had *romance* questions. And those were something Kaito wasn't prepared to answer.

While Hiro spoke, Kaito stared mutely at his son, irritation plain on his face. He had no opinion on whether the fact that Sakumi Eisho had saved Hiro a seat in the cafeteria at lunchtime meant she liked him or not. Especially since she had spent the whole meal looking over at the table where Yoshi Animoto sat with his friends. Yoshi was a year older than Hiro, and did kendo for two hours every day after school.

Finally, in lieu of a response, Kaito got up and walked out of the room, returning a few minutes later holding the book his wife had given Hiro's sister, Kimiko, a few years earlier, when *she* had turned thirteen.

"Here," he said abruptly, setting the book down on the dresser. "This will answer your questions."

He left without another word.

Hiro picked up the book, which was called *I Like Me: A Growing Guide for Girls.* His curiosity piqued, he leafed through it.

It blew his mind.

The book was incredible—from the descriptions of girls' bodies, to the explanations of the changes they were going to go through, to the *photographs* . . . Hiro couldn't believe it.

And he couldn't believe his father had given it to him.

With each page he turned, he felt as if he were growing more mature, even becoming, dare he think it, cocksure.

Thanks to this book, he understood women now. He could talk to them and, um, *pleasure* them in ways they had never dreamed possible. He would take everything he was learning and unleash it, like a force of nature, on Sakumi Eisho.

Thanks to this brilliant book, Hiro was going to become a bona fide *stud.*

The feeling lasted for two wonderful hours, right up until his sister stuck her head in his room to call him down to dinner. Kimiko noticed what he was reading and let out a little scream.

"Oh my God, where did you get this?" she asked, pouncing on the book.

"Father gave it to me."

"Did you read it?"

Hiro nodded, holding his breath. Now his sister would realize that her baby brother was grown up, that he was about to become not just a teenager, but a *man,* an equal. Someone to be taken seriously.

Maybe she'd set him up with one of her friends. How amazing would *that* be?

Instead she started to laugh.

"Can you believe how *lame* this is?" she exclaimed. She riffled through the pages and stopped, reading a passage out loud. "Seriously—do you know any girl who would be caught dead *celebrating her menses with a personal monthly ritual?*"

She flipped the book shut and made a *how-retarded-is-that?* face at Hiro, who was lying back against his pillow, thoroughly deflated.

"God, it's just like Dad to make you read it. I mean, what century is he living in?"

"I know, right?" he agreed weakly.

She tossed the book back down on the bed.

"Anyway, dinner's ready, so come on." She flounced out of the room, leaving Hiro a muddle of doubt and self-loathing.

He should have known better. Most likely his mother had hoped the book would help guide her daughter down the proper path. Given the crowd she had begun to hang around with it hadn't served its purpose.

As for Hiro, he was more confused about girls than ever.

"I'm so glad you're here!" Charlie said—in Japanese, of course—throwing her front door open wide and giving Hiro a hug.

She had asked him if he wanted to come over after work to watch a movie, and he thought about it for, oh, about a tenth of a second before giving her an enthusiastic yes.

He'd stopped at the drugstore on the way over and bought the biggest Whitman's Sampler they had. He wasn't sure if bringing a girl a box of candy was delightfully retro or hopelessly corny, but either way, it was chocolate, so he knew it would make Charlie happy.

He handed it to her, and she ushered him inside.

This was the first time he'd been to her place, even though it was only a few miles away from his. Her apartment smelled wonderful, like oranges and almonds, and the air-conditioned chill was a welcome relief—even though it was barely summer, the West Texas weather was living up to its reputation.

The living room looked like a Hollywood set from some 1940s movie about a world traveler, the sort that would feature Katharine Hepburn as Amelia Earhart. Every inch of wall space was plastered with vintage travel posters featuring far-flung destinations. Jakarta, Dubai, Krakow, Morocco.

A string of fairy lights, shaped like miniature airplanes, bedazzled the big picture window. The bookshelves, painted cool tropical colors, held a variety of seashells, almanacs, Russian nesting dolls, Swiss cuckoo clocks, Indonesian teak boxes, a family of carved wooden elephants, and other souvenirs people had brought back for Charlie from their trips to places she had only ever dreamed of going.

A nonworking fireplace housed an iron candelabrum with a dozen lit ivory spires. The mantel was crowded with the sorts of knickknacks Hiro loved—geodes, hunks of quartz, Indian arrowheads, a rock with a two-inch-long fossil of a fish. And hanging above it was an absolutely terrifying mask, made of straw and fur and what looked like slivers of bone, grimacing out over the room.

"Yikes!" Hiro took a step back.

"That's a Zapotec shaman's mask," Charlie said, following his gaze, a laugh playing around the corners of her mouth. "It's from Oaxaca."

"How can you relax in here with it staring at you all the time?" Hiro asked, only half joking.

"I like it. He keeps me company. Besides," she added, "I bet Takezo Kensei wore masks that were even creepier."

True. But Hiro still wasn't getting any closer, even though he would have loved to go examine the geodes and fossils on the mantel beneath it. "Is Oaxaca on the itinerary for your trip?"

"Definitely. But that's as far south as I'm going to go, at least in this hemisphere."

"Really? I always kind of wanted to go to Brazil for Carnival," Hiro said.

"Rio would be fun," she agreed, wrinkling her nose, "but definitely not the Amazon."

"Why not?"

"The world's biggest spider lives there," she said, and shuddered. "The Goliath bird-eating tarantula. They can grow to be up to a foot long!"

"Yuck," Hiro said agreeably.

"They *hiss*. They're the only spider that makes any noise." At the very thought, Charlie gave a squeamish little shimmy, like she could feel one crawling on her. "I *hate* spiders. I'm scared to death of them."

"I kind of like them, ever since I saw *Spider-Man*."

"Ugh." Charlie shimmied again. "They're the only things I was afraid of."

"*Was?*"

It had been so long since Hiro had to correct her Japanese that he wasn't sure if her use of the past tense was a grammatical mistake or not.

Charlie rolled her eyes self-deprecatingly. "Ever since I started remembering everything, it seems like there's so much more out there to be scared of."

Hiro's stomach clenched. If she only knew how afraid she really should be . . .

But there was nothing he could do about it tonight, and he didn't want to ruin the evening. So he tilted his head toward the Zapotec mask.

"If you're not afraid of *that* guy, then I'd hate to find out what *does* scare you," he said lightly. "So, what movie are we watching?" he asked, changing the subject.

"Well, speaking of scary—" Charlie said with a laugh. She plucked a DVD from the shelf next to the TV and held it up so he could see it. "I'm afraid the Video-a-Gogo's selection of Japanese-language movies is a tad limited. The only one I could find was the original version of *The Ring*. So don't be surprised if I end up in your lap."

If only.

She stuck the movie in the DVD player, then headed into the kitchen for snacks.

Hiro walked over to the battered red suede sofa and sank down onto it. An old-fashioned traveler's trunk served as a coffee table. Piled on top of it were a couple of photo albums, a bronze pig with a clock in its belly, and a heavy art book from the Alte Pinakothek Museum.

Hiro chose one of the photo albums. He opened it up and nearly had a heart attack. The very first page held an eight-by-ten color photo of a sixteen-year-old Charlie wearing a Catholic school uniform.

Pleated plaid skirt, tight navy V-neck sweater over a white blouse with a round Peter Pan collar, knee socks . . .

He was still staring at the photo when Charlie came back in. She was carrying two longneck bottles of root beer and a sombrero-shaped platter of guacamole with tortilla chips piled around the brim.

She set the goodies down on the table, then plopped herself down next to Hiro, folding her knees up under herself. "Whatcha looking at?"

"Oh—" Hiro said guiltily, feeling like a pervert, "this was on the table."

Charlie leaned against him, putting a hand on his shoulder, so she could look at the pictures, too. Various soft parts of her body pressed up against him, and Hiro gulped hard, feeling as if he was going to faint.

"Oh my God, I look like such a dork," she squealed, covering the picture with her hand.

Yeah, right.

"That was my sophomore year at Saint Nicasius's," she said, taking the album away from him and turning the page. "I can't believe you saw that!"

As the picture went away, Hiro was unable to stop himself from letting out a sad little sigh—which Charlie, thankfully, ignored. He picked up his bottle of root beer and pressed its cool side against his forehead while Charlie chattered away, identifying the people in each picture.

"This is Debra, my best friend from elementary school. She lives in Austin now." She pointed to a photo of a sandy-haired girl with buck teeth that jutted out from her mouth at an angle perpendicular to the floor. "Oh, and here I am at Lynette's pool party last summer." Charlie in a black bikini—*nice.*

She flipped another page. "And here's me and Lloyd at my aunt's wedding last year." Charlie wore a purple sequined bridesmaid's dress that made her nose look weirdly red, while Lloyd mistakenly thought he was in a Gap ad.

On the facing page was a picture of a laughing woman in a poufy white dress.

"Oh, this is my aunt Erika!" Charlie told him, gazing down at the picture fondly.

"She looks like you."

"I know—everyone says that."

She turned to the next page and paused. Hiro looked down at the photo—a tall man with dark hair and a kind face, sprawled in an upholstered armchair, balancing a tiny baby with a bright shock of red hair on his knee.

"Is that you?" Hiro asked.

Charlie nodded. "With my dad. That's the only picture I have of him."

"Just like Robogirl," Hiro breathed.

"What?"

"The only connection Robogirl has to her past is a picture of a man holding a little red-haired girl. She thinks it's her father but she doesn't know for sure. It's part of Robogirl's lore."

"Well, I know for sure this is my father," Charlie said.

Hiro couldn't read the emotions behind her voice. "Of course," he hurried to agree. "I just meant—"

"—that Robogirl and I both have red hair?" she said, and this time she was definitely teasing, so Hiro grinned.

"Can we go back to that picture of you in the bikini?" he asked.

Charlie laughed. "No."

She flipped the page and said, "Last picture."

On the back leaf of the book was an old photo, its colors washed out. It was a picture of the Burnt Toast Diner, draped with a big festive banner that read GRAND OPENING. A dozen smiling people in pink aprons and chef's whites stood in front, smiling for the camera, their arms around one another.

Hiro looked at it, fascinated. "When was this taken?"

"In 1976," Charlie said. "The year the diner opened. I think we still have some cans of lima beans from back then, somewhere in the storeroom!"

"Oh my, is that Lynnette?" Hiro exclaimed, pointing at an only slightly smaller teenage orb with a blond beehive.

"Yep, she's been here since the beginning. And there's Bob, back when he still had some teeth," she said, pointing out the cook. Then her finger moved to the girl Bob was standing next to, his arm slung around her shoulders, and Charlie sighed.

"That's Barbie Travis—it's so sad."

"Why?" Hiro asked, looking at the girl's happy face.

"She's a waitress who was murdered at the diner."

Oh. My. God.

Hiro's jaw slammed down onto the coffee table. Or at least it seemed that way.

"*What?* What happened?"

"It was a couple of months after the diner opened. Barbie was dating one of the line cooks, a guy named Merle Eckels. He was a bad guy, had been in and out of Brownsville—that's the prison—and had lied about his past to get hired."

Charlie grimaced, then took a sip of root beer as if she was washing away the bad taste his name left in her mouth.

"He got jealous of the way she would talk with the customers, said she was flirting, accused her of doing a whole lot worse . . . and when she tried to break up with him—" Charlie gave that same little shimmy of revulsion. "—he killed her."

Good Lord.

"How?" Hiro asked, praying she wouldn't say anything about cutting out her brain.

Charlie's eyes grew wide, and she drew a finger across her throat, making a *krrrrrsssch* slicing sound.

"Holy cow!" *At least it wasn't her forehead. But still!*

"I know, horrible, isn't it?"

"Did they ever catch the guy?"

Charlie nodded. "Caught him, convicted him, and gave him a date with Old Sparky."

"Who?"

"The Huntsville Prison electric chair. That's its nickname. Eckels was the second-to-last inmate in Texas who was executed that way—in 1977 they switched exclusively to lethal injection." Charlie stopped herself, and he guessed that she had been close to reciting a long list of facts about the electric chair. Instead she just shrugged. "We had a field trip in the sixth grade, so—"

"You went on a field trip to see someone executed?" Hiro boggled.

Charlie shook her head. "We went to the Texas Prison Museum. The chair's on display there. I told you I'm remembering scary stuff now!"

She bumped her shoulder against his, then smiled. "Okay, enough talk about murder—let's watch *The Ring!*"

With that she picked up the remote and pressed PLAY. Hiro obediently turned his eyes toward the images that started flickering across the TV screen, but he wasn't really seeing them. Inside, his mind was racing, reeling, thinking about Barbie Travis.

Was there a connection between her murder and Charlie's?

Were they both somehow connected to the Brain Man?

Was all this a part of his mission, and was finding this information out somehow linked to him saving the world?

Or could it be just a coincidence? That seemed hard to believe. Although a lot of things had happened lately that Hiro never thought he would have believed.

A million questions, and no answers.

Hiro just hoped he wasn't supposed to go back and save this Barbie girl, too. He was having a hard enough time figuring out how he was going to save the girl he already had.

A scary scene in the movie made Charlie jump. She burrowed her face into his shoulder, squealing, then lifted his arm around her for comfort.

Hiro rested his arm across her shoulders, and she snuggled up against him. But while this usually would have been an occasion that would have made him leap around with glee, right now, his heart wasn't in it. He wished they could shut the movie off, even if it meant Charlie moving back to her own side of the couch.

He didn't need to watch murders on TV. He had enough of them to deal with in real life.

17

T HE SPRING BEFORE HIRO STARTED NINTH GRADE, HIS FATHER
brought him along on a six-day business trip to Madrid. Hiro hadn't
wanted to go—the trip coincided with the *Batsu-Batsu* Gaming Con-
vention in Akihabara, and Hiro had been looking forward to going for
months.

But Hiro's mother was visiting her cousins in Nagoya, Kimiko was
spending the break from school at the beach with a group of friends,
and Hiro's father wouldn't hear of letting him stay home alone.

So despite his protests, Hiro was dragged along to Spain.

It was a miserable trip across the board. Every day Kaito had meetings that ran well into the evening, and Hiro, who managed to get lost
in Tokyo, even in neighborhoods he had been to dozens of times before,
was afraid to explore the city on his own.

So he spent his time hanging around the hotel, playing his Game
Boy and sulking.

The low point of the trip came the day before they were supposed to
return home. Kaito's business associate invited Hiro and his father to go
see the bulls fighting at the Correo Topalo, in the center of town.

Hiro flat-out refused to go.

First Kaito tried to convince him.

"Senor Manfredi went to great trouble to get us tickets," he told his son. "It would be disrespectful not to go. Besides, you enjoy going to see kabuki—this is much like that. It has pageantry and spectacle. Tradition. I think you'll enjoy it."

"I *don't* like kabuki, I hate it," Hiro said incredulously. He was always amazed at how little his father knew about him. "And they don't kill a bunch of poor, dumb animals in kabuki, anyway."

"Well, I'm going, and you will accompany me," Kaito said, reverting to his usual tactics. "This discussion is ended."

It was one of the worst afternoons of Hiro's life.

The bulls seemed small, and stupid, and more confused than angry. The matadors seemed small, too, and thoughtless, like playground bullies. The bandilleros drove their knives into the shoulders of the first bull, and the instant Hiro saw its blood spilling onto the sand, he knew he wouldn't be able to take it.

He thought he was going to be sick, and stood up, but the noise and the heat, and his father's warning stare, made his legs wobble so that he sank back down into his seat.

He couldn't stand to watch, but anytime he shut his eyes, Senor Manfredi would poke a sharp elbow into his side and laugh, saying things in Spanish that Hiro couldn't understand, but he knew were insults, slurs to his masculinity.

In desperation, Hiro finally lifted his video camera and watched the fight through the lens, and was mildly comforted by the protective layer of artifice it created between himself and the death in the ring.

The camera let him pretend that the destruction he was seeing wasn't real, that the matadors and the screaming crowds and even the bulls themselves were just actors in a movie, something he could shut off whenever he felt like it. The illusion gave him the distance he needed to make it through the rest of the afternoon.

For the past few months, every time Hiro thought about Isaac Mendez, the painter he'd found murdered the first time he ever teleported, he felt that same protective layer of artifice shuttering down in front of his eyes. But now he wasn't achieving that distance through a camera lens, but through the lens of time.

If Hiro actually allowed himself to think about that day, the moment of finding the painter's body, he would probably go crazy. Or have a nervous breakdown, or go back to Japan and hide under his bed. It was so brutal and terrifying.

So he *didn't* think about it, at least not in a way that would allow the reality to come through. Instead he pushed that knowledge into a tiny room in the back of his mind, and locked the door.

Yet even though it was shut away, he couldn't forget it entirely. It was like living with violence, a blank, unfeeling violence that was always there, but that he would never see coming. It made the world feel dangerous all the time.

So when the gruesome images of that day tried to scuttle forward—*flash!*—the shutters would drop down, and he'd turn his mind instead to the happier parts of the memory. Because that whole experience had started out very happily indeed.

One second he had been on the Tokyo subway, heading home from the karaoke bar where he'd been unwinding with Ando. The next second Hiro found himself in New York, in the middle of Times Square, with no idea what he was doing there, and even less of an idea what he was supposed to do next.

For the lack of a better option, he'd started walking down 42nd Street, and nearly strolled right past that newsstand with the rack of American comic books on display, but something out of the corner of his eye made him stop and go back. Moments later he'd picked up the issue of *9th Wonders!* that revealed his destiny.

On the cover of the comic book, in perfect four-color detail, was an illustrated image of Hiro himself, wearing the same clothes he had on at that exact instant. He was standing in the middle of Times Square with his arms outstretched in overjoyed wonder, the exact same way he had thrown his arms out moments earlier, when he'd realized that he could teleport.

That he had a superpower.

Hiro had sagged against the side of the newsstand, inadvertently knocking a stack of *Celebrity Hairdo* magazines to the ground, but he didn't even notice. His eyes were riveted to the images in the comic book.

Page after page, each panel showed Hiro's journey, from the moment he stopped the clock in his cubicle at Yamagato Industries to his explaining time travel to Ando in the karaoke bar in Shinjuku. It showed him standing here, slumped against the side of the newsstand, the fallen magazines getting trampled by businessmen hurrying to catch the 1-2-3 trains uptown.

Hiro started shaking as he flipped through the pages. How could this be? What did this mean? And—what was on the next page? What would happen next?

He was afraid to look.

Instead he closed the comic book, flipped it over, and looked to see where it had come from, who had published the story of his life. On the bottom of the back cover was a small caption:

Published by Isaac Mendez, Inc., 215 Reed Street, #7, New York, New York.

Okay, so that's what he'd do: go find this Isaac Mendez and get to the bottom of everything that was happening.

Only—*was* that what he should do?

Well, there was one way to find out.

He opened the comic book again. Screwing up his courage, he picked up where he had left off. On the next page was a panel showing Hiro's head peeking around the door of a loft-style apartment, with a speech bubble that said, "Mr. Isaac Mendez? Hello?"

Awesome—then that was the plan.

He was tempted—scared, sure, but tempted just the same—to flip one more page, but before he could the surly newsstand owner, who had a face like a boil, barked, "Hey, pal. This isn't a library."

Hiro looked up from the comic book.

"No pay. No read."

Hiro pulled out his wallet. It was full of yen. He hesitated for an instant, but—*money is money, right?* And he really needed that comic book. So he tossed a handful of yen down on the counter, then ran away, as fast as he could, *9th Wonders!* clutched in his hand, on his way to Reed Street and whatever the next page held.

"Mr. Isaac? Hello?"

He walked around the room, taking in all the paintings, absolutely flabbergasted at what he was seeing.

Sketches for a comic book—a panel of Hiro talking on the phone, the dialogue bubble over his head reading, "Ando, it's me, Hiro. I'm in New York."

Another sketch showing Hiro's eyes, wide with shock at something he was seeing.

The floor covered with a mural of fire, smoke, Armageddon. The paint on the floor was still wet, a trickle of red oozing toward him.

Hiro stared down at it realizing—that wasn't paint. It was blood.

He followed the thin stream around the corner to its source, unwilling to look but unable to stop his feet from carrying him there. And that's where he found Isaac, the top three inches of his head cleaved clean off, his skull an empty cup where his brain had been.

In any other circumstances, the sight would have done him in. Finding the body alone would have been more than Hiro could handle, but just as bad were the images of destruction Isaac had painted before he died—images of Hiro's destiny.

If Hiro let his mind accept that these things were really happening, or going to happen, he would have fallen apart, hero or not.

But anytime he thought about it—the reality of the bomb, the way his shoe had skidded in the puddle of Isaac's half-congealed blood—*flash*—the protective shield of distance shuttered down. Events became just pictures, panels in a comic, no matter how portentous they seemed. None of it felt real, the same way the bullfight in Spain wasn't real.

But Charlie?

Charlie *was* real. And the closer he grew to her, the less distance he was able to achieve from the reality of what had happened in New York.

He *had* seen Isaac's body, not just in an illustration, but with his own two eyes. That murder was going to happen—for real, and soon.

And so was Charlie's.

The more time passed, the more he realized that he couldn't keep fooling himself. Telling himself that all he had to do was keep Charlie away from the diner the day of the murder. That idea seemed foolish and simplistic now. There were too many coincidences, too many pieces of the puzzle Hiro just wasn't seeing, to think that the Brain Man would be dissuaded that easily.

He needed to wake up and realize that time was running out. It was the middle of June, for God's sake, and a third of his time had slipped away. The only progress he'd made so far had been romantic, and not even much of that.

What a great superhero he was!

What a Bushido!

He'd spent two months becoming a busboy with a crappy apartment, convincing himself that he was making progress with his mission, but in actuality he was no closer to saving Charlie than he'd been the day he arrived. What a terrific way to fulfill his destiny.

No, it was time to get serious. Isaac had really and truly died, and the same thing was going to happen to Charlie unless he stopped mooning around like a lovesick otter and figured out a real, concrete plan to save her life.

Okay, but how? Where to start?

With no other ideas springing to mind, Hiro decided he would start again at the same place he had started last time—the Music City Mall.

18

"FIFTY THOUSAND VOLTS, MAN. HOW MESSED UP IS THAT?"

PJ, the gangly sales kid at the comic-book store, poked Hiro on the arm with a chewed-down fingernail and shook his head in disbelief.

The pimple was gone, replaced by an angry scarlet crater, raw and oozing. Hiro tried not to stare, but his eyes kept straying involuntarily to PJ's forehead.

"Just goes to show you—you gotta be honest with the ladies."

When Hiro first walked into the shop, PJ had greeted him like a long-lost cousin, giving a happy shout of recognition. Comic-book salesclerks led a lonely life. The kid had zipped out from behind the counter and physically dragged Hiro over to the shelves that held the Japanese manga, practically vibrating with excitement.

PJ had pulled a copy of *Robogirl* #215, which the store had just gotten in. He snatched it out of the stacks and presented it reverently to Hiro.

Hiro opened it up, recognizing it instantly as the one he'd read in Tokyo a couple of weeks before he and Ando had left for America.

In it Robogirl thought she'd finally found true love, but it turned out to be a double cross. When she discovered the deception, she got the guy back by turning her hand into a metal probe and jamming it into an electrical outlet as she kissed him good-bye, the current coursing from her lips to his, instantly frying what little heart he actually had.

PJ seemed especially taken with this story line. He flipped through the pages and shook his head again.

"You can't lie to women, they'll see right through it," he said, like he was auditioning to take over for Dr. Phil.

"You think about that, son."

After he paid for the comic and headed back out into the busy shopping mall, Hiro actually did think about it.

Maybe he *should* just be honest with Charlie. Warn her what was going to happen, so she could be prepared, or at least aware and alert. Maybe he should just come clean with her.

But how could he tell someone she was about to be murdered?

Hmm. He couldn't. For a couple reasons.

First of all, he mused, *one of the principal rules of the space-time continuum is that you aren't supposed to know too much about your own future.* Hiro wasn't exactly sure why not, but since practically every science-fiction movie Hiro had ever seen had agreed that no good could come from it, he figured it was a rule he should probably follow.

But even if telling her *didn't* mess with the laws of time and space, Hiro wouldn't know where to begin.

"So, how attached are you to your brain?"

No.

But no matter what he said, whether it was gentle or straightforward or cautionary, it was bound to freak her out. Like with seriously endless screaming and weeping, or a complete catatonic shutdown.

If he told her what was going to happen to her, she'd be utterly terrified. Not just of the Brain Man, but of Hiro, too.

Of course she would be, Hiro thought as he strolled past the food court. He stopped to buy a cup of lemonade, sipping it as he wandered aimlessly down the passageway.

People blame you if you tell them they're going to have a bad performance review at work, he considered. *There's no way she won't shoot the messenger over this.*

If she believes me, she might think I'm in cahoots with the killer. And if she doesn't, she'll think I'm insane, and call the police.

Hiro couldn't bear to have Charlie afraid of him. He couldn't imagine anything worse.

Of course, that was if she believed him in the first place.

And why would she? He hadn't told her about his powers yet. She didn't know he was from the future, so why would she even consider the idea that he'd know what was going to happen to her?

Hiro stopped abruptly in the middle of the corridor, the hamster waking up and starting to spin the wheel.

A woman who had been walking behind him, pushing a triple-wide stroller containing three sticky toddlers, bumped into him when he stopped, cracking him hard in the back of the knees.

Hiro yelped and doubled over, trying to rub the pain out of both of his calves at once.

"Watch it!" the woman snarled, conveniently overlooking the fact that it was *she* who had crashed into—and possibly crippled—*him.*

The little kid on the left waved a partially sucked Tootsie Pop at him.

"Watch it, watch it, botch it, potch it, snotch it!" he singsonged, making his sisters laugh.

Hiro straightened up painfully.

"Excuse me," he said politely to the woman, but she just scowled and muttered something he couldn't quite catch.

"I am sorry," he continued, and she stalked off, all three kids chorusing "Potch it, fotch it, watch it!" They kept it up the whole way down the hall until they turned the corner and were finally out of earshot.

Hiro limped over to a bench and sat down, absentmindedly massaging his bruised legs as his mind returned to the Charlie problem.

Or actually, he realized, the Charlie solution!

He would tell her about his powers. It was as simple as that.

He would tell her that he was able to bend time and space, and once he'd convinced her that he was from the future, he would tell her she needed to stay away from the diner on October 9th, and just not tell her why.

She'd seen lots of sci-fi movies, so she would understand not to question him too specifically about her own future, right?

Hiro stood up—the pain in his legs forgotten—and nodded a couple of times, agreeing with himself that this was a very good plan.

An *excellent* plan.

He would start by convincing Charlie he could stop time, and then work up to him being a time traveler, and just kind of skip over the whole harbinger-of-her-death thing altogether.

It shouldn't be that hard to get Charlie to believe him. After all, he'd managed to convince Ando, who was about the biggest skeptic in the history of the world.

Either way, he didn't care. He finally had a plan, concrete steps he could take to succeed at his mission and fulfill his destiny, and he felt better than he had in ages.

He drank the last sip of his lemonade, then headed back to the food court to get a refill. Maybe he'd buy a cup for PJ, too, take it over to him at the comic-book store, just to say thanks. After all, the kid had solved his dilemma.

A cup of lemonade was really the least he could do.

19

"*ABRACADABRA!*" HIRO SHOUTED, ALTHOUGH HIS HEART WASN'T really in it.

He froze time, rooted around in one of the three brown paper shopping bags he'd brought along until he found the white stuffed bunny rabbit, then crammed it into the black silk top hat. Then he unfroze time and pulled it back out with a flourish.

His audience, a dozen wide-eyed eight-year-olds, burst into astonished applause.

"Ta-da!" Charlie said, giving him a secret little wink. She took the props from him, then turned to the dazzled crowd. "What amazing trick will The Magnificent Hiro perform next?"

Hiro kept a smile plastered on his face as he held up the toy clown he was about to make magically disappear. At least he got to see Charlie in her cute Magician's Assistant outfit, he thought glumly. At least that was something.

It hadn't been as easy as Hiro had hoped to convince Charlie that he had superpowers.

For the past two weeks he had done everything he could think of to try to persuade her that he had the ability to stop time. He changed his clothes fifteen times in the blink of an eye. He moved furniture and even once physically picked up Charlie herself and carried her from the kitchen to the living room.

But nothing worked.

Charlie simply and steadfastly refused to believe that what she was seeing was anything more than a magic trick or sleight of hand.

At first Hiro had only stopped time when they were alone, so he wouldn't inadvertently reveal his powers to anyone else, but he got so desperate to make Charlie believe that what she was seeing was real that he finally decided, *Screw it*. He needed to go all-out to prove to her, once and for all, that she wasn't just seeing things, that he didn't have her under some kind of hypnotic spell.

He'd waited until the lunch rush at the diner, when every table was packed. All the waitresses were overwhelmed with customers clamoring for their meals; Bob was dinging the hell out of the bell as their orders all came up at once. And right when Charlie was completely swamped, Hiro concentrated and stopped the chaos, freezing time as he delivered all the orders to her customers, refilling their water glasses, replacing dropped forks, belting a squirming baby tighter in his high chair, taking care of anything and everything anyone could possibly need from her.

And when he was finished, when all of Charlie's work was done, he stood in front of her with an expectant smile, sure that this time she would have no choice but to believe that he had his powers.

He unfroze time, and Charlie jumped, looking from table to table at her happy, fulfilled customers, then turning her wide eyes on him.

"Hiro," she said, her voice impressed and uncertain, causing Hiro to grin.

Finally!

But then she turned to the other waitress and called, "Lynette, you've got to see this. Hiro's a magician!"

Hiro's spirits plummeted as Lynette waddled over. She'd managed to keep from smoking for the past month by replacing her cigarettes with candy. As a result, she was no longer round so much as egg-shaped.

"Oh my gosh, I just had an idea," Lynette said. "You know Sammy's turning eight next weekend." Sammy was her son, whom Hiro had yet to see when he wasn't throwing a tantrum. "You should come do a magic show at his party!"

No.

No way.

Not a chance.

"That's a *great* idea," Charlie said, her eyes lighting up. "I'll help—it'll be so much fun."

Unh-unh.

Nope.

Never going to happen.

"So, whaddaya say?" Lynette had asked him.

NO!!!

Hiro smiled weakly.

"Sure."

Well, *that* had been counterproductive.

Hiro slumped down in the passenger's seat of Charlie's car, a little rainy cloud of despair hanging over his head.

If he was trying to persuade Charlie that his ability to bend time and space was a *super*power, not just a magic trick, then that afternoon's performance had certainly gotten him off to a hell of a start.

The magic show had actually been a gigantic hit—parents of three of the party guests had booked Hiro's act for their own kids' birthdays. Apparently Hiro could look forward to a lucrative future as a magician.

The problem was, of course, that it wasn't an act, it was real, and now Charlie seemed less convinced of that fact than ever.

A couple of times during the afternoon, astonished at the stunts Hiro was performing, she'd asked him how he was doing it. But each time he told her the truth, that he was freezing time, she would just nod in mock-seriousness and say, "I understand. A magician never reveals his secrets."

It was so frustrating that he wanted to scream.

Instead he just swallowed his vexation and tried again.

And again and again and again.

"You're so quiet," Charlie commented now.

Hiro twisted his mouth up into a smile as she glanced over at him, then let it fall the instant she turned her eyes back to the road.

"Bending time and space takes a lot out of a person."

She chuckled, even though he hadn't been joking.

"You were amazing," she said. "I swear, I don't know how you do it. Those tricks seem so real."

"Because they *are* real," he said for the millionth time. "I have a power. You have a power, too—your memory. It will only get stronger in the future."

"The future. Right. Keep forgetting that's where you come from," Charlie said patiently.

Maybe he *should* scream. Maybe that would startle her into believing him.

Instead he sighed, suddenly so exhausted he could barely keep his eyes open.

He leaned his forehead against the smooth glass of the car window and stared out at the dark Texas countryside that was passing by. At night the land's flatness, so endless and open during the daytime, seemed oppressive, suffocating, with no hills or trees or houses to break up the unending sameness. Anything could be out there, in the dark.

Anything or anyone.

"Don't you understand?" he asked quietly, almost under his breath. Even though he knew she didn't understand at all. "I'm trying to save your life."

But Charlie didn't hear him, or maybe just didn't answer. She flicked on her turn signal, merging off Old Alamo Road onto the highway.

And Hiro went back to staring out the window, at the nothing that was out there, as the car carried them down the dark streets toward home.

20

Hiro idly reached for the paper airplane lying on the counter by the doughnut case. Someone had folded it out of a lunch receipt and left it behind.

Charlie had needed to swing by the diner on their way home to grab a sweater she'd left there, and while she headed into the storeroom to search for it, Hiro sat down at the counter to wait for her.

He smoothed the paper airplane's wings, folding the tips up slightly to give it loft. *Nice and easy,* he thought, pulling his hand back to launch it into the air. He let go, and the plane sailed over the counter and skittered to a stop next to the soda fountain.

If he bent the nose down a touch he might get it to travel the whole way into the kitchen, he thought, going around behind the counter to pick it up again. He was fiddling with the tip, trying to get the angle just right, when—

BAM!!!

A gigantic crash came from the storeroom, accompanied by the sound of Charlie shrieking.

In a flash Hiro dropped the paper airplane and vaulted over the counter, flying toward the storeroom.

He didn't have time to stop time, it was faster just to run—*it's only June it can't be the Brain Man not yet it's too early*—and a moment later he was hauling ass through the door.

In the storeroom Charlie was on her knees, gathering up half a dozen cans of fruit cocktail that were scattered around the floor. She looked up sheepishly when Hiro came bursting in.

"I saw a spider," she said, "and knocked over these cans trying to get away."

Good grief!

He stared at her in disbelief, bending over and resting his palms on his knees, sucking wind.

"You scared me half to death!" he panted.

"I'm sorry. It's just"—she grimaced—"spiders."

Oh my God.

That was the final straw. He couldn't take this anymore.

He straightened up, fighting to get air into his lungs, and felt his eyes filling with tears. He didn't know what to do. He couldn't quit, but he didn't know how he was going to go on.

He didn't want Charlie to see him cry, so he turned and staggered back out into the dining room.

He heard her as she jammed the cans back on the shelf and hurried after him.

Charlie walked over to where he was standing, trying to get hold of himself, and put her hands gently on his shoulders.

"I'm sorry," she said softly, looking him in the eyes. "I didn't mean to scare you."

Hiro looked at her helplessly. It was the bottom of the ninth. If he couldn't convince her of his power now, he never would.

He wished—he wished—

Charlie was still looking at his face, searching, and he wrested his eyes away from hers in shame. His gaze fell on the paper airplane he'd been playing with, lying on the counter, starting to come unfolded—

—and an idea shimmered into his mind.

He *wished.*

He looked back at Charlie, his face serious, desperate. Hopeful.

"There is an ancient Japanese tradition," he said slowly, praying this would work. "Origami. Folding paper."

Charlie looked interested, and Hiro's confidence pinged up a notch.

"In Shinto, cranes were considered sacred birds, and an origami crane was a sign of good luck."

Recognition sparked on Charlie's face, and she nodded eagerly. "I read about that! It's said if a person folds a thousand cranes, they'll be granted one wish."

"Yes," Hiro said, then he shut his eyes and concentrated.

He could feel the earth slipping out from under his feet, feel it spinning round and round, pinning him against its surface, as he focused on bringing it to a stop.

A second later, he opened his eyes.

Charlie was still gazing at his face when she noticed something over his shoulder. Her eyes flickered and she gasped. Then her hands dropped from his arms and she turned around in a little circle, hushed and astonished at what she was seeing.

The diner was filled with a thousand cranes.

Crimson cranes, golden ones, green, plum, yellow. Cranes the color of the sky, the sun, every color imaginable, folded from paper that glistened and sparkled, pale and bright and dazzling, a thousand strong.

They hung from invisible threads, swooping and gliding around the room, transporting it on fragile wings from dusty hot diner to a place magical and sublime.

They flew, carried by ancient winds, over vast seas, lush forests, foreign lands.

Fog rolled in, saline waves crashed against unknown shores, the stars flickered and sparked, blazing hotter and brighter than ever before.

The cranes flew to Mount Koya, Mount Hiei, Mount Nantai San, to where barefoot Shingon monks picked up their mallets and struck their gongs, the chimes echoing across six thousand miles from the mist-shrouded scared spires to the hot baked capacious earth of Midland, Texas.

Charlie flew with them, transfixed and delighted, then she threw back her head and laughed. And when she turned her face once more toward Hiro's, he could see in her shining eyes that she finally believed him.

She believed him.

Hiro's heart tooted horns and banged on drums, throwing great handfuls of confetti joyfully into the air.

"How did you—" she began wonderingly, then shook her head, spellbound. "You did this."

"Yes."

"So it's true. You—you can stop time. You're from the future."

"*Yes.*"

Charlie looked at him, an emotion Hiro couldn't read playing across her face, then turned away, gazing around again at the intricate paper birds, brushing the ones closest to her with light fingertips, setting them swaying.

"A thousand cranes," she said softly. "Did you make a wish?"

Yes. And it had already had come true—she believed him. But—

He shook his head.

"Not a thousand cranes. One is missing."

Charlie cocked her head, a question in her eyes, and he smiled. "You need to make the last crane. The wish is for you."

Her face lit up, and she reached for the gilt square of paper he held out to her. "Show me."

Hiro put his hands on hers and guided her through the folds: bringing the four corners of the paper together, creasing the edges into a triangle, carefully flattening the layers inward, then bending them back; the crane's body emerging like a miracle, Hiro's strong slender hands and Charlie's small soft ones coaxing the wings from the paper, then the tail, the head.

Finally all that was left was the beak, and Hiro reluctantly let go of Charlie so she could fold the final point down alone, creasing it carefully with a polished pink fingernail—and then it was done.

Charlie cradled the thousandth crane tenderly in her hands, her lips moving in the same silent wish she had made on her birthday, two months earlier.

She walked over to the cash register and perched the tiny golden bird on top of it. Then she turned back to Hiro, her eyes unexpectedly wet.

Hiro held his breath.

Charlie walked back over so she was standing in front of him again, and this time she placed both of her hands very lightly on his chest.

"You're so nice to me," she said, with an embarrassed little laugh that said how ridiculous she thought it was that she was crying.

He could feel his heart thudding wildly against her palms, which were pressed, flat and warm, against his shirt.

"No one's ever been this nice to me."

Hiro reached out and gently brushed a tear off her cheek, completely blown away by the softness of her skin beneath his fingers. He let his hand linger there, caressing her face.

"I can't imagine anyone not being nice to you," he said, his voice barely a whisper.

Charlie smiled at him, the tears threatening to spill over again.

Then slowly, excruciatingly, she leaned forward and brushed her lips against his, gently as a butterfly flapping its wings.

Hiro felt a dizzying rush, happiness and desire colliding inside him.

He had just kissed a girl!

And not just any girl, but Charlie.

Charlie!

His first true kiss.

He moved his hand from her cheek to the nape of her neck, his fingers tangling in her hair, pulling her close.

For the first time since he had met her, for the first time since he had discovered his powers and started this journey, Hiro wasn't thinking about the mission, not even a little bit. His entire mind, his *soul,* was focused on Charlie.

Emotion welled up inside him, and he shut his eyes, leaning forward to capture her mouth with his again . . .

. . . and when he opened his eyes an instant later, he found himself sitting in his cubicle at Yamagato Industries, six thousand miles away.

21

No.

NO!!!

Hiro looked around wildly, his whole body overflowing with dismay. He was back in Tokyo.

How could this have happened?

He could still feel the lingering pressure of Charlie's lips, taste their sweetness against his own, but Charlie was—

Oh God.

The blood drained from Hiro's face as the thought struck him. The last time he had accidentally teleported, he had ended up in the future. What if—

He lunged for the computer on his desk and frantically pounded on the keyboard to bring the sleeping screen to life, praying he hadn't gone forward in time, praying he wasn't too late, praying the clock in the corner of the screen wouldn't reveal a date past October 9—

June 28.

Thank God. It was the same day. He hadn't traveled through time, just space.

Which still wasn't *great,* but at least Charlie was still alive. He still had plenty of time to save her, he just needed to get back to Texas.

He shut his eyes, focusing his concentration . . . and then thought better of it. He didn't know how or why he had teleported here—did he really want to risk trying to bounce back to Midland?

He turned back to his computer and brought up the Google window. *Flights from Tokyo to Texas,* he typed.

There was a JAL flight leaving in four hours—awesome. He clicked on it. There were last-minute seats available, and he could have one for only . . . $8,756.

Oh.

He opened his wallet and pulled out the Yamagato corporate credit card he was only supposed to use for emergencies. He was pretty sure this qualified.

But even if it didn't?

The memory of Charlie's kiss—and his eagerness to get back to her and kiss her some more—was worth every penny of his father's wrath he might incur.

He clicked BUY NOW, then left his cubicle and walked down the corridor to the printer he shared with three other drones.

Having retrieved the tickets, he was heading back toward the exit when—

"You're back!"

Hiro turned. Ando was standing behind him, looking surprised. Hiro blinked. Did Ando know he had been in America?

"I am?" he asked uncertainly.

"Was the movie sold out?"

Huh?

Hiro looked even more confused, and Ando laughed.

"What have you been doing for the last thirty minutes, getting wasted on sake? You left here half an hour ago to go see *Ran* at the Shinjuku Bunka Cinema."

Holy cow! Hiro remembered the night he had gone to see that film. He had been sitting next to a girl who was chewing roughly eighteen pieces of bubblegum at once. She kept reaching into her mouth and pulling one end of the gum out into a long string, which she'd wind up around her finger before popping it back into her mouth and chewing a few more times. She did this over and over again, completely distracting Hiro from the movie, not to mention putting him off bubblegum forever.

But that meant that he had just missed running into himself. He gulped. If he had teleported just half an hour earlier, he would have completely screwed up the space-time continuum!

Did this mean he was at the movie right now? Could he literally be in two places at once? His head spun just thinking about it.

Ando tossed him a funny look. "What's the matter with you?"

"Nothing—I'm okay. I just decided to skip the movie."

"How come?"

As much as Hiro wanted to confide in his friend about everything that was happening—the teleportation and the mission and the murder, all the overwhelming things that he was dealing with alone—he knew that he couldn't. This wasn't the right time. Ando was a part of their mission *in the future*. Hiro wasn't sure what would happen to their time line if he told him now, but he couldn't take any chances.

Besides, if he took the time to convince Ando all over again, he'd miss his plane.

But there *was* one thing he could tell Ando. In fact, he could hardly wait to tell him.

"I met a girl," he said, unable to keep the satisfied grin from spreading across his face.

"You're kidding!"

"Unh-unh. And guess what else? I *kissed* her!"

Ando's mouth dropped open in shock. "No way! Good for you!" He grinned and slapped Hiro on the back. "This calls for a celebration. C'mon, let's go get some food and you can tell me all about her."

Hiro was *dying* to tell someone all about Charlie. But—

"I can't. I'm on my way to go see her right now."

Ando looked disappointed. "Well, maybe tomorrow night."

"Maybe."

Hiro started to walk away when Ando stopped him. "Wait a minute—you're going to go meet her empty-handed?

"No you're not," he answered himself, before Hiro got a chance to. "You have to bring her something."

"I don't really have time—" Hiro started.

Ando shook his head. "Find the time. Seriously. If you want to get in good with this girl, you need to make an impression."

Hmm. Hiro considered this. Maybe he should freeze time and go buy Charlie a present. As eager as he was to get back to her, he certainly could find all the time he needed. And Ando had a lot of experience with women—he knew what he was talking about.

"It's like with me and Niki."

Then again—

"But . . . she's on the Internet," Hiro said, not quite sure how to put it without being insulting. Niki was an online stripper who ran a website where Ando spent most of his free time and disposable income. "You pay her to take her clothes off for you."

"Doesn't matter," Ando said smugly.

Okay, guess he wasn't offended.

"If a girl doesn't like you," Ando continued, "she's not going to get naked, no matter how much money you have."

Oh God. Hiro couldn't even think about Charlie getting naked. He was still reeling from the kiss; he could hardly even imagine her taking off her clothes.

Oh boy.

He had to get back to her *this instant.*

22

Hiro discovered that the ability to stop time comes in handy when you're trying to catch a flight at rush hour, so he found himself at the departure gate at Narita Airport ready to go a good two hours before his flight was scheduled to leave.

He thought about calling Charlie to let her know what had happened, but he was pretty sure—*wait, is Tokyo fourteen hours ahead of or behind Texas?*—that it was the middle of the night in Midland, and she was probably sound asleep.

Well, he'd see her soon enough.

Waiting for his flight, he spent the time browsing through the little terminal gift shop, looking for something to read on the plane and—since Ando really *did* know a lot more than he did about women—searching among the paltry selection of souvenirs, trying to find a present he could buy for Charlie.

He was back-and-forthing between a T-shirt printed with a picture of the Nippori subway station and a pencil box shaped like a tray of sashimi when his eyes fell on the perfect thing. A reproduction of one of the Kensei Tapestries from the Meiji Museum, mounted on a rectangle of heavy card stock, showing the legend of Takezo Kensei and the Dragon, Hiro's favorite of the stories about the great Bushido warrior.

Charlie will love this. It was exactly the right thing to show her how he really felt about her. He picked up the print and smiled, finding himself uncharacteristically calm.

He could feel tremendous things happening to him, as if he was on the brink of something powerful and life-altering and gigantic. It reminded him of when he had first discovered his power to bend time—although that had felt external, a gift bestowed on him by outside forces. This was visceral, a long-dormant part of himself finally stretching its legs and coming to life.

He and Charlie had a true connection, like a rubber band that was pulling him back to her.

A *love* connection.

So he paid for the print and then glanced at his watch, hurrying back to the gate.

It was time to go.

The diner was just closing up by the time Hiro, grimy and exhausted from his thirty-four-hour trip, finally arrived.

As much as he would have liked to go home, take a shower, and freshen up, he could think about nothing except seeing Charlie. He paused outside the door and replayed in his mind for the millionth time the moment when he and Charlie had kissed, the feel of his hands on her face, his lips against hers.

He wanted to jump up and down at the memory of how fantastic it was that she kissed him, and that she believed him, and that he still had nearly four perfect wonderful months to spend with her while he convinced her to stay away from the diner on the day the Brain Man was coming.

He could see her clearly through the brightly lit front window of the Burnt Toast, wiping down the counters and chatting with Bob, who was relaxing with a beer, his chef's hat crumpled on the stool next to him. Lynette was toddling around with a broom, and there didn't seem to be any customers left.

Good.

That way Charlie wouldn't be shy if she wanted to, say, hurl herself into his arms and shower him with kisses. Or anything else like that.

Hiro took a deep breath, the excitement burbling up inside him, then pushed the front door open.

"I'm back!" he announced, the majority of his face taken up by a smile.

He threw open his arms—*okay, Charlie, come 'n' get me!*—and waited. And waited.

And . . . waited?

Lynette and Bob—his co-workers, his *friends*—barely glanced up.

"I gotta go clean the grill," Bob mumbled, grabbing his hat and disappearing back into the kitchen.

Lynette shook her head, then turned. She pushed her broom back toward the storeroom, stopping briefly to put her hand on Charlie's shoulder and murmur something into her ear. Something Hiro couldn't catch. Then she also hurried out of the dining room, and Hiro was left alone with Charlie.

Charlie, who didn't even look up from the counter, suddenly very intent on scrubbing at a stain that Hiro was pretty sure was a permanent part of the Formica.

"Charlie?" he said uncertainly, taking a few steps toward her.

She ignored him, abandoning her sponge in favor of her fingernail to work at the stain.

Okay, this wasn't even close to the reaction he was expecting. He walked all the way up to the counter, bewildered, and touched her sleeve.

"Hey. It's me. I'm back," he repeated.

Charlie yanked her arm away and turned her back on him, still furiously swabbing at the counter. "Okay, you're back. So what?" she replied, her voice low and angry.

"Wait—what? What's wrong?"

She finally looked up at him, and he could see that her eyes were red and puffy, as if she'd been crying. What in the world was happening?

"What do you want, Hiro?"

"I—I want to know what's going on," he said, surprised and hurt. "Are you *mad* at me?"

Charlie's eyes narrowed incredulously. "Oh, why would I be mad? You kiss me and then disappear for two days without a word. Why would *that* make me mad?"

A wisp of hair had come loose from her neat ponytail, and Hiro had to fight the urge to tuck it behind her ear.

"I'm so sorry," Hiro said. "I accidentally teleported to Tokyo, and I had to fly back." He kept his voice low, and glanced around to make certain no one else was near enough to hear, even though he was speaking in Japanese.

"Oh, so you can fly, too?" she snarked.

"No, I—I had to take an airplane. I didn't want to risk teleporting, in case I couldn't get back." He twisted his hands together, stung by her anger and desperate to make her understand it was all a big misunderstanding. "I'm so sorry—I don't know how it happened. One instant I was here, the next I was back in Tokyo."

"I thought you'd left for good," Charlie said furiously, the tears welling up again. "I thought—I didn't know what to think! You made those cranes appear and it felt so perfect and then you were just—*gone*. I didn't know what happened to you, or why you left."

"I don't know, either," Hiro said, trying to sound gentle, and fighting panic. "But all I could think about the whole time I was gone was getting back to you."

He touched her sleeve again, and this time she didn't pull away. But she didn't rush to embrace him, either.

"I was really worried," she said, the anger gone from her voice.

"I know. But I'm here now."

Charlie looked down. She took a deep, shaky breath.

"I look terrible," she said, wiping the back of her hand across her reddened eyes.

"You look beautiful," he answered, because it was true.

She gave him a small smile. Relieved, he smiled back. Maybe they could move past this now, and Charlie could give him a welcome more like the one he had been expecting.

But before they could move a muscle, the men's room door banged open, and Lloyd came out, still tugging on his zipper.

Uh-oh.

Lloyd did a double take when he saw Hiro; then his face hardened, and he came storming over to where they were standing.

"Hi, Lloyd," Hiro said weakly. "I'm back!"

POW!

Lloyd responded by punching Hiro squarely in the face.

Hiro's eyes rolled back in his head, and he crumpled to the ground.

Lloyd stood over him, cradling his fist, Charlie's knight in shining armor.

"*That's* what you get for hurting Charlie!" he said.

It was the last thing Hiro heard before blacking out.

23

"DO YOU THINK IT'S GOING TO LEAVE A MARK?" HIRO ASKED, gingerly pressing the ice pack against his eye, which was swollen shut and already an alarming shade of purple.

"Yeah, but don't worry—it makes you look like a badass," Charlie said.

Hiro was still sitting on the floor of the diner where he'd landed when Lloyd decked him. What was it about America, he wondered, that he kept getting this sort of reaction from every jerk who came along?

At least Lloyd was gone now. As were, presumably, Bob and Lynette. Hiro wasn't sure.

When he had come to, the only person left in the diner had been Charlie. She was crouched in front of him, holding a bag of frozen peas wrapped in a clean dish towel. She held it out to him, an indecipherable little smile on her face. He tried to figure it out.

Serves you right?
Boys will be boys?
Chicks dig bruises?

Whatever—even if it was *chicks dig bruises,* he really didn't care. All that mattered to him was that she seemed to have forgiven him.

"Aren't you glad you came back?" she joked now, sitting down on the floor next to him, with her legs sticking straight out in front of her like a little kid.

But Hiro nodded, dead serious.

"Yes. Especially since I never meant to go in the first place."

She wrinkled her forehead, looking deep in thought.

"So, your leaving? That was part of your—" She hesitated before she said the word, like she couldn't even believe they were discussing this. "—your superpowers? Like stopping time, and being from the future?"

He nodded again.

"Okay. So—did you time-travel somewhere?"

"No, I just teleported. I moved through space, not time. To Japan."

"Why?"

"I don't know why," he admitted, a sinking feeling starting in his stomach as he thought about it. One minute he had been kissing her, swept up by the happiness, the rightness of the moment, and the next—*poof!*

"I didn't do anything; I wasn't trying to use my power at all. It just . . . happened."

"But—if it's an actual power, a *superpower,* shouldn't you be able to control it?" Charlie asked uncertainly.

Well, yeah, he *should,* but—

"Usually I can," he said anxiously. "At least, I can control the ability to freeze time." He gave a sad little shrug. "But the time-travel part is—"

Totally screwed up.

"—a little unpredictable."

He shifted the improvised ice pack, pressing a cooler part against his blackening eye, and his shoulders slumped as despair welled up.

"Hey." Charlie chucked him lightly on the arm to get him to look at her. "Freezing time is the most important part," she said encouragingly. "*That's* the real superpower."

"You think so?" Hiro asked in a small voice.

"Well, sure. Definitely. I mean, who cares about time *travel*—" She waved a hand and rolled her eyes disparagingly. "Being able to *stop* time is a thousand times cooler."

Hiro smiled a little, letting himself be convinced.

"Come on. Even *Superman* wasn't able to freeze time."

"I guess it is pretty cool," he agreed.

She grinned at him. "Do it now."

"What do you mean?"

"Show me. Stop time now and change something. Please?"

He grinned back at her.

"Okay. Shut your eyes."

She did.

"Now open them."

Charlie gasped—suddenly, instantly, she was at her apartment, with Hiro sitting next to her on the couch, the small green bag from the Narita Airport gift shop on her lap.

She looked around, shaking her head in wonder, then stared at Hiro.

"You—carried me here?"

"Um . . . actually, I—" He hesitated. "—I may have borrowed your car. But there was no traffic."

"You didn't, like, *peek* or anything, did you?"

He looked horrified, and she laughed.

"I'm just kidding," she said, though the expression on her face showed a hint of concern.

"I wouldn't!" No matter how much he wanted to.

"I know," Charlie said with a smile. She picked up the bag from the gift shop. "What's this?"

"Open it."

She reached into the bag and brought out the picture of the tapestry.

"Oh! Takezo Kensei!" She ran her fingers reverently over the front of it. "Which legend is this?"

"Takezo and the Dragon. It's my favorite of all of them."

Charlie got up and propped the picture up on the mantelpiece, next to the gruesome Zapotec shaman mask, where they both could see it. Then she came and sat back down on the couch, but closer this time, right next to Hiro, so she was leaning back against his chest and he had no choice but to wrap his arms around her.

Which he did willingly.

"Okay, now tell me," she said, gazing up at the picture.

"When Kensei was a young man, after he had found his sacred sword, he longed to unite Japan. So he went to the dragon and asked it to teach him the secrets of the sword. The dragon agreed. With the skills the dragon taught him, Kensei fought his enemies and won, saving his people. But the dragon came to the palace and demanded payment—the life of the princess whom Kensei loved."

Hiro tightened his arms, drawing Charlie closer against him.

"Kensei drew his sword and plunged it into his own heart, which he handed to the dragon, saying, 'My love is in here—take it.' Then he died."

"Oh no," she said, and she whimpered softly.

"To save what was important to him, Kensei had to be strong enough to lose his heart."

Together they looked up at the image on the mantel: the dragon fierce and terrible, Kensei proud and stoic as death crept up on him, the muted red of his blood staining the sword.

"Another sad ending," Charlie said softly.

Hiro bent his head, acknowledging that she was right, but knowing that for Kensei, it was all a part of finding *gi*. *To the Bushido, death comes in its course.*

"Do you like your present?"

"I love it."

She leaned back into his arms and let out a big sigh.

"I'm glad you came back," she said. "I wouldn't want *our* story to have a sad ending."

"Are you kidding?" Hiro said, his arms still around her. Her thin body felt comfortable and familiar next to his. She felt like home.

"Our story's just beginning."

24

"When I was in middle school, I used to drive the nuns crazy by begging them to start a 4-H club at Saint Nicasius's," Charlie said as she led Hiro across the wide grassy avenue of the Midland Fairgrounds toward the barns. She had already explained that they housed the animals local farm kids had raised and entered in the fair. "But they said none of the other girls were interested in joining, so we couldn't have one."

"Poor Charlie."

"I know." She gave a brave little *on-the-bright-side* shrug. "I pleaded so much that Sister Hilda finally arranged for me to go horseback riding every Saturday. So that was something, at least."

Hiro was unable to hold back a grin.

She swatted his arm playfully. "I'm just letting you know that going to see the animals is a very moving experience for me," she said. "So if I start crying at the sight of the baby goats, you'll know why."

Hiro nodded. "I feel the same way about Super Nintendo," he said sadly. "When I was eight, my parents refused to buy me one—they said I had to make do with my Atari 2600. Now even the *thought* of Super Mario gets me all choked up . . ."

Charlie grinned and swatted him again, then disappeared into the first barn.

Hiro happily tagged after her, still unable to believe his good luck. He and Charlie were on a date—a real, bona fide, no doubt about it *date*. He had asked, she'd accepted, and here they were.

It was incredible!

He had the power to go anywhere in the world, but there was no place on earth he'd rather be than right here, right now, at the Midland County Fair, with Charlie by his side. Or rather, in front of him and pulling away fast.

Hiro and Charlie had burned their fingers on funnel cakes and gotten dizzy riding the Tilt-A-Whirl and clapped along with the oompah band belting out Sousa marches on the main thoroughfare. They examined a display of antique quilts and cheered for a cowboy performing rope tricks on a small stage and watched, fascinated, as an auctioneer sold off a score of cattle, calling out bids in a voice so swooping and fast that, even if he'd understood English perfectly, Hiro still wouldn't have been able to decipher it.

They had barely even scratched the surface of everything there was to do and see.

At the moment Hiro wasn't sure if they'd get to see anything else, because Charlie looked like she could spend the rest of the night in the barns, cooing over all the animals.

"Oh, a Flemish lop-eared rabbit," Charlie exclaimed, pulling Hiro over to a pen containing an enormous brindle-coated ball of fuzz hopping around inside.

A very small boy wearing a pair of muddy overalls sat in a metal folding chair next to the pen, proudly guarding his pet. The boy's pant legs were rolled up into cuffs the size of life preservers, but they still bagged and drooped on the straw-covered floor.

"Look how adorable!" Charlie said, nodding toward the bunny and the boy both.

"His name is Quincy Carrot-Muncher," the youth told them happily. He stood up and heaved the rabbit, which was practically bigger than he was, out of the pen, holding it up so they could get a better look at it. "He won a blue ribbon this morning. Best in show."

"Congratulations," Hiro said. He reached out to stroke the bunny's soft little nose with his fingertip. Its sleepy brown eyes were calm, but the whiskers were trembling.

"Oh, I would never hurt you!" he reassured it, then marveled to Charlie, "I've never seen such a big rabbit!"

"He's still a baby," she said. "Full-grown Flemish rabbits can reach up to twenty-five pounds."

"Wow," Hiro said appreciatively.

The little boy gave the bunny a quick smooch on top of its head, then set it gently back down in its pen. It hopped a few feet away and sat down to scratch furiously at its ear with a big hind paw.

Hiro and Charlie waved good-bye and continued down the row, looking at the other, lesser, bunnies.

"Did you know rabbits can be housetrained?" Charlie said, carefully averting her eyes from a pale beige one that clearly wasn't.

"Really."

"Yes! They're actually excellent pets, although in most cultures rabbits are considered livestock, not pets, and are primarily raised for food."

"Huh."

"Yeah. In a single year, a rabbit can produce over a thousand times its body weight in offspring, which makes them a sustainable source of—" Charlie caught herself. She blushed self-consciously. "I sound like a dork, don't I?"

Hiro nodded.

Her eyes opened wide in mock-outrage. "Hey!"

"Well, you asked," he said, then added, amazed at his own courage, "a *cute* dork, though."

Charlie gave him a wry smile.

As they headed out of the barn, a couple of preteen girls, giggling like crazy, careered past them, jostling into Hiro. His arm bumped against Charlie's, sending a lightning bolt of electricity all the way down to his toes. He rubbed his hand off nervously on his jeans, then reached out and took hers.

She laced her fingers through his, like it was the most natural thing in the world for them to be holding hands. After another half an hour of perusing the various livestock, they wandered back across the wide fairgrounds.

Hiro peered around in wonder at the twirling, flashing lights, so

happy that he felt like a balloon, so buoyant and light he was pretty sure
he could just bob up and away.

But then he saw something that let all his air out.

They were strolling hand in hand along a corridor lined with carnival games when they saw Lloyd coming toward them, two heavy-
browed, squinty-eyed henchmen in tow.

Great, thought Hiro. *Just great.*

"Hi, Charlie," Lloyd said with a huge smile, holding out his arms.

Charlie dropped Hiro's hand and gave Lloyd a cursory embrace,
then nodded to his two companions. "Hello, Lloyd. Dwayne. Willie."

Hiro's heart dropped in his chest.

Lloyd smirked at him. "Hey, buddy. Sorry 'bout that shiner," he said,
in the least sorry voice Hiro had ever heard.

Hiro involuntarily reached up and touched his eye, which was still a
Crayola box of greens and purples.

"It's getting much better," he replied meekly.

Charlie looked from one man to the other nervously.

"Be nice, Lloyd."

"I'm always nice, aren't I, guys?" Lloyd grinned at his two friends,
who hung over his shoulders, staring at Hiro like hungry hyenas. Taking advantage of the lull in the conversation, she turned to leave, and
Hiro prepared to follow.

"Hold up, Charlie," Lloyd said quickly. "Hasn't your friend bothered
to win you a bear yet? What kind of a man is that?"

Charlie's eyes narrowed, and she grabbed Hiro's arm. "We're going
now."

"No, wait," Hiro said, confused. "What is he talking about?"

With a sigh, she pointed to a nearby game booth, where a teenage
girl was trying—and failing—to win a prize by tossing baseballs into a
clown's mouth. Stuffed animals in every shape and color hung on the
wall. Baseballs were lined up on the counter.

"Charlie's got a whole collection of teddy bears I've won her here,"
Lloyd bragged. "One for every year since we were kids. C'mon, Charlie,
I'll win you another one for your collection. The biggest one yet."

What an idiot.

"*I* will win one for you," Hiro said stiffly.

"You don't have to, Hiro," Charlie said in a kind voice, still trying to
pull him away.

But Lloyd interrupted again. "Of course he does!" he said. "C'mon, son, show us what you got. I hear the Japanese are good at baseball."

Hiro scowled at him, then stepped up to the counter.

"How many for that one?" Hiro asked the vendor, pointing to a bear almost as big as Charlie herself.

"Three in a row," the vendor replied. "If you get two, you get one of these." He reached under the counter and produced the saddest, scabbiest little stuffed animal of all time.

Still, Hiro couldn't let Lloyd get the best of him. He gave the vendor a dollar, and the man handed him three balls.

He shot Charlie a look—*here goes nothing*—and felt her squeeze his arm. Not expecting much, he threw the first ball.

It went in.

He grinned at Charlie, who beamed back at him.

Lloyd looked surprised, but shrugged it off and stepped forward for his turn.

"Did I mention I was a three-time all-American pitcher in high school?" Lloyd said. His henchmen guffawed like this was the funniest thing they ever heard.

Winding up like the Sasaki Kazuhiro of Midland, Lloyd threw his first ball. It sailed cleanly through the clown's maniacal grin. Lloyd's friends cheered like he'd just clinched the series.

Hiro felt his heart pounding, his blood rushing in his ears, and for a minute he worried that he might just disappear, teleport away to God-knew-where, leaving Charlie behind with Lloyd.

But he took a deep breath and with every fiber of his being calmed himself.

He picked up the ball, focused, and threw.

Beauty!

Two down, one to go.

Lloyd wasn't smiling now. "Guess anyone can get lucky," he said, taking aim. Lloyd's second throw went in easily.

"The home team always gets an advantage," he said, "so I'm gonna go ahead and take my third throw now." Before Hiro could even respond, Lloyd wound up, his forehead wrinkled in concentration, then released the ball.

Hiro stopped time, freezing the ball in midair.

He needed time to think. He thought about nudging the ball off course, only—Charlie knew about his powers. He didn't want her to think he was a wuss who had to cheat to win.

On the other hand, no way was he going to be beaten by Lloyd.

Hmmm. What would his favorite Tokyo Swallows player, Yao Ayakawa, do in this situation?

Hiro knew the answer to that question.

He unfroze time, and the ball sailed on.

And on his own, with no interference from Hiro at all, Lloyd *missed.* He stomped his foot in the dirt, cursing.

Hallelujah! Now all Hiro had to do was make the last pitch. Charlie would have her bear, and he would've gotten the best of Lloyd.

The cop's friends did their best to console him.

"Don't let it get to you, buddy."

"No way that shrimp can hit three in a row."

Hiro just ignored them. Charlie grinned at him and gave his arm a quick squeeze. That was all he needed. With her support, he could do anything. He was invincible.

He picked up his third ball.

"Choke!" Lloyd said, covering the taunt with a cough. His friends laughed and picked up the chant. "Choke! Choke! Choke!"

Hiro closed his eyes. He could feel Charlie's soft breath on the back of his neck, and the sweetness of that melted his heart.

He thought of the ballfield at Ueno Park, a peaceful place where he'd played with his father as a child, before things got so strained between them.

He opened his eyes.

Took a breath.

Threw the ball.

Swoosh!

It went in. *Victory!* Hiro threw his hands up in the air and shouted for joy.

"You did it!" Charlie squealed happily, jumping up and down and clapping her hands.

The vendor just smiled at her. "Which one do you want, darlin'?" he asked.

She pointed at the big bear, and he brought it down for her. She buried her face in its fur.

I wish I could freeze time right now, thought Hiro, *and stay right here, in this perfect moment, forever.*

"Nice throw," Lloyd said to Hiro, his lips a hard, straight line. He gave him a slap on the back, a little harder than he needed to, and then leaned in to Charlie, putting his hand on her waist and kissing her cheek.

"See you later, babe," he added.

"Cut it out, Lloyd," she said, her voice irritated as she shoved him away, then wiped off her cheek with the back of her hand.

Lloyd just smiled, unfazed. "Call me," he said, raising a cocky eyebrow, then he turned and sauntered off, his friends skulking after him.

Charlie shot Hiro an apologetic smile. "He's such a jerk," she said.

Hiro shrugged, determined to remain the picture of nonchalance. But inside, his heart was in chaos.

Charlie could knock Lloyd all she wanted, but he knew they had dated. Maybe they still *were* dating. Lloyd certainly acted like they were.

Hiro groaned inwardly, confused and overwhelmed. Wasn't he supposed to have learned this sort of stuff by now? What was *wrong* with him?

Charlie started up the thoroughfare, staggering a little under the weight of the bear. But Hiro wasn't sure he could help her carry it.

He was too busy struggling under the weight of his own heart.

25

ONE OF THE FEW TIMES HIRO HAD EVER COME CLOSE TO HAVING A real relationship with a girl was when he was eleven, with Tami Oyoki. She was his sister Kimiko's best friend, but the two girls couldn't have been more dissimilar.

That was before Kimiko's wild phase, so she was studious and practical and still shaped like a bento box, her entire body a precise lean rectangle with no bumps or ridges or curves anywhere. Tami, on the other hand, was an explosion of noise and activity and sleek scoops of flesh, piled up in a way Hiro found absolutely mesmerizing.

Tami would come over after school most days to do homework and hang out with Kimiko, and Hiro spent fully a semester doing nothing but spying on them. He didn't go so far as peeping through keyholes or "accidentally" walking in on her in the bathroom. But he managed to always be around—on the periphery, sticking to doorways and the edges of the room—as close as he could get without his sister yelling at him to stop bugging them, or slamming the door in his face.

Tami would *never* close a door in Hiro's face.

She was always nice to him. So nice, in fact, that it seemed to Hiro she might actually like him.

When Tami and Kimiko were playing a game of Go, Tami invited him to play the winner, and when the girls rented a movie, she patted the cushion next to her and invited him to sit down. When she saw him eating a green-tea mochi ice cream, she asked if she could have a bite, which she took from the place he'd already been chewing, which made it almost like their mouths had touched.

It was practically like she had kissed him, or at least *wanted* to.

And one night, when his sister and Tami were having a slumber party and Kimiko had ordered Hiro to *"stop hovering, you pest,"* Tami had said, "Leave him alone, Kimiko. He's cute."

Score! He was in!

He'd dragged his Transformers sleeping bag and some paper and a box of newly sharpened colored pencils into the hallway outside Kimiko's door. He lay on the floor, listening through the crack under the door while Tami talked and giggled, and drew a picture for her of him, dressed like a ninja, saving her from the clutches of an evil dragon.

He spent hours on it, carefully rendering the dragon's scales to give them the right shading that would make it look as if it was writhing. Erasing and redrawing her features half a dozen times to make sure they were accurate enough to pay homage. Endowing his ninja with considerably more muscles on one arm than Hiro currently had over his entire body.

When he was finished, when he looked down at his masterpiece and got a little thrill up his spine from how real and sexy and courageous it was, he carefully wrote a caption along the bottom of the picture.

"Princess Tami is rescued by her devoted Hiro."

Then, holding his breath, he slipped it under the door.

He listened as feet padded over, the paper rustling as it was picked up, then his sister's voice, amused and mocking, saying, "I think my little brother's got a crush on you."

"Oh, that's precious," Tami's voice said, and even though she was on the other side of the door, Hiro felt as if she was looking into his soul.

He grabbed his art supplies and sleeping bag and raced back to his own room, suddenly shy, worried that she'd open the door and see him. He spent the whole night wide awake, staring at the ceiling, radiating love for her.

The next morning, he awoke remembering that the two girls had plans to go shopping in Shimo-Kitazawa with a gang of their friends.

Just after breakfast, Kozumi, a snout-nosed idiot a few years ahead of them in school, swung by to pick them up. Kozumi pulled up in front of their house in a battered van, and the two girls piled giggling into the front seat next to him.

The instant the door shut behind them, Hiro snuck into his sister's room to absorb any last molecules of Tami that might still be lingering in the air. And that's where he saw his picture, balled up and tossed carelessly into the trash can. All his effort and love forgotten and discarded, nothing more than a piece of garbage.

He fished the picture out of the trash and smoothed it flat. Tami was only nice to him because he was her friend's geeky little brother, he realized. She had never really liked him.

Hiro ripped the picture up, shredding it into little pieces and dumping them back into the trash can.

He had been fooling himself. Tami was probably in love with Kozumi, who was bigger and meaner than Hiro, and drove her places in his car. He couldn't really blame her, though. Honestly? He blamed Kozumi, even though he knew it was irrational.

Hiro *hated* Kozumi.

After they wrestled the teddy bear into the trunk of Charlie's car, she announced that she didn't think they had eaten a sufficient amount of junk food at the fair, and suggested that they stop by the Dairy Queen for a little dessert.

Hiro nodded, not wanting to seem petulant, but completely absorbed in the question of how Charlie felt about Lloyd. A short time later they pulled up to the ice cream parlor.

They paid for their hot fudge sundaes, then she led the way over to one of the battered picnic tables.

Hiro sat down on the bench across from her, which gave him a perfect view, over her shoulder, of the fauxhawked and eyebrow-ringed teenage boy at the next table. He was kissing a girl, and seemed intent on swallowing his date's entire head. He lathed her mouth and cheeks with long gooey swipes of his tongue, and unhinged his jaw anaconda-style to fit more of her face into his mouth.

Hiro's eyes widened in fascinated horror, and Charlie swiveled her neck around to see what he was looking at.

"Oh my God," she said, turning back to Hiro and hunching over her ice cream, giggling. "I should have warned you—this is one of the prime make-out spots in all of Midland for teenagers."

"Really?"

"Yeah. We used to come here all the time when I was in high school."

"Oh." Hiro said quietly. He must have looked horrified, and she laughed.

"Not like *that,* silly," Charlie said, balling up her napkin and tossing it at him. "I'm a nice Catholic girl. I barely even held a boy's *hand* until I was eighteen."

She rolled her eyes at him and took a bite of her ice cream.

"I'd just come here with my friends and we'd try to flirt with the boys we had crushes on. I was never much good at it, though."

"Me neither," Hiro admitted. "I'm still not."

Charlie smiled at him. "Oh, I'd say you're doing a pretty good job."

Hiro felt a million tiny tremors spark through him.

Oh my God. What does that mean? Did it mean she liked him? Or was it a subtle way of telling him to back off?

No—it had to mean she liked him. But what about Lloyd? Was she involved with him, too?

What did she want?!

She was looking at him like she was waiting for a response, but he had too many questions to come up with any answers, so in desperation he flickered his eyes away from hers. They landed on the teen couple behind her.

Big mistake.

Fauxhawk grabbed his girlfriend's hand and brought it to his lap, pressing it against his jeans.

Hiro swallowed hard and tried to focus away from them, back on Charlie, who had apparently realized she was dealing with a complete dimwit who would be hard-pressed to tell her his own name, let alone how he felt about her.

"I guess it's my own fault," she was saying, a sad look on her face. She lifted one shoulder in a little self-deprecating shrug. "Even when I did manage to find a boyfriend, I'd always end up breaking up with him after about two dates over something stupid, some insignificant little thing he did that drove me nuts."

Like . . . teleporting away in the middle of their first kiss? Hiro rumpled up his face. Was this her way of letting him down easy?

"I once dumped a boy because he listened to reggae," she continued.

Or maybe it wasn't about him at all. *Ooh, please let this just be an anecdote, and not a parable.*

"I thought you liked reggae," he said, carefully keeping his tone casual.

"I don't mind it, but when he listened to it, somehow it was annoying. Besides, he breathed through his mouth and the combination was just too much." She noisily sucked air in through her teeth, then shook her head.

"Everybody's done that," Hiro said, through a mouthful of whipped cream and hot fudge sauce. "Broken up with someone for a really bad reason."

"Yeah, but I do it all the time. Because, like, one guy had these tiny pale useless little hands. Like a *Tyrannosaurus.* I couldn't take it. The thought of him touching me with them—" She broke off, giving a little shiver of revulsion.

"But that was stupid of me." Charlie shook her head. "That was no reason for me to dump him. He was so nice . . ."

Hiro made a sympathetic face. "Nice doesn't make up for *Tyrannosaurus* hands."

"No, I guess not."

Hiro looked up, involuntarily meeting Fauxhawk's gaze. He smiled at Hiro, then very deliberately lifted his middle finger. His girlfriend captured it in her mouth, sucking aggressively on his knuckle.

Gah! Hiro winced, not sure if he was grossed out or jealous. *Both, really.*

"Sometimes I feel like Sakurazawa," he said.

Charlie scrunched up her forehead. "Who?"

"He was a kidnapper who tried to blackmail Robogirl in issue ninety-four."

"Oh, of course." She tossed him a strange look, but didn't stop him.

"Robogirl was in love with him—she's always falling in love with the wrong guy—and he broke her heart," he told her, warming up to the story. "It was so awesome—she didn't want to kill him, 'cause he wasn't one of her actual targets, so she turned her arm into a trephine—a surgical blade—and jammed it underneath his eyelid, lobotomizing him."

"That *does* sound awesome." She was actually beginning to look interested now. He took that as encouragement, and pressed on.

"Sakurazawa spent the rest of his life in a psych ward, stumbling around in little circles, hugging and kissing this old sock puppet, 'cause he thought it was her."

Charlie looked confused. "Wait—why do you feel like that?"

Hiro shrugged, suddenly a little embarrassed. "It sometimes seems like everyone else in the entire world is having relationships and falling in love and just—moving forward, you know? And I wandered off the path somewhere and am just stumbling around in little circles, like Sakurazawa."

Charlie nodded. "I know exactly what you mean. I swear, all my friends from high school are married and having kids. And I'm—what? I'm in the exact same place I was in five years ago."

Huh. Where was she five years ago? *At the prom with Lloyd.*

Okay, that was it. This was torture. He had to know one way or another.

"So, you and Lloyd . . ." he started, then stopped, instantly regretting having brought the subject up. Now Charlie would admit that she only liked Hiro as a nerdy little brother.

And then he would have to kill himself.

The world's longest pause, then—

"Me and Lloyd what?" Charlie asked innocently.

"Nothing."

He jabbed at the bottom of his dish with his plastic spoon, a little sickened at the way the melting ice cream swirled together in a brown, streaky mess.

"Hiro—"

He jabbed harder.

"Hiro!" Charlie touched his arm, laughing but nice. "Are you trying to murder that sundae? Here—"

She took the dish out of his hands, then carefully spooned up a small bite.

"This is how you're supposed to do it." She popped the ice cream in her mouth, then closed her eyes, a dreamy expression on her face. "Mmmm. *Oishii!* Delicious!"

She scooped up another spoonful and held it out to him. "See? Now you try."

Hiro grinned despite himself, obediently opening his mouth and taking the proffered bite. "Mmmm!"

"That's more like it," Charlie said. "And by the way? Lloyd and I went out a couple times, but we're just friends, nothing more."

She tilted her eyes up to meet his.

"I guess I've just been waiting for the right guy to come along, because I've never really been serious about anyone—" She gave him the sweetest smile he had ever seen. "—until now."

Hiro shut his eyes, cold sweet happiness flooding through him, and when he opened them, Charlie was in front of him, her gorgeous face, her heart-stopping smile.

And then he was kissing her again, kissing her for real this time, without teleporting or stopping time or disappearing. Her lips were light on his, then harder, as she leaned across the table, her hands coming up to wrap around his neck.

He felt her tongue slip past his lips, lightly tickling his. He'd always thought French kissing sounded a little gross, but it wasn't gross at all. It was the opposite of gross.

It was spectacular.

He reeled at the overload of sensation, feeling her mouth sealed against his, her hands warm on his skin, her hair soft beneath his fingers.

She let out a noise, an involuntary little *mmmm,* a soft private sigh or groan of such wanton desire that—God, he really was like a fourteen-year-old—Hiro had to pull away from her before he literally exploded.

He moved his head back, just a fraction of an inch, keeping his hands on her, catching his breath. Charlie's eyes were closed, but he opened his—just for a second—and saw Fauxhawk watching them.

Hiro grinned at him, sticking out his thumb and pinkie and shaking a rock-and-roll fist at the kid.

Then he returned his attention, and his lips, to Charlie.

26

LATER, DRIVING HOME, HIRO LEANED BACK, DROWSY AND CONTENT, in the comfortable passenger's seat. His hand held fast to Charlie's, resting on the seat between them. He only stirred when Charlie cut the wheel hard to the left, swerving to avoid an animal that went skittering across the road in front of the car.

"Was that a white-tailed desert jackrabbit, indigenous to the American Southwest, identifiable by the black spots on its front paws?" he teased.

Charlie shot him a sidelong glance. "*No.* It was a groundhog." She returned her eyes to the road and drove in silence for a minute before adding, "Or, as it's formally known, a *Marmota monax.*"

Hiro laughed.

He waited until Charlie had pulled the car up to the curb in front of his apartment at 40 Progress Street, then said, "You know, I was thinking—you really seem to know an awful lot about rabbits."

"It wasn't a rabbit!" Charlie protested.

"Still, at the fair you were a regular expert."

"I can't help it!" she wailed. "I read a book about rabbits when I was, like, in the third grade, and when I saw that bunny back there, it all came back to me. Every word, every picture. I even remember the publisher, the copyright. The Library of Congress number. It's a curse!"

"It's a *gift.*"

"Yeah, right." She didn't look convinced.

Hiro turned in his seat and peered at her in the darkness. "It seems to me, if you wanted to become a rabbit farmer, knowing all that stuff would come in handy."

"Why would I want to be rabbit farmer?" she asked, wrinkling her nose and completely missing his point.

"Or a veterinarian," he said pointedly. "Or a humanitarian aid worker, one who knows that rabbits are a source of protein, and knows which places where people are starving but also have the sort of climate where rabbits could thrive . . ."

Charlie stared at him for a long silent second.

"You're saying I could make a difference," she said in a soft voice.

Her face changed, realization blooming on it like a flower.

"If I read about agriculture, livestock, soil composition—I could take all that knowledge and . . . and try to fight the world hunger problem."

Hiro nodded. *Exactly,* he thought.

She gripped his hand tighter.

"Or—I could read about *anything*—medicine, law, diplomacy—"

"You learned Japanese in about ten minutes," he reminded her.

"My memory is a *gift.*" She said it with authority, sounding more firmly convinced with each passing moment. "I could do anything I wanted."

"You can."

"I could change the world."

Hiro grinned. *Yep. She sure could.* Right after he saved it.

"I never really thought of my memory as a *power,*" Charlie said, "I mean, not the way stopping time is."

An hour had passed, and they were still sitting in the front seat of her car, just talking.

Thirty minutes earlier Hiro's landlord had walked out to the sidewalk to make sure they weren't prowlers casing the joint. But when he had seen who it was, Mr. Roiz made a big show of dramatically covering his eyes, just in case they were doing things they would be better off doing in private. Then he went back inside, making lots of *You-got-a-room-why-not-use-it!* harrumphing noises.

Every few minutes since then, he'd flicked his porch light on and off, just to remind them that they were in an essentially public place, so they shouldn't get too carried away . . .

But Hiro and Charlie were so caught up in their conversation they barely noticed.

"At first I thought it was just a trick, you know?" Charlie said. "Or like, maybe I was just finally getting enough sleep or something. Eating enough fish so that my brain was getting all the vitamin E it needed for the first time ever. Because I'd remember stuff that I read in the paper, the names of people I hadn't seen in years, numbers for a bank account I hadn't had since I was a teenager. But then I started to realize it was bigger than that."

Hiro put his hand lightly on her knee, making the connection between them physical. He knew how she felt.

"I wasn't just remembering things I'd read that morning, but books I'd read *years* ago, word for word," she continued. "It's like—it's like my memory was a long corridor with a million rooms, and all the doors were being flung open at once. I could go into any room I wanted and see exactly what was in there." She frowned. "And sometimes I'd find myself in a room I didn't choose, and see things I didn't want to remember."

"Like what?"

Charlie gave a little shrug. "Just—little things, mostly. A girl making fun of me on the playground. Having to admit to a mean teacher that I hadn't done my homework, when I knew she was going to yell. Liking a boy who didn't like me back."

"Yin and yang. Light and darkness." He tightened his grip on her knee, squeezing it. "All superpowers have both good and bad sides."

"Does your power have a bad side?" she asked.

Hiro shuddered at the thought, and didn't want her to feel him trembling, so he pulled his hand away from her leg. Charlie immediately reached out and laid her hand on his arm, keeping the connection alive between them.

If she ever knew how bad the dark side of his powers was, the things he'd seen, things he'd seen done to *her*—

He shook his head, disconsolate at the thought.

"You've seen it yourself," he said lightly. "My teleporting away at the worst possible moment? Definitely a downside. But a hero has to face both the good and the bad in his powers, if he wants to fulfill his destiny."

Charlie shook her head, a little smile on her face. "But I'm not a hero."

"Yes, you are!"

"Don't tease me, Hiro," she said softly.

"I'm not! Destiny brought us together. Destiny gave us these powers. That makes us special."

"Destiny, huh?"

Hiro nodded. "My destiny said I was supposed to come to America . . ." He hesitated—how best to say this? "And find you."

Charlie was looking equal parts skeptical and captivated.

"So what's my destiny, then? Super rabbit farmer?"

Hiro wasn't sure what her destiny was, but he knew she had one. That's why he had come back to save her.

"You need to discover that for yourself. But you'll find a calling, and your power will lead you to greatness."

"Ooooo-kay," Charlie said, without a whole lot of conviction.

He had to try harder. "It's like with Robogirl," he said, trying to explain what seemed so obvious to him. "When she first was reprogrammed so she could feel, she didn't think she was a hero, either, but she—"

Charlie held up a hand. "Um, Hiro?"

"Yes, Charlie?"

"Could you please shut up now and kiss me?"

Yes.

Hiro could definitely do that.

27

Thus began Hiro and Charlie's Summer of Love.

Finally. Finally it was happening to him, the way love was supposed to happen, the way he had read about in books. His terrible luck was over—this was it. This was love.

Days passed, and Charlie got more perfect each time he saw her.

It was all made even more amazing by the fact that Hiro finally—*finally!*—figured out a way to ensure that Charlie would be nowhere near the Burnt Toast Diner on the day the Brain Man came.

They were spending the afternoon at the park and had wandered up past the duck pond to a row of stone tables with checkered boards painted on their surfaces.

Half a dozen older men were sitting at them, furiously moving chess pieces around, slamming their hands down on timers, making bets and slipping crumpled five- and ten-dollar bills across the tables to one another.

Hiro and Charlie stood for a moment, watching them in fascination. "Want to play?" Hiro asked.

Charlie looked at him, thrilled. "You know how?"

Hiro nodded. His father had taught him how to play chess when he was very young, and while he had never seriously played competitively, he had kept up an interest in the game long after Kaito had stopped inviting him to set up the board in the evenings after dinner.

In its own way, chess was almost as good as video games. Sometimes better. You were the samurai, the soldiers, the generals, planning attacks, protecting your lord, battling for honor. What was not to like?

Charlie clapped her hands. "Yay! I have a set at home, we should go get it—"

"Where at home?"

Charlie looked confused. "On the shelf in my hall closet, but—"

Hiro blinked fiercely—then held the set out to her.

She laughed. "I am *never* going to get used to you doing that!"

They walked over to an empty table and sat down. Charlie carefully pulled each chess piece from the silk-lined box Hiro had fetched, and set them up in rows on the board. The pieces were beautiful, covered with heavy swirling cloisonné.

"My aunt Erika gave me these as a wedding present," Charlie said. "Even though she was the one getting married. I think someone gave them to her, and she really wasn't a chess person."

He smiled, admiring the deep enameled colors of the king as he set it in place.

"You must be serious about chess," he remarked, "to have kept them so pristine over the years."

Charlie blushed. "Actually, when she gave these to me, I'd never played before in my life. But she thought I might like it, because most other games had stopped being fun for me."

"Why is that?"

"Do you know how impossible it is to lose even a single round of *anything* when you have a perfect memory?" she asked, rolling her eyes sardonically. "I'd go to Shelby's weekly poker game and remember every single card that had been dealt. We'd play Trivial Pursuit and I'd have won the game before anyone else got a single pie piece. Even stuff like Charades—since I remember the title to every movie I've ever heard of, I guess the right answers on the very first try." Her mouth turned down in a little pout. "It gets boring winning all the time!"

Hmmm . . . That wasn't exactly a problem Hiro was familiar with.

"So I should prepare for an ass kicking?" Hiro asked, pushing his pawn forward a square and starting the game.

Charlie grinned. "Well," she said, moving one of her own pieces, "You may have a better chance than you'd think. Since I didn't want to ruin another game for myself, I've made a point not to read any books on chess—"

Hiro moved his bishop out of the back row.

"—but every time I play I end up memorizing all the moves the other player makes, so—" She quickly captured it with her queen. "—yeah. Get ready to be crushed."

Hiro grinned and took her rook.

Charlie beat him fairly quickly, although Hiro put up a good fight, making a couple of moves that Charlie had clearly never seen or expected. That made her laugh with happiness at finally having a bit of competition.

While they played, a few of the other players gathered around to watch, and when Hiro finally knocked his king over in defeat, a white-haired guy who was all chin leaned over to Charlie. "Wanna try your hand against a *real* player, missy?"

Charlie raised an eyebrow, giving Hiro a look that clearly said, *NOW you're going to see an ass kicking!*

"Sure," she replied, and Hiro got up to let Chin sit down in his place.

"Twenty-dollar bet," he warned.

Charlie's smile widened. "Good. That'll help pay for my trip around the world."

Charlie dispatched Chin with no trouble at all, and by the time the sun was starting to set and she was packing her chess set lovingly back into its box, she had taken on and beaten every player in the park and had earned $140. Each time a player would tip his king and hand her a bill, Charlie would name the place she was going to spend it—breakfast in Brussels, a rickshaw ride in Jaipur, an offering to the Oracle of Delphi. And with each foreign place she named, the plan grew more solid in Hiro's mind.

He'd thought long and hard about how he was going to keep Charlie away from the diner on October 9. He knew just telling her to stay home wouldn't work. Even though she believed him about his powers, he couldn't figure out a way to tell her he had seen something happen to her in the future without having to tell her exactly what it was.

And he just couldn't tell Charlie she was going to be murdered.

He couldn't do that to her.

But none of the ideas he'd been able to come up with so far seemed solid—as he turned each one around in his mind, he always thought of a way in which it would fail, and Charlie would end up going to the diner and being killed.

In one wildly off-the-wall scenario, he thought he might be able to get her arrested. Frame her or accuse her of some crime and have her locked up tight behind bars, where the Brain Man wouldn't be able to get to her. Only what if she convinced Lloyd to let her out? He'd probably do it, too, if he thought it'd give him another chance with her. Plus there was the fact that everyone in town loved Charlie, and would never believe that she'd break the law.

If anything, they'd arrest *him* for accusing her, falsely or not, and if he was the one in prison, then he really couldn't save her. Not to mention the fact that there was no way he'd be able to survive even ten minutes behind bars. Just going through the *delousing* would probably finish him off.

And, of course, Charlie would hate him if he tried to get her arrested, so forget it. That idea was out.

Maybe he could burn down the diner. That would keep her away from work. Except then the Brain Man would probably just track her to The House of Pies, or wherever, and kill her there. Hiro was pretty certain Charlie had been targeted because of her abilities. So that was no good, either.

Chain her up in the basement?

Drug her?

Clunk her over the head with a leg of lamb, like in that Roald Dahl story, so she'd be safe in the hospital while he ate the evidence?

No, no, and no. None of those was any good. He needed to get her away, maybe go to visit her aunt in Phoenix, or somewhere—anywhere—out of Midland altogether.

But as he listened to Charlie tell the chess players of the exotic places she was going to spend their money, it came to him: if he was going to take her away, why not take her all the way to Japan?

It was brilliant. The Brain Man wouldn't be able to get her if she was six thousand miles away. It would eliminate the chance that she would be called to fill in for one of the other waitresses, or even that she might stop by work to pick up something she'd left. Or any of the million other little things that might put her and the Brain Man in close proximity to each other.

And if she's in Japan, he mused, *even if she does get called in to work, it will take her so long to get there that by the time she arrives, it will already be October 10, and the murder will have been avoided.*

His enthusiasm was beginning to make him silly, he realized then. Nevertheless, he knew she wanted to go to Tokyo. He just hoped she'd want to go there with him.

Right away.

28

"MAN, AM I HUNGRY!" CHARLIE SAID, LIFTING HER SHIRT SLIGHTLY to rub her tummy in a way that made Hiro feel like he needed to lie down in the parking lot and let her back the car over him a couple of times, just to calm him down. "How 'bout you?"

Honestly, Hiro was way too excited to eat.

He had run out to the library during his lunch break and used one of their public computers, logging onto the Japan Airlines website and reserving two plane tickets to Tokyo.

He would like to have left for Japan immediately—would happily have swept Charlie away that very night—but he wasn't sure if she'd be willing to stay away from Midland for three full months, and the whole point of taking her to Japan was to make sure she wouldn't be in Texas in October.

So he had decided to look for flights closer to the terrible date. He was pleased to discover that, by buying the tickets so far in advance, he would knock thousands of dollars off the ticket price. That didn't hurt, either.

So he scrolled ahead through later flights, and sucked in his breath when he saw one scheduled to leave on September 23, *Shobun No Hi,* the autumnal equinox. That day was a holiday in Japan, a celebration of long and lasting life. A lucky day.

Perfect.

He reserved two seats. The computer remembered his corporate card from the last emergency ticket he had bought, and he said a silent *thank you* to the gods—or the accountants at Yamagato Industries—for not cutting off his credit.

He'd printed out the tickets, his mind tumbling with all the different ways he'd be able to invite her on the trip. When he arrived at his decision, he froze time while he got everything ready, then spent the rest of the afternoon grinning like a maniac, unable to contain his excitement as he waited for the lunch shift to end.

Finally, after what seemed like the longest afternoon of his life, everyone finished wiping down their tables and tallying up their receipts, and Hiro and Charlie were in her car, heading home.

Charlie had skipped lunch, so she was starving to death, and as they headed up the front walk from the driveway to her apartment she kept suggesting restaurants they could go to.

Hiro shook his head no to each one. All he wanted to do was get inside, to the surprise he had waiting for her there.

"Well, what do *you* feel like eating?" she finally asked, exasperated, after he'd vetoed yet another suggestion.

"How about some sushi?"

"I wish," she said, fumbling with her front door key. "Too bad the most exotic meal in this town is pizza and beer at the bowling alley."

She pushed the door open and took one step inside, then stopped, amazed. Hiro beamed as she looked delightedly around her.

He had transformed her apartment into a Japanese garden. There were flowers everywhere: branches of delicate white blossoms in tall vases, and water lilies floating in great glass bowls. Glowing paper lanterns hung over a beautifully set table, with intricately folded napkins, ebony chopsticks, and glowing white tapers in crystal prism candlesticks.

"Hiro!" she exclaimed, dazzled, and threw her arms around his neck in an impromptu hug.

Hiro could smell the perfume on her neck, and the warm softness of her body pressed up against his almost made him forget about the evening he had planned.

He held her tight for a moment, then reluctantly let her go. Stepping in front of her, he took her hand and led her into the kitchen. There he pulled out an elegant pot of tea and poured them each a cup, and gestured to the counter, where he'd set up a sushi bar.

"I wanted to give you a little taste of Japan," he said.

Charlie clapped her hands together in delight. "Can I help you make it?"

"*Help* nothing—you'll be doing most of the work!" he teased.

She smiled and reached into a cabinet, searching for a cooking pot. "I don't have a *hangiri*, so we're going to have to make the rice on the stove, but it should still be okay," she said, measuring water, sugar, salt, and vinegar into the pot. "Oh—did you buy any kombu, to give it some texture?"

Hiro, who was reaching into the fridge for the platter of fish he had stowed there earlier, looked over at her, surprised. "How do you know all that? You said the most exotic thing to eat in Midland is pizza."

She smiled a little sheepishly. "Well, if I'm going to have a Japanese boyfriend, I should probably memorize a few Japanese recipes, right?"

Hiro blinked. Wait a minute—did he hear that right? Did she just call him her *boyfriend*?

Charlie was grinning at him, her face blushing pinkly. *Yep. She said "boyfriend" all right!*

"Wah-hoo!"

Hiro threw up his arms, sending tiny red fish eggs flying everywhere like confetti at a parade. Charlie laughed, ducking her head to avoid being showered.

"Oops, sorry," he told her, wiping a fleck of *tobiko* off her cheek with the tip of his finger.

Charlie didn't seem to mind at all.

They drank a cup of tea while the rice finished cooking, and after it cooled Charlie reached for a sheet of nori, positioning it on a bamboo mat, ready for her first lesson.

Hiro showed her how to roll up the sushi, carefully keeping a tight, even pressure on the nori to make a plump, even log.

Charlie mimicked him, clumsily rolling up her sushi into a tilted, misshapen lump. She cut it into sections, looking down sadly at the lop-sided slices.

It was the most adorable thing he'd ever seen.

They carried the plate of sushi into the dining room and sat down at the carefully set table. Charlie reached for the napkin folded on her plate, and Hiro held his breath. Here it was—the moment of truth. He bit his lip, light-headed with anticipation, certain he could feel his heart knock into his tonsils as it leapt up into his throat.

Charlie set her napkin neatly across her lap, then noticed the flat white envelope that had been hidden beneath it.

"What's this?" she asked, with a puzzled smile as she opened it.

Hiro—sweating so much he thought he was going to dissolve completely away—leaned forward, watching as she pulled out one of the plane tickets to Tokyo.

"Oh . . . my . . . God," she said, her voice catching. "A trip to Japan!"

He nodded. "I know you wanted Munich to be the first stop on your trip around the world, but I was hoping Tokyo might be okay instead."

Charlie gazed down at it, shaking her head in disbelief. And when she looked back up at him, her eyes were shining. "Only one ticket?"

Hiro pulled the other one out of his pocket, his hands shaking, feeling happy and nervous and relieved and completely, totally, overwhelmingly in love. He held it up to show her. "In case you said yes."

Charlie smiled at him, looking just as happy and nervous and—did he dare think it?—in love as he was.

"Yes!"

29

"WHAT'S THE MATTER WITH YOU?" LYNETTE ASKED HIRO, HER voice equal parts amused and exasperated.

He looked up from the table where he sat, marrying ketchups, and blinked. "What?"

"You keep sighing."

"I do? Huh. I did not even realize it."

She gave him a funny look. "I don't know what's happening to you," she said.

Hiro didn't know, either, but it was great.

He shrugged, and Lynette went back to rolling silverware up into paper napkin bundles. "You're driving Lloyd crazy, mooning around here with that big smile on your face."

"Sorry."

She smiled. "Well, don't stop on my account."

Hiro nodded.

He couldn't stop. Even if he wanted to.

30

"EXCUSE ME!" HIRO SHOUTED, TRYING TO MAKE HIMSELF HEARD
over the raucous country song that was belting out of the speakers
hanging in every corner of the Jackalope Ice House. The Ice House was
a divey little honky-tonk on the outskirts of Midland.

He waved at one of the sexy bartenders, who was dancing a modified
two-step on top of the long wooden bar, trying to get her attention.
No dice.

He finally caught the eye of a lanky blond bartender who was taking
a breather between "Ring of Fire" and "Friends in Low Places," and motioned her over.

"What can I get you?" she asked, leaning across the bar.

Hiro glanced over at Charlie, who was standing beside him. She
looked perfect. But then again, when didn't she? She had on a light cotton dress covered with tiny flowers. It swished softly around her bare
legs, and she was wearing a leopard-print cowboy hat he couldn't imagine anyone else in the entire world pulling off—but it looked amazing
on her.

Hiro looked around the joint, happily bopping his head to the pulse
of the music. A small wooden dance floor was jam-packed with men
and women in cowboy boots and hats and fringed western shirts, all

moving and gyrating to the song being belted out by the live band, rocking out on a stage in the back of the room.

Then he returned his gaze to the bartenders dancing on the bar, strutting and grinding to the fast-thumping music.

He stared up at them, mesmerized, then caught himself. He didn't want Charlie to think he was enjoying the sight too much.

But when the bartender slapped their drinks down in front of him and he turned to hand one to Charlie, he saw that she was watching the dancers, too, shaking her hips to the music.

A pretty brunette bartender dancing in painted-on jeans and a sparkly rhinestoned shirt looked over at them. She smiled, then reached out a hand and pulled Charlie up onto the bar.

Without skipping a beat Charlie got up and—what was that phrase—*dropped it like it was hot.*

Hiro cheered along with the crowd. He couldn't believe how cool it was having a girlfriend. He watched her dance, awestruck. Not only did he get soft, sweet Charlie, he got wild and crazy Charlie, as well.

When the song ended, she stretched out her arm for him to help her down, and he felt like the luckiest guy in the bar. He wished Miyoki Akayawa, that mean little gymnast from the eighth grade, could see him now!

Nothing could ruin the magic of this night—

"Wanna dance, Hiro?"

—except that.

He shook his head, terrified at the thought.

"I'll just watch you," he said, trying not to show his fear.

When they were kids, Kimiko used to make Hiro practice dancing with her to a Hanson CD she'd gotten for her tenth birthday. They'd gotten pretty good at it, jitterbugging and b-boying across the thick shag carpet in her bedroom, cranking the volume on her stereo higher and higher, until their father finally stuck his head in the room, shouting at them to stop. He claimed they were trying to raise their ancestors from the grave.

But Hiro had apparently used up his entire life's supply of rhythm back then. Because ever since, every time he'd ever attempted to dance in public he'd ended up flailing around like he was being electrocuted, arms and knees disregarding any signals his brain sent to them, hurtling themselves willy-nilly out from his body, whacking into people's noses and knocking over expensive vases and generally doing their damnedest to detach themselves from Hiro altogether.

He'd developed a very subtle front–back rocking movement that he would occasionally trot out in karaoke bars if he was singing a particularly uptempo song, but that was it. He wouldn't even get on the Dance Dance Revolution machine when he'd go out to game centers with friends.

So—sorry, Charlie, but there was just no way.

"Come on," she wheedled, batting her eyelashes seductively at him. "It'll be fun."

Unh-unh. He'd step on her and break her foot. Or break his own foot. Or break *both* their feet.

He opened his mouth to refuse, when—

"I'll dance with you in a heartbeat, pretty lady," a deep voice said over the din.

Hiro turned to see a tall, handsome cowboy who looked like Butch Cassidy's long-lost twin, smiling down at Charlie.

Go away, Hiro silently commanded him.

Butch didn't listen. He tipped his hat to Charlie, giving her a come-hither half grin.

No, no, NO! That is NOT happening, thought Hiro. He wasn't going to lose Charlie, not even for a second, especially not to this rodeo clown. Even if he did look like he ate guys like Hiro for breakfast.

Hiro reached over and slung his arm around Charlie's shoulders, puffing out his chest a little.

"She's dancing with *me,*" he informed the cowboy, in an ice-cold *I-will-hurt-you* voice.

Charlie smiled at Hiro, and then, to his astonishment, gave Butch a wink.

"Sorry, Jake. Guess I'm taken."

She grinned and led an incredulous Hiro over to the dance floor.

"You know him?" he exclaimed.

"It's a small town. Everybody knows everybody! And it got you dancing, didn't it?"

For just a moment, he wondered if he might have been set up. But then he had more important things to worry about.

On the dance floor, everyone was lining up as the band busted out the opening bars of their tongue-in-cheek rendition of "Achy Breaky Heart."

Charlie dragged Hiro into the line across from her. "Just do what I do," she said. "And have fun!"

Don't I get at least one private lesson? he thought, panic beginning to well up inside him. *This is like jumping into the ocean before you even know how to swim.*

The crowd started to move, and he watched Charlie for guidance. She knew the steps perfectly, slapping her boot and clapping at exactly the right moment, in sync with the other dancers and in time with the music.

He was so busy watching her that he forgot to keep dancing and bumped into the guy next to him, who smiled good-naturedly.

Still apologizing, he didn't notice when the whole line jumped to the left, and a stringy-haired woman nearly flattened him.

Hiro glanced at Charlie, embarrassed. Why couldn't he have super-*dancing* powers?

Wait a minute—he didn't have to look like a fool. He could freeze time, practice the steps, and come back once he'd learned them. He was about to do just that when he caught the look on Charlie's face.

She didn't look like she was embarrassed by him. In fact, she was gazing at him like he was the cutest thing on two legs. He didn't need superpowers to be smooth enough for Charlie, he realized. She liked him exactly the way he was.

Just like that, dancing became fun. He wasn't any better at it, but at least he was enjoying himself. He hopped and swung his way through to the end of the song, and applauded enthusiastically along with the rest of the dancers.

"We're going to slow it down a little now," said the lead singer, a middle-aged woman with a smoker's rasp that was surprisingly sexy. "This is a song by Alison Krauss."

As the first low, sweet notes started to play, the crowd on the dance floor thinned out a bit. Hiro started toward the bar, following the other people who were heading that way. But Charlie caught his hand.

"Not so fast," she said, pulling him back to her. "I'm not going to let you get away that easily."

Let him?! Hiro thought, wrapping his arms around her, matching his movements to hers. Slow dancing was a million times easier than line dancing. To say nothing of the fact that it gave him a great excuse to be close to her.

If he had his way, he would hold her like this forever.

31

"So glad y'all could make it!" Lynette said as she opened the gate.

"Like we'd miss one of your parties!" Charlie answered, bussing Lynette on the cheek and handing her the tray of brownies she'd made the night before.

Lynette was hosting her Tenth Annual Labor Day Barbecue Blowout, and Hiro and Charlie had arrived sunscreened, bathing suits under their clothes, and ready to have fun.

In her blue-and-green tie-dyed sarong, Lynette looked like a topographic globe complete with tall peaks, bumpy ridges, and deep valleys. She shut the gate with a clang, then revolved from Ecuador to Uganda, leading the way to the backyard.

Half of Midland was there, mingling around the pool, drinking out of yellow plastic cups. Smoke poured from the barbecue, and country music blared from a pair of beat-up speakers.

Hiro looked around, and suddenly he felt panicked. All these guys with their shirts off! He hadn't even considered the fact that Charlie was going to see him shirtless for the first time, especially around all these enormous rippling Texas farmhands.

Erp.

With a quick glance at Charlie, he quickly excused himself to use the bathroom. Once there, he dropped to the ground and knocked out a hundred—well, at least twenty—push-ups to fire up his guns.

Out of breath and sweating, he stood up and flexed his biceps. *Hmm.* Still not quite satisfactory. He wouldn't want Charlie to think that he—

Wait a minute.

He thought about Charlie, and realized that she wasn't the only one who was going to get a chance to check out the other in a swimsuit. Any second now she was going to be stripping down to her bikini.

Forget the guns, he thought. *Let's get this party started!*

He hurried out to the pool and sure enough, just a few moments later, Charlie started taking off her clothes. She walked over to a striped plastic deck chair by the pool and dropped her purse on it. She shimmied out of her shorts, kicking them off her slender ankles. She flipped the skinny strap of her tank top off one shoulder. Then the other.

Then, in one swift graceful motion, she whisked her whole top off, revealing the sleek white bikini underneath.

Holy cow.

Oh God. It was too much; she was way too gorgeous for him.

Hiro scuttled back into the house.

He slammed the bathroom door shut behind him and leaned against it, trying to calm down and take control of himself.

So he was seeing her in her bathing suit for the first time. He could keep it together, right?

Um. Sure he could.

He and Charlie hadn't had sex yet, they had barely done anything more than kiss, but Hiro didn't care. They had been going out less than a month, and he didn't want to rush things, didn't want to tempt fate by moving too fast.

He had never done this before, never fallen in love like this, never known what it was like to meet someone who made him feel as if the world suddenly made sense, like things would actually turn out right. It was all new to him, and it was wonderful. Charlie was the one. She was what he'd been waiting for his entire life.

And maybe sex shouldn't be a part of it. At least not yet.

After all, Hiro's entire sexual history could be summed up in the four weeks he and Charlie had been going out. And while Charlie had a bit more experience with the opposite sex than he did, from what she'd said she didn't have much. Hiro knew she'd dated several guys, but she'd always taken things glacially slow.

At this point, he and she were pretty well matched, in terms of knowledge and expertise. And while he liked to think of himself as a ho-taming gangsta, deep down inside he had to admit that he was just as happy to ease into the physical side of things.

For now it was enough to hold her hand across the booth at the diner, to enjoy it when she leaned her head against his shoulder while they sat on her couch, watching TV, to touch her face and look in her eyes and know she was feeling the exact same thing as he was.

So no matter how hard it felt at times, they could wait.

Hiro splashed his face with cold water, took a few deep, regulating breaths—*take it slow!*—and went back out to join the party.

They had plenty of time to move their relationship forward, since they no longer had the threat of the Brain Man hanging over them.

They had her whole life.

32

The arrival of Charlie's passport in the mail—the first she'd ever had, pristine now but ready to be groped and fondled by various customs agents—was a cause for great celebration, with corks popping and sparkling cider pouring.

"I can't believe it's really happening, that we're really going to Japan!" Charlie said, giving her passport a ridiculous little kiss.

Hiro clunked his hip against hers lightly.

"Believe it!" he said, even though he personally wouldn't stop worrying until they actually were on the plane and it had taken off. Until then, a persistent little gremlin would keep knocking on his brain, somewhere right behind his eyes, hissing, *She's not safe yet, you haven't saved her yet, it could still fall apart.*

So despite his outward appearance, he didn't relax—he couldn't.

But as the trip grew closer, and their days and night were filled with preparations—reading guidebooks and drawing up itineraries and making packing lists—it became easier and easier to coax the gremlin into lowering his voice a little bit.

. . .

One evening, a couple of weeks before their scheduled departure, they were at Charlie's house and had just finished dinner. Hiro was loading the dishwasher and Charlie was in her bedroom, digging through her closet to find a red leather hatbox that, she said, used to belong to her grandmother, and she wanted to bring along.

Hiro didn't quite understand why she'd want to haul around such an impractical piece of luggage, especially since she wasn't planning on bringing any hats, but he certainly wasn't going to stop her.

He was just rinsing the last traces of spaghetti sauce off the blue pottery serving bowl when he heard Charlie let out an alarmed shout from the bedroom.

"Charlie? You okay?" he called, setting the bowl down and shutting off the water. When she didn't answer, he wiped his hands against the sides of his jeans and headed toward the hallway to check on her. He was halfway there when Charlie came out of the bedroom, clutching her right forearm, her face pale.

"What happened? What's wrong?" he asked frantically.

"I just got attacked."

"Attacked!" Hiro's entire body went cold with dread.

The Brain Man.

Only—she was standing in front of him, her head still irrefutably intact.

"Wait—you were just attacked right now? By who?"

"A brown recluse spider," she said, her voice trembling.

Oh, for the love of . . .

"A what?"

"A brown recluse spider. *Loxosceles reclusa.*" Charlie brushed a strand of hair back from her face with a trembling hand. "It's one of the world's deadliest spiders."

"And you just saw one in your closet?"

She nodded. "They like dark, isolated places. Abandoned barns, vacant haylofts, deserted toolsheds—"

"Cute girls' apartments—"

"Don't make fun of me, Hiro. This is serious."

"I'm not."

He was.

"You know I've been terrified of spiders my entire life," Charlie said, sniffling. "And the venom of the brown recluse spider is nearly eight times as toxic as rattlesnake venom. It can cause *paralysis*. People can *die*."

"I'm not making fun of you," he said again, more seriously, giving her a comforting hug. "What should we do, put some calamine lotion on it or something?"

"I really think I should go to the emergency room." There was an edge of panic in her voice. "Will you come with me?"

"Of course. Should we—call an ambulance?" Charlie had been teaching Hiro how to better drive her old Ford station wagon, doing circles around the parking lot at the big Kroger's grocery store, but he had never driven with other people on the road, or on the highway, so—

She shook her head. "I can drive. I just don't want to go alone."

"Okay," he said, grabbing his jacket. "Just—are you positive it was a brown recluse?"

"Yes," she said, though somewhat uncertainly. "They're very dangerous."

"Did you get a good look at it?"

"I didn't have the chance," she said, indignation in her voice. "It happened too fast."

"Maybe it was a roach," he said, trying to reassure her—and himself, to some degree. "I mean one of those big ones."

"It wasn't a *roach*," Charlie said. "Look, you don't *have* to come with me if you don't want to."

"Are you kidding?" Hiro said. "The hospital on a Saturday night? What could be better than that?"

The triage nurse at the hospital was a short, fat, frowning gnome of a person. She had streaks of sweat down the armpits of her white shirt, and beneath her polyester skirt her legs were unshaved. She scowled at them when they first walked through the sliding double doors of the ER, which didn't exactly inspire confidence, but when they arrived at her desk, Hiro saw that the name tag she was wearing said CHARLIE.

That had to be a good sign, right?

"Same name!" he crowed, giving the nurse a big grin. Her expression didn't change. "She's Charlie, too," he explained, pointing at Charlie, who smiled weakly. "You have the same name."

Scowling-Charlie handed Sweet-Loving-Perfect-Charlie a clipboard and a gnawed-on ballpoint pen.

"Fill this out and have a seat," she ordered in a voice that matched her face. Charlie grimaced in pain as she lifted her arm to take it. Hiro moved quickly to grab it for her.

"I think I've been bitten by a brown recluse," Charlie said. "I need to see a doctor."

"Honey, unless I see you passed out on the floor, you're not seeing anyone until you fill out that form. So you'd better get moving."

"Thank you," Hiro said meekly, and they headed over to the waiting area.

"God, I haven't been to the doctor in years," Charlie said, looking down at the paperwork asking for her medical history and insurance information. "They used to make us get a yearly physical in high school, but that was just one of the nuns taking your temperature and making sure your spine wasn't growing in crooked. The last time I was actually *sick* was January '98."

Hiro raised an eyebrow.

"Strep throat. I had a hundred-and-two-degree fever and couldn't eat for three days. But we were in the middle of intramural volleyball play-offs, and I played outside blocker, so I went to school anyway." She started to throw her hands up in the air in a cheer, then remembered her arm and stopped. "It was worth it, though. Catholic League District Champs!"

"Ah." Hiro didn't quite understand this mentality; he himself tended to be the sort of kid who had a lot of earaches, and would beg to stay home from school if it so much as drizzled outside. "That's very . . . athletic of you." Somehow, he didn't think he sounded enthusiastic.

"Shut up," Charlie said, whacking him with the clipboard.

"I see your arm's feeling better," he said, and she instantly crumpled her hand back into her lap.

"Shut up," she muttered again, then started rapidly filling out the form.

Hiro grinned, reassured that her injury wasn't life threatening, then looked around the waiting room.

Other than a geezer slumped across three seats, snoring, and a couple of drunken roughnecks who looked like they'd stopped by on their way home from Fight Club, the place was deserted. Maybe that meant they wouldn't have to wait too long.

There was a TV bolted to the ceiling in the corner of the room, with a remote control attached to it by a long grimy chain. Hiro walked over and grasped the remote.

"I turn this on, okay?" He addressed the room in general.

No one responded, so he shrugged and hit the POWER switch.

Static.

Static.

Some football movie. *Rudy*, he thought—the movie about the Notre Dame football player.

Static.

Jerry Springer.

More static.

Hiro shrugged and flipped back to *Rudy*. *Eh. Whatever.* Better than watching the drunks, he mused halfheartedly.

Adorable-Charlie got up to give her completed paperwork to Grumpy-Charlie, then came back and sank down next to Hiro, leaning against his shoulder. She watched the movie in silence for a few minutes, then let out a gigantic sigh.

Hiro looked over at her. "How you doing?"

"It hurts to talk. I can't move my face. My face is on fire."

"That's tetanus. You don't have that. Unless the spider that bit you was rusty."

"I think the venom is spreading. The poison is circulating through my body."

"You know, Rudy undergoes all *sorts* of hardship, but he *never* complains."

Charlie shot him a sideways glance.

"I hate this movie."

Two hours later. The drunken roughnecks had long since been patched up and sent home, the sleeping geezer had woken up and wandered out into the night, Frowny-Charlie had abandoned her desk and was no-where to be seen. On the screen Rudy had just sacked the other team's quarterback and was being carried off the field by his teammates, and Hiro and Charlie had both dissolved into tears.

"I never cry at movies," Charlie sobbed. "Not even *Bambi*. Not even *E.T.*"

"They wouldn't let Rudy play," Hiro told her, "but he didn't give up, and now he's won."

A doctor in a white coat so new it still had the creases in it came strolling past the empty triage nurse's desk and saw Charlie and Hiro in the waiting room, weeping. He angled over to them, looking concerned. "Are you okay?"

"I was bitten by a brown recluse spider," Charlie told him, wiping away her tears with the back of her hand.

The doctor sucked in his breath. "Ouch." He looked over at Hiro. "Did he get you as well?"

Hiro snuffled, feeling like an idiot. "No, I cry because of movie."

The doctor glanced up at the TV, where the end credits were play-ing, and made a face. "I went to USC," he said, then turned back to Charlie.

"Okay, where'd the spider bite you?"

"On my arm." Wincing slightly, Charlie pulled up her sleeve and held her arm out to show the doctor.

He studied it for a second. "Where?"

She pointed. "Right there."

He leaned closer, peering intently. "I don't see anything."

"Are you kidding? I was attacked by a poisonous spider, and you're telling me you don't even see the bite?"

The doctor shook his head.

"It's right there. Right there! You're telling me you don't see that?"

The doctor shot a look at Hiro, who shrugged helplessly.

The doctor shrugged, too.

"Don't give me that!" Charlie said indignantly. "I know what hap-pened to me, and I'm not going to die just because you need glasses."

"Well, your symptoms aren't severe, so you're not going to give up the ghost right away," the doctor said, his voice reassuring. "Why don't you give us a blood sample. We'll send it to the lab, see if they find anything. Right this way—" He looked at the clipboard he'd picked up from the desk. "Right this way, Charlene."

Hiro squeezed her hand tightly before Charlie followed the doctor off into an exam room. He picked up the remote and started flipping through the TV channels again, settling back in the uncomfortable plastic chair.

"I told him the article I read said an antivenin had to be given in the first three hours, but he cited a study at Baylor that refuted that."

"Wait—how many articles have you read about brown recluses?"

"There was another one in the paper this morning."

Okay. No wonder she'd been freaking out.

"Maybe next time, when you see an article about spiders, you could just flip the page, not read it," he suggested gently.

Charlie's eyes widened, and she shook her head. "You've got to know what's out there. It's the only way to stay safe. There's nothing worse than not knowing."

Hmm—he didn't think he really agreed with her. Why live in fear? Especially if you've got a Hiro to save you? But he didn't want to press the issue.

"You want to come in for a while?" he asked as she pulled the car up in front of his house. He glanced at his watch. "It's not even ten."

"Night's a puppy," Charlie said, and shut off the engine.

33

THEY TRIED TO RE-CREATE THE *RUDY* MAGIC WITH *VARSITY BLUES,* but it just wasn't the same, even though Hiro personally found the thought of whipped cream bikinis inspiring in a completely different sort of way.

By the time it was finished neither of them could stop yawning.

"God, I don't feel like driving home," Charlie said, stretching and carrying their soda cans over to the sink.

"You should stay," Hiro said, looking around the tiny room, which was without a couch. "I could sleep on the floor."

"No, that's silly," Charlie said.

Damn. It would have been nice to wake up with Charlie there.

But she wasn't finished.

"It's a big bed. We could both sleep in it, I think that would be fine."

Holy cow.

"I mean, just—*sleep*—" she said, sounding a bit awkward now.

"Of, of course, absolutely," he agreed immediately. "Don't worry—"

"I'm not," she said with a smile. "Besides, it'll be good practice for Tokyo."

Very true. Hiro had avoided thinking about the sleeping arrangements for the trip. He'd hoped that they would be staying in the same room, but hadn't known how to bring it up with Charlie without sounding either lecherous or, even worse, priggishly chaste.

"This'll give you a chance to get used to my snoring," she said.

Hiro laughed. "You don't snore." She was perfect, and perfect people didn't snore.

"Like a lumberjack," she said, nodding solemnly. "You better pack some earplugs."

She walked over to the shelves where he kept his clothes. "Mind if I borrow a T-shirt?"

Hiro shook his head, his throat suddenly dry. Charlie grabbed one, then walked to the door to the hall leading to the bathroom. "I'm going to go get changed."

" 'Kay," he managed to choke out.

While Charlie was in the bathroom, Hiro made a mad flurry of sleepover preparations. Fluffed the pillows, switched the old pillowcases, flipped the top sheet over to give it a somewhat-fresh feeling.

Then he ducked into the kitchen—in case she came back in while he was undressing—and changed into his most alluring pair of boxer briefs and a clean, fitted black T-shirt.

Nice.

Hiro Nakamura, sex machine.

Or not. He pulled a pair of shorts on.

He didn't want to already be in bed when she came back in—that would be too presumptuous—so he settled for leaning against the wall with one elbow, his other fist on his waist, one leg slightly forward to elongate his body. He'd learned that particular pose from watching *America's Next Top Model.*

A minute later, the door opened and Charlie shyly peeped in. Hiro forgot to hold his pose as he stared at her.

Oh God, she's cute as a bug in that shirt. Even though it was about six sizes too big for her, she made it look insanely tantalizing. The hem came halfway down her thighs, and the neckline kept slipping to the side, exposing one perfect freckled shoulder. DON'T MESS WITH TEXAS was emblazoned across the front—he hoped it was a coincidence that she'd picked that one, and not a warning.

She gave him a bashful smile as she walked over to the bed and sat down. "It's so weird having you see me in my pajamas," she said.

"I can turn the lights out."

"I'm just being silly. I mean, you saw more of me in my bathing suit at Lynette's party."

Gulp!

He lunged for the lights, hit the switch, and the room was plunged into darkness. He felt his way over to the bed, climbed in, and lay down, shy and horny and petrified. He was both dreading and looking forward to sleeping next to her, terrified of what they might do, and also of what they might not.

He didn't want to move, was scared to death that any part of him might accidentally brush against any part of her, in case she got the wrong idea and thought he was trying to molest her. So he lay frozen, flat on his back, hyperconscious of the way the bed jounced every time he breathed.

Inhale—jiggle.

Exhale—jiggle.

Inhale—jiggle.

Exhale—jiggle.

Damn, the bed was rocking so much she'd probably think he was molesting *himself.*

Okay, he would just take shallower breaths, little light tiny motionless breaths.

That worked for about thirty seconds, until he realized he wasn't getting enough oxygen and thought he was going to pass out. Finally he couldn't control it anymore and gasped for air, his lungs convulsing, his breath a buzz saw, the bed rocking and bouncing so much he was afraid she might need to take a Dramamine.

God, he was such a loser. Charlie was probably trying to figure out the fastest escape route out of his apartment. He snuck a peek at her. His eyes had adjusted to the dark, and she was barely visible in the faint glow coming through the curtains, cast by the streetlight outside. Then he felt the bed shift as she turned to face him.

Here it comes, he thought. Just—take it like a man when she says she has to leave. Don't cry in front of her. Wait until she's gone to start bawling.

"Sorry if I was such a pain at the hospital," she murmured.

Oh! That was unexpected. *Rock!*

"You weren't."

He also turned, just slightly, so he was facing her, careful to keep his hands pulled in tight against his body.

"Besides, when we get to Tokyo, I'm going to make you come with me to the optometrist's. *Then* you'll see some drama. When they blow that little puff of air in your eye . . . Ugh!"

He gave an exaggerated quiver.

Charlie laughed. "Hey, you can't be too careful around little puffs of air," she said, and gave him a little shove on the shoulder.

She didn't pull her hand back, though. She kept it there, and Hiro was glad it was too dark for her to see the absolutely seraphic look on his face.

"Watch out, here comes the scary air!" she teased and, leaning forward, blew softly in his ear.

"Stop!" he giggled. "Or else I'll get you back with—the spider!"

He scrabbled his fingers across the mattress between them, scurrying them up her arm, and she shrieked and giggled and somehow magically moved closer to him.

So he spidered around to her back, and then they were kissing again.

Only this time, they were kissing *lying down*. In a *bed*. And whatever Hiro thought he knew about pleasure hopped on the short bus and went back to remedial classes, because what he was feeling now was so much more advanced and sexy and urgent than anything he had ever known before.

He could feel every inch of her body against his, their bare legs sliding across each other's, their heartbeats syncopating, separated by only thin layers of fabric, his hands moving across her back, down her sides, touching the softness of her body through the T-shirt.

"Oh!" he couldn't stop himself from gasping, and although he instantly turned a glowing neon red, blushing so fiercely he lit up the room like the molten core of a reactor, she didn't pull away.

Miraculously, she rolled onto her back and pulled him closer.

Holy cow!

Her T-shirt had ridden up just a little—there was that smooth flat strip of tummy he had admired so many times. He brushed his fingers across it, sure he was going to leave a trail of sparks, then slowly, carefully, slipped his hands up under her shirt, sliding their way up her stomach until they were touching her breasts.

Oh my God! He was touching her breasts! For real! In person! He couldn't believe it! They felt—they felt—

Well, actually, they felt a lot like the way her arm felt—soft warm smooth skin. But the fact that he *knew* they were breasts, and he was the only one who was allowed to touch them, made it five million times better than touching her arm.

Well, *duh.* Hiro rolled his eyes in the dark.

She let out a little breath.

And then he leaned over and tenderly brushed his lips across the strip of her exposed stomach. Her skin felt like it was on fire; he could feel the heat lustering off it. He kissed it again, and now it was Charlie who made the *oh!* sound, the muscles in her stomach clenching.

The sound and the movement together were so erotic that he forgot about his nerves, forgot about his naïveté.

He traced his lips over her flat stomach, branding a circle around her belly button with the tip of his tongue. Moving higher, her shirt floating upward, exposing what his hands kept covered, kissing a line up the sweet hollow of her sternum, breathing in the warm mysterious scent of her skin.

Charlie moaned, her fingers tightening in his hair, pulling it sharply, and Hiro felt his whole body *tug.*

A wave of emotion and desire crashed down over him, feelings so irresistible and overpowering and just plain *good* that he—

—teleported away. Instantly. Accidentally. Inadvertently.

Again.

Shit!

34

H E WAS FREEZING.

Even before he opened his eyes, he knew it had happened again, that he had teleported again despite himself.

Why? Why now?

He was enraged, he felt cursed—why did his powers always malfunction right when Hiro was happiest?

Why did he keep *doing* that?

Discomfort began to overcome his anger, though, and he decided he would figure it all out as soon as he got out of this absolutely ice-cold place.

Finally he opened his eyes. He was lying on a counter, in a steel room full of medical instruments and machinery all clustered around a steel examination table, on which there was a body draped with a sheet.

Instantly he slammed them shut again.

He was in a morgue!

He screwed his eyes even more tightly shut, concentrating, trying to teleport away as fast as he could.

Take me back take me back take me back.

But it didn't work.

He tried again, concentrating harder—

Nothing.

The goose bumps on his arms and the hair prickling up on the back of his neck made it all too clear that he was still in that steel room. And that covered body was still lying on the table.

Oh God, I have to get out of here!

Trying again and again . . .

. . . but it still didn't work.

He started to hyperventilate. Why weren't his powers working? What was happening? Why couldn't he escape?

He was starting to feel light-headed, so he ordered himself to calm down.

Breathe.

Relax.

Of *course* he couldn't control his focus if he was panicking. It was like the time—during one of the first driving lessons Charlie had given him—that the car wouldn't start when he turned the key. Instead of waiting, he had turned the ignition over and over, pressing the gas pedal again and again, trying so hard to make it start that he'd ended up flooding the engine.

I've flooded my own engine, he decided. *That's why I can't teleport. I just need to calm down and wait for my focus to return.*

He kept his eyes shut, controlling his breathing the way he'd learned in the morning tai chi classes Yamagato Industries had offered its employees. Slow deep breaths, his body and mind relaxing, until finally he felt ready to try again.

Okay.

He concentrated, focusing all his energy and emotion on Charlie, on teleporting back to her—

And still nothing happened.

What's going on? Why couldn't he get back to Charlie?

Hiro finally opened his eyes again, and they fell on the sheet-covered body. He sucked in his breath. What if he couldn't get back to Charlie . . . because he was already with her?

What if the body on that table is her?

He didn't want to look, but he had to. He had to know. So he sat up and slowly lowered himself off the counter, self-consciously remembering that he was still barefoot and wearing shorts.

A dozen shuffling steps brought him to the foot of the exam table. With a trembling hand, he grasped the edge of the sheet and slowly pulled it back until a pale, hairy foot came into view.

A *man's* foot.

Hiro staggered back, sagging with relief. It wasn't Charlie. *Thank God.*

A heavy slip of oaktag was tied around the man's toe. Hiro glanced at the name written on it: WALKER, JAMES.

Hmmm. Hiro didn't know anyone named James Walker. Poor guy, whoever he was, but that didn't help explain what was happening.

Why had he teleported here, to this place, to this room? There had to be a reason—the way he saw it, there were no coincidences. Every odd occurrence and unexplainable experience he'd encountered had been another piece of the puzzle, another step on his journey; all inexorably linked to his mission, his destiny. So this man, this body, must be connected in some way, too.

His glanced back down at the tag, and froze, noticing for the first time the date written under the name: AUGUST 19.

Twenty days ago.

Unless James Walker had been lying on this table for almost three weeks—and, not that he was any kind of expert on forensics, but there was no way that foot had been dead for that long—Hiro had unknowingly and unintentionally traveled back in time.

Why? *Why?*

He was fairly certain the answer was lying right in front of him.

He might not recognize the name *James Walker,* but there was a chance that maybe he'd recognize the face. So while the thought of looking into the dead man's eyes filled Hiro with horror, he felt some unseen force prodding at him, moving his hands forward to grip the sheet next to the man's head.

He took a deep breath and pulled, exposing the man's head and upper body.

Instantly, he dropped the sheet, stumbling backward, retching, groping blindly for a trash can. As soon as he found one, he threw up into it.

The top three inches of James Walker's head had been sliced off, and his brain had been removed.

Hiro heaved again and again, his body spasming as the full implications of what he had seen hit him.

He didn't recognize James Walker's face, but he certainly understood now how he was connected. It wasn't just Charlie and Isaac Mendez who were victims of the Brain Man. James Walker had been killed by him, too. And who knew how many others were out there, men and women, all perilously close to being hemicapitated at this murderer's hands.

Hiro felt icy tendrils of fear clamp around his throat, suffocating him, testing his resolve, as the sudden realization of his own carelessness raced berserker-like through every nerve in his body.

How could he have let his mind stray, even for one second, to anything other than the mission?

No wonder his powers weren't working right. He'd screwed up, gotten off track, lost sight of his true purpose. His destiny wasn't to fall in love with Charlie, it was to *save* her.

His mission had always been there, looming next to him, hanging over his head. *Save Charlie from the Brain Man.* Twice he had forgotten it, had let himself get so caught up in the emotions of falling in love that he had put it out of his mind entirely, and twice he had accidentally teleported away.

But he couldn't afford to forget it a third time. October 9 was right around the corner.

Time was running out.

35

HIRO FROZE TIME AS HE LEFT THE MORGUE, BOTH TO KEEP ANYONE from seeing him and to make sure—thank heavens—that at least one of his powers was working again.

On the way out he found a locker with some clothes that almost fit him. He spotted a man who was particularly well dressed, and borrowed some money from his wallet. He was careful to write down the man's name and address, so he could mail back the money when he got home.

Even so, he felt guilty.

But then he focused again.

He figured destiny had been giving him a wake-up call, to remind him not to let himself get distracted from his mission again. And he was going to heed that warning.

He didn't want to risk teleporting to an even more inconvenient time, so he took a Greyhound back to Midland, slouching in his seat with an Anaheim Angels baseball cap pulled low over his eyes, interacting with no one. He was dying to run straight to Charlie, but since he was still three weeks in the past, he was afraid of what might happen if he did.

The way he figured it, based strictly on *The Terminator* and the *Back to the Future* movies, time was both circular and progressive—everything that had already happened was still happening, and it was just a matter of rejoining the chronology at the right moment. The Hiro who was in bed making out with Charlie would teleport away, and he'd step in to take his own place.

Sadly, he realized he wouldn't be able to pick up *exactly* where they left off. He resolved to rejoin her the next morning, just to be safe.

He knew that he couldn't do anything to mess with the space-time continuum, so he had to avoid *himself* at all costs. Thus he checked into a different motel than the one he'd stayed in back in April, one where he was pretty sure he wouldn't be recognized, and he waited for time to catch up.

He spent the next twenty days in complete isolation, being overly cautious about being seen, afraid to let himself get sidetracked again. At the same time, he was full of fresh determination and resolve to spend the weeks thinking solely and fully about the mission, about destiny, about Charlie.

By the third day he was going stir crazy, and ended up passing the bulk of the time by composing an epic poem, an ode to Charlie's beauty, as well as by eating candy from the vending machine, practicing standing on his head, getting irrevocably hooked on *All My Children*, reminiscing about the wonder of Charlie's breasts, drawing up an imaginary guest list for their dream wedding, circling items he wanted to order in a dog-eared L.L.Bean catalog someone had left in the room, and picking balls of lint off the nasty pilled bedspread.

Hiro could hardly wait for time to catch up so he could rejoin the world, but when the day arrived he was so desperately overeager that he started to second-guess himself.

Wait, does August have thirty days or thirty-one?

He managed to psych himself out. So by the time he finally convinced himself that *Yes, today is the right day*, he ended up being nearly three hours late for his morning busboy shift.

He burst through the front door of the diner, so excited to see Charlie that he could hardly contain himself—and was crushed to discover that she wasn't in the dining room.

She wasn't in the kitchen, storeroom, or break room, either. He had halfway talked himself into venturing into the ladies' room to look for her there when Lynette spoke up.

"She's not here today, babe. She called in this morning, said she needed to go to the doctor."

"Oh my God, what happened? Is she okay? Is she sick?"

"She said she got bit by a spider and needed to pick up the results of the blood test they gave her."

Of course!

Hiro sank down onto one of the counter stools, gasping in relief. Even though weeks had passed for him since the evening they had gone to the hospital, for Charlie the spider bite had happened less than a day earlier.

"Is she coming in to work the lunch shift?" he asked.

Lynette shook her head.

"I told her to go ahead and take the day off." She gave him a sly grin. "You came in so late, I thought you might be playing hooky with her."

Hiro smiled back. He wished he was.

Well, he'd already waited twenty days to see Charlie. He guessed a few more hours wouldn't hurt.

He tried calling her during his break, then again when he finished his shift, but she wasn't home either time. So he decided to go back to his own apartment and change his clothes, then head over to her house and wait for her. The nice thing about being in such a small town was that he knew the person he was looking for was bound to come home soon—there weren't that many places to go.

In his own apartment he noticed with satisfaction a few small signs of Charlie's having spent the night: his DON'T MESS WITH TEXAS shirt crumpled in the hamper, a coffee cup in the sink, the bed made far neater than he'd ever managed to make one on his own.

He showered, then put on his thin blue jacket, the one with the kanji lettering spelling out "I don't belong here" on the front pocket. Even though she still wasn't home, he decided to walk to her apartment. It would be nice to be out in the fresh air, anyway, after being cooped up in that motel room for so long.

He got to her house while it was still pretty light out, and settled down on her stoop to wait.

The streetlights were already winking on and the sun was dropping fast by the time he saw her car pulling up to the curb.

She came up the walk, rooting around in her bag for her keys, and stopped short as he leapt up to greet her. A fleeting look of resignation or sadness or tolerance moved like a cloud across her face.

But maybe it was a trick of the failing light, he thought, because when she reached him on the steps, she put her arms around him and gave him the sort of kiss he would have expected from someone he hadn't seen, or wasn't going to see, for a very long time.

"How's it going, Mary Jane?" he said.

"Don't call me that," Charlie said, joking but not really. She opened her door then turned to face him, moving her body to block him from trying to come in with her. "Turns out it wasn't a brown recluse, or if it was, he didn't bite me."

"Well, that's awesome news, right?"

She nodded but didn't say anything, and didn't invite him in.

"Where were you all day? I tried calling a bunch of times."

"Just running some errands."

"Oh, where'd you—"

"You know what, Hiro? I'm really tired and just want to get inside." She held up a carry-out bag of burritos, gave it a little shake. "Dinner's getting cold."

He stared at her, bewildered. Was she mad? Was it because he'd teleported? Did he do something wrong? Had he smooshed a butterfly weeks ago in LA that led to her being mad today?

"So, do you want me to go?" he asked, trying hard not to sound petulant.

For one heart-stopping instant it looked like she was going to say yes, but then she shook her head, giving him a smile that didn't quite reach her eyes.

"Then I'd have to eat all these burritos myself."

And she led the way inside.

36

INSIDE HER HOUSE THERE WAS MORE EVIDENCE THAT HE HADN'T messed with the chronology when he'd teleported—her passport was still propped up on the bookshelf, the spaghetti bowl he'd been washing was still in the sink, a cork was on the floor under the table where it had whizzed, but still, Hiro could definitely tell there was something wrong.

Charlie had a quietness about her, a stiffness he'd never seen before, and that made him very nervous and very sad. She was definitely upset about something, even if she said she wasn't.

God, maybe she thought their relationship was moving too fast. Maybe she was pissed off that he'd been so forward with her, so presumptuously handsy.

"Um, so last night—" he said, not sure where he was going but figuring he'd get there eventually, "when we were at my house, in bed and all—"

For the first time all night, some of the warmth came back in her eyes.

"That was wonderful," she said.

Hiro Nakamura, sex machine!

"I thought so, too," he replied.

He moved a little closer to her on the couch, waiting for her to elaborate on his masterful skill and irresistible magnetism, or at least express a wish for him to put his arms around her.

But instead she just took a bite of burrito and moved away from him, ostensibly to reach for a napkin.

Okay, something is definitely wrong.

"Um, so I accidentally teleported again last night—"

"So I noticed."

Oh God, no wonder she's acting like this.

"I'm really sorry."

"It's fine. I'm just glad you got back so quickly this time." She grinned at him. "I spent the whole morning figuring out a cover story for the folks at the diner in case you'd ended up in Japan again, and had to take another plane home."

Huh, okay, maybe she wasn't mad. Maybe he'd just been imagining the whole thing.

"Bus. I just landed in LA."

"Well, good. Least you weren't gone too long."

"Yeah, but I wish I'd been here to go with you to get the results from the spider bite."

Charlie didn't answer. She got up and carried her plate, her burrito only half eaten, into the kitchen.

Hiro got up and followed her.

"Charlie? Is everything okay?"

"I told you, turns out I wasn't bitten after all," she said.

Yeah, but—"Is everything else okay?"

She shrugged. "Sure. I haven't been to a doctor in so long that I figured while I was there this morning, I might as well let them do a physical, just to make sure everything else is fine."

"And is it?"

"Is what?"

"Is everything fine?"

Charlie laughed. "Yes, Hiro. I told you I never get sick. It was just a checkup."

"Routine scheduled maintenance."

She turned away from the sink and gave him a funny look. "What?"

"Oh, in *Robogirl*? She has to go once a month to visit this guy called The Mechanic—he's this mysterious old Japanese guy who has sick mechanical skills—he can fix any kind of machine or computer or motor that's broken. He's the only one who's able to repair Robogirl, and he's also, like, her only friend. So she goes in for these checkups, just to make sure all her parts are working smoothly. They call it routine—"

He looked up and saw that Charlie had folded her arms in front of her chest and was peering at him with narrowed eyes.

"—routine . . . scheduled . . . maintenance," he finished. Then, innocently, "What?"

"Only I'm not a robot," she said, still glaring at him.

"What?" he repeated, confused.

"I'm not Robogirl!"

Huh? "I know that."

"Do you? 'Cause you're always going on about how I'm sooooo much like her, but I'm not her, and I'm sick of you trying to turn me into her."

What the hell?

"I know you're not her," he said, feeling a little peeved himself, and not quite knowing why.

"If you love Robogirl so much, why don't you just go home and read about her in one of your stupid comic books!"

Ouch.

Okay, what was going on? He took a deep breath.

Charlie was acting, well, to be perfectly frank, she was acting like it was that time of the month. Hiro had grown up with an older sister, and had been forced to learn to accept being yelled at irrationally. But he had also learned not to *ever* suggest that maybe the reason she was yelling was due to anything Tampax-related.

"I'm sorry," he said, managing to sound more sincere than annoyed. "I never meant to imply that I wanted you to *be* Robogirl."

Because he hadn't. Not really. Sure, they were a lot alike, but Hiro would choose flesh-and-blood Charlie over ink-and-paper Robogirl in a heartbeat.

"Good," Charlie said, still sounding miffed. "I wouldn't want to disappoint you by actually being human, and not some superpowered robot."

Okay, the fight wasn't over.

Hiro suddenly, desperately wished he'd hung on to that copy of *I Like Me: A Growing Guide for Girls*. He bet that it would have some suggestions for how to defuse this argument. But without it, he was just going to have to handle it himself. So he said what he thought would be the cheeriest possible answer. "Are you kidding? I could *never* be disappointed by you." Her face softened a bit. Good. He'd meant it, too. "Here, come on, I'm sorry."

He walked over and gave her a hug, and she sighed, the tension leaving her shoulders as she hugged him back.

He stood there with his arms around her for a long minute, until he thought he felt the anger drain completely out of her, then gave her a little smooch on top of her head.

"That's better. You okay? I'm sorry."

She nodded, her head against his chest, still holding him tight.

"Besides," he added, "you might not be a robot, but you do have superpowers."

And for some reason, that was the worst possible thing to say.

Charlie instantly went rigid, and she pushed away from him, staring at him like she'd been hugging a Goliath bird-eating tarantula.

"Screw this power," she shouted. "I *hate* it. I wish I didn't have it."

Okay, this was more than PMS.

"But your memory is a gift—you can do great things with it—"

"It's *not* a gift! I don't want it anymore. I wish it would go away!"

"Part of being a hero is accepting—"

"Oh my God, do *not* lecture me about yin and yang again!" Charlie said, slapping her hand on the kitchen counter with a bang.

Hiro winced, as stung as if she'd slapped his face.

"It's *bullshit*, and I'm sick of it," she said, and her eyes filled up with tears. "Don't you think there are things I don't want to remember? Don't you think there are things I'd rather keep shut away?"

"You'd said that," Hiro said quietly, shaken by her outburst. "Playground bullies, kids being mean—"

"I can remember my parents dying!" she interrupted angrily. "I was only *six months old*, but I remember every detail of the car accident—the noise, the broken glass, the *blood*." Her voice was hoarse, and Hiro swallowed hard, shocked and distressed, not knowing what to do.

"It never really felt real to me before, never felt like an actual tragedy, because I was so young when it happened, I was too little to know them. But now, thanks to this stupid power, I remember them." She started to cry for real. "I remember them, and I *miss* them."

Hiro stared at her, helpless. He desperately wanted to hold and comfort her, but she seemed so fragile he was scared to touch her, and completely at a loss for words.

Charlie took a deep shuddering breath, swiping at the tears on her face as she looked straight into his eyes. "So I don't want this power. I wish it would *go away*!"

It?

Or *him*?

Hiro hesitated, a million thoughts jumbling through his mind. What had brought this on? Had being at the hospital reminded her of being taken there with her parents after the accident? He wanted to talk to her about it, wanted to help her, and even if she wanted him to go away, there was no way he could leave until he knew that she was going to be okay.

"Charlie," he said softly, reaching out and not quite touching her arm. His hand hovered uncertainly a few millimeters over her sleeve.

"I'm sorry," she said, turning away from him to face the sink again. She turned on the cold water and soaked a clean dishcloth. Then she pressed it to her eyes, calming herself down and wiping every trace of the tears away.

Hiro watched her, his entire body a question mark.

She looked over at him and smiled, but with difficulty, and her eyes were shadows in her face.

"I'm sorry," she said again. "It's not you, I'm just—it's been a long day."

"What can I do?" he asked. "How can I help you?"

"I just need to take a nice hot bath and go to bed," she said. "I'm just tired. But I'll be fine tomorrow."

She moved across the room, gently shepherding him toward the door.

"I don't want to leave you when you're upset," he said, his shoulders hunching.

"I'm fine," she answered, her face twisting into an expression she probably meant to be reassuring. "I'll just see you at work tomorrow, okay?"

"Okay," Hiro said, since he didn't really have any other choice.

Then, even though every impulse inside him was screaming at him to stay, he did what Charlie wanted. He turned around and walked away.

37

THE NEXT MORNING CHARLIE CAME INTO THE DINER AND HUGGED Hiro hard, whispering "sorry" in his ear, then gave him a kiss so wickedly passionate Hiro was almost able to forget how upset she'd been the night before.

Almost, but not quite.

Because even though she acted and looked like everything was back to normal, there was an odd energy about her, and a distance he'd never felt before, that made his chest grow tight for no apparent reason.

She still laughed and chatted with him at the diner, and hung out with him after work, but it felt a little forced. Over the next few days Hiro tried to see if she was acting this way with anyone else at work, but because he couldn't pinpoint the way she was being weird, it was impossible to tell.

What was definitely weird, though, was the fact that she suddenly had less time to spend with him. They'd hung out practically every night the entire summer, but now she was suddenly needing nights in by herself, or "out with the girls," and there were several days when she didn't come in to work until the lunch shift. One day she didn't come in at all.

He tried to ask her about it, but he wasn't sure what to ask her, because anytime he asked if she was okay, she either blew it off with a hasty "of course" or made a joke. Neither of which provided a satisfactory answer, but at least she wasn't yelling at him again, so he didn't want to press his luck.

Besides, they'd be in Japan in a matter of days, and then he could stop worrying. Because even if she was still acting funny, at least she'd be funny and *alive*.

So for now, he decided the best thing to do was just act the same way he always had. If she could pretend nothing was wrong, then so could he.

"Guess what?"

Hiro bounded up to the counter where Charlie was wiping down all the equipment after the shift, getting things clean and ready for the morning. "They're having a Samurai Film Festival at the Drafthouse in Austin!"

"Austin?" Charlie said with a little *oh-that's-right-you're-not-from-around-here* laugh. "That's over three hundred miles away."

"So what? If we leave right now, we can make it in time for *Yojimbo*, *Seven Samurai*, and *Hidden Fortress*. This is going to be so awesome—you're going to love them!"

Her face fell.

"Hiro—I can't leave right now—"

"Hmm. Tell you what—how about I 'help' you finish up your side work? I bet I can get it done in no time," he joked.

But she shook her head. "No, I mean, I can't go out with you *tonight*. I already have plans." She turned the corners of her mouth down in a sad little frown. "I'm sorry."

The hell? He and Charlie had gone out together every single Tuesday night since they met, because they both had Wednesdays off. Tuesday night was *their* night. How could she possibly make other plans?

And an even bigger question: who did she make them with?

At that moment, to Hiro's abject horror and disbelief, Lloyd came in, his hair pomaded into a sleek glinting helmet, vast clouds of Stetson stirring the air around him into a rolling boil, the collar of his stupid polo shirt turned up like it was proclaiming to the world: *Hey, everybody! Here comes a big pretentious asswipe!* He came up behind Charlie and put his big greasy paw on the small of her back.

"You about ready, babe?"

Lloyd! Was she kidding? Was this some kind of sick joke?

"Five minutes," she answered quickly, refusing to meet Hiro's eye as she assiduously polished the milk shake machine.

Lloyd had no such qualms, and gave Hiro a grin so triumphant and self-satisfied that there must not have been a canary left in the entire state of Texas.

"I'll go pull the car around," he said, and then swaggered out, leaving the stench of his drugstore cologne behind.

Hiro glanced around wildly, certain that Ashton Kutcher was about to pop out from behind the deep fryer to inform him that he'd been punked, because there was really no way in heaven or hell or anywhere in between that Charlie was actually going out tonight with Lloyd. Right?

Right?!!!

Charlie still wouldn't look up at him.

"It's not a date or anything," she told the exceptionally shiny milk shake machine. "It's just dinner. As friends."

Hiro's face crumpled. He tried to answer her, but his throat was rapidly closing up, so all that came out was a rasping little wheeze of air.

Charlie finally looked at him, and he managed a casual little *whatever* shrug.

Seriously, he needed a tracheotomy or something, because his throat had swollen shut. He couldn't breathe, let alone talk. So when she said, "I'll see you tomorrow," in a quiet funny voice as she headed out to Lloyd's waiting four-by-four, he just sketched a wave at her, then sank onto a stool, laying his head down on the bleach-scented counter.

The Formica was blissfully cool against his burning cheek as he waited to black out from the lack of oxygen.

Hiro Nakamura was no stranger to pain. In his twenty-four years he had experienced practically every type of pain there was: physical, psychological, emotional, existential.

He'd been whacked in the bazookas by a Little League fastball clocking in at over thirty miles an hour.

He'd gotten turned down by his high school's Physics Olympics team because, as Matsu Bekku, the team's captain, told him, "Just because you look like a total geek, it doesn't mean you're smart."

He'd let his beloved Daisho, the fourteenth-level dwarf cleric he'd spent three years creating, get killed within the first five minutes of a weekend-long D&D tournament at summer camp.

And he'd had to stand alone on stage in front of the entire school, in the middle of a production of *Romeo and Juliet,* dressed in a foppy tunic and tights, lines memorized, lips puckered up and ready to go, while in the wings, his costar informed the play's director in a voice loud enough for everyone to hear that if being Juliet meant that she had to kiss that *creepy little freak,* then *she quit!*

But as painful as all of those things were, they couldn't hold a candle to the devastating anguish he felt seeing Charlie and Lloyd drive off together.

He wasn't just jealous—although he *was* jealous, so terribly jealous he felt like he was going to burst into flame. But that wasn't the part that really hurt.

The real agony was in not understanding *why.* Why didn't she like him anymore? What did he do wrong? He felt stunned and brokenhearted, like a little puppy who expects to be cuddled but instead gets swatted with a big Stetson-scented newspaper.

What in the world had gone wrong?

38

HIRO STAYED CEMENTED TO HIS STOOL AT THE DINER, HIS HEAD down on the counter like a little kid who'd been caught talking too much in school, silently praying for death to come, while the sounds of the restaurant being closed up for the night swirled around him.

But death didn't come. Lynette did.

He heard the jangle of her car keys, then felt her hand—like an over-filled hot-water bottle—touch his shoulder.

"Need a ride home, hon?"

Hiro nodded. If he was going to die, he might as well do it in his own bed. So he got up and followed Lynette out to her car.

She unlocked the passenger's door of her green Taurus station wagon and he got in. The inside of the car was filled with Beanie Babies, piled in the back hatch, lined up along the dashboard, carefully sitting up straight in the backseat.

Hiro accidentally sat down on one when he got in, a little fuzzy bull-frog with a squeaker inside it that went *REEEP!* so loudly he jolted and banged his head on the ceiling of the car.

"Sorry," he apologized to the frog, and sat more carefully, perching it gently in the cup holder and rubbing his sore head.

Lynette glanced over at him. "Where do you live, sweetie?"

"Forty Progress Street," he mumbled. Ha! Lot of good that so-called lucky address had done him.

Lynette started the car and pulled out of the parking lot. The radio came on, tuned to a country station, and they sat quietly as Lynette drove, without talking, listening to it.

A song started that Hiro recognized, a syrupy woman's voice singing something about taking forever in vain.

Hiro's throat started to close up again. That was the song he and Charlie had danced to, back in the beginning of the summer.

Back when they were happy.

Back when the lyrics meant nothing more than a chance to hold Charlie close.

"Can we shut that off?" he asked Lynette, and she reached over and hit the button.

"Charlie really cares about you, you know," she said.

"Sure." She cared enough about him to go out with Lloyd.

"Hiro." Lynette's voice was uncharacteristically sharp. "I've never seen her this happy. I've also never seen her get this close to anyone before."

Hiro stared out the window. "Except for Lloyd."

"Please. Lloyd doesn't have a chance with Charlie. Besides, she's already taken. By *you*."

Hiro leaned his forehead against the glass. That would be a lot easier to believe if she hadn't been acting so strangely all week.

"Just give her time."

He sighed. For six months now, that was all he'd been trying to do.

Lynette dropped Hiro off in front of his apartment, then tooted her horn twice as she drove away.

The noise roused Mr. Roiz, who had been dozing in a lawn chair on the front porch, a bucket of chicken planted in his lap.

The landlord peered at Hiro as he shuffled up the path, scuffing his shoes on the dusty sidewalk. "What the hell happened to you?"

Hiro shrugged, the picture of dejection and confusion and self-pity.

"Where's that little redhead you used to go out with? Haven't seen her around in a while."

Hiro shrugged again, unable to hold back a little mewling peep of despair.

"Say no more," Mr. Roiz said, even though Hiro hadn't said *any-thing*, and clambered up out of his chair.

He tossed the remaining contents of the fried chicken bucket out into the yard, to the delight of a dozen neighborhood cats that appeared out of thin air. Then he wiped his hands off on the thighs of his droopy jeans and beckoned to Hiro.

"Come on inside," he said, opening the patched screen door and standing back to let Hiro go through. "We'll get you straightened out."

Hiro wasn't particularly in the mood to be straightened, but anything was better than the prospect of going alone up to his tiny room and facing the endless black void of loneliness that was the first night of the rest of his godforsaken life, so he went along willingly.

Mr. Roiz led him into the kitchen. Hiro sat down at the breakfast table while Mr. Roiz hefted a two-liter bottle of RC out of a bottom cabinet. He poured it into a couple of dusty glasses and set one in front of Hiro. Then he grabbed a teaspoon from the draining board next to the sink and stirred his own glass vigorously, ridding it of its carbonation.

"For digestion," Mr. Roiz told him, taking a long swig.

Ah. Hiro picked up his own glass and politely lifted it to his mouth, making sure not to let the glass touch his lips, and not actually drinking.

"So what's the problem?" Mr. Roiz asked. "Not enough tang in your poon?"

What?

"Can't get the pig out of the sty?"

Hiro stared at the landlord, baffled. He was so used to having Charlie around to translate any English he didn't know that he had almost forgotten about the language barrier that stood between him and the rest of the world.

Mr. Roiz saw his expression and leaned closer. "Have you porked your little girlfriend yet?" He enunciated each word carefully and provided a visual aid by popping his right index finger in and out of his closed left fist.

Crystal clear.

"No," Hiro mumbled, not sure how to explain what the problem was, but pretty certain he didn't even want to try.

"Ha! I got just the thing for you."

Mr. Roiz rocked back and forth in his chair a couple of times to build up momentum to roll up onto his feet, then he tottered over to lift a plastic pillbox off the kitchen windowsill.

"Viagra. Daddy's Little Helper." He dumped a pill into his wrinkled palm and held it out to Hiro. "Here, take it."

"I do not think—"

"Go on! Take it!"

He waited, his hand held out patiently, until Hiro took the little blue pill and slipped it in his pocket.

"Trust me, that'll put a little wasabi back in the old California roll." He let out a big lascivious chuckle.

Hiro blanched. "Thank you," he said with as much sincerity as he could muster. "I need to go now."

He stood up and gave the landlord a formal little bow, then practically bolted for the door.

Ew, ew, and *ew!*

He ran upstairs and dropped the pill in the toilet, flushing twice to make sure it was gone for good.

Okay, *that* had been helpful. Not only did he not feel any better about Charlie, now he also wanted to move.

He sank down on his bed. He wished Ando were here, so he could talk to him. Or Kimiko. Hell, he would give his right arm just to talk to his *father*.

This despite the fact that the one time Hiro did confide in his father about his romantic troubles—when he was sixteen and was feeling particularly blue about a girl he liked—Kaito had simply pointed at his goddamn THIS IS NOT A FAIRY TALE plaque, as if the answers to love's mysteries were hidden there. Like it was a cipher Hiro could decode, or some kind of Zen koan upon which to meditate.

Hiro hadn't really needed to be reminded that life wasn't a fairy tale. The girl, Yuki Shirakawa, had responded to his invitation to go get some ice cream after karate class by kicking his ass in front of the whole dojo. But at least his father had listened to his problem, even if he hadn't offered much of a solution.

At least back then he wasn't entirely alone, the way he was now.

Wasn't there *anyone* in Midland whom Hiro could talk to?

. . .

"Dude, I know just how you feel."

PJ carefully dangled the shot glass of whiskey over his mug of beer, and Hiro hesitantly copied him. At the same time, they dropped the depth charge, then raced to guzzle down the drink in a single pull, before it fizzed up all over the bar.

Hiro slammed his empty mug down, nearly choking on the drink before uncrossing his eyes and peering at PJ.

The gangly comic-book sales kid drained the last drop of his boilermaker, then let out a satisfied burp.

"Same thing happened to me with this girl I was dating, out of nowhere she started acting like a real my-country-'tis-of-thee, and I didn't know why."

"Why?"

"I didn't know!" PJ swayed precariously on his stool, waving to the bartender for another round. "One minute she's all over me, next minute she acts like I've been secretly developing the Kuma River Zombie Virus in my basement lab—"

PJ goggled at him, giving him a huge expectant grin as Hiro perked up.

A Robogirl reference! Awesome!

He *loved* PJ. And he loved Robogirl—sorry, Charlie-out-on-a-date-with-moron, but he *did*, so *shut up*. And he especially loved depth charges.

For the second time, he dropped a shot of whiskey into a beer and drank it all down, nearly passing out in the process.

"So what happen? You cut her loose?" he asked PJ, slurring just a little.

PJ shook his head. "I couldn't, man. I loved her. Plus she was my third cousin, so I knew I was going to have to see her at Christmas and all, and I didn't want it to be weird."

Good point, Hiro thought. He didn't want to cut Charlie loose. He loved her, even if he wasn't related to her. And whether she loved him back or not, he had to save her.

"So what you do?"

"I told her how I truly felt, deep down in the bottom of my heart. I said I loved her and couldn't live without her, and we talked about why she was mad, and you know what happened?"

"She forgive you?"

PJ nodded.

"Plus she gave me the best hummer I've ever gotten."

Huh.

"Charlie'll forgive you, too, man. She's got to. Just talk to her."

Okay, as much as he missed Ando and all, PJ was a freakin' *excellent* wingman.

"You really think it work?"

"Sure, I mean—what'd you do to make her mad in the first place?"

Hiro shrugged, reaching for his beer glass to see if there were any drops left. "I teleport into future. Saw her murdered with brain cut out."

PJ stared at him, then shook his head slowly.

"Maybe you better bring her some flowers, too."

39

"READY TO GET CLOBBERED?"

Hiro tossed Charlie a smile, his arms loaded with a bag of sticky buns and two paper cups of coffee.

"You're the one who should be nervous," Charlie answered, opening the door for him.

She had sounded hesitant when he called to see if they were still on for their weekly chess game, like maybe he was going to demand an explanation about Lloyd, but he didn't. Hiro didn't mention Tuesday night at all.

The chessboard was already set up, and Hiro sat down behind the white pieces as Charlie fetched a plate for the pastries. Hiro was good enough at chess that it still held some challenge for Charlie, especially since they had worked out a system to throw her knowledge of every chess move ever made off balance. Every third turn, Hiro would get to move twice in a row. This kept her from being certain which pattern he was going to follow, and gave him a much-needed opportunity to pick off some of her chessmen.

They played one game which Charlie won, then another where Hiro managed to eke out a win at the last possible second. He jumped up and did his victory dance—shake, shake, boom!, step, turn, turn, boom!—as Charlie laughed and set up the board for a tiebreaker.

All afternoon Hiro had been waiting for things to feel close enough to normal that he could talk to her about what had been bothering her, and he finally saw his chance.

"Hey, so the Samurai Film Festival has been extended a week," he said, casual-but-careful. "I was thinking maybe we could go on Saturday."

Charlie set down the pawn she was holding and looked down at her lap, hugging her arms around herself.

"I just thought—it'll be perfect practice for our trip to Japan, to get us in the mood."

She looked up, and her eyes were filling with tears. Hiro's heart flopped over, quietly expiring inside his chest.

"You do still want to go?" he asked, knowing and hating the answer.

"I can't," she said, her voice barely audible.

He shook his head. "You have to. Please, it's so important." He seized her hand, looking into her eyes, desperate to make her understand.

"I came back here from the future to do this, to make sure you would go. I'm trying to save you, it's my mission, my *destiny*. So, *please*—" He clung to her more tightly, her hand a lifeline, his voice raw and urgent. "—I don't care if you believe me, just tell me you'll go. *Please*."

"It's not that I don't believe you, Hiro. Because I do."

"Then why won't you go?"

Charlie's eyes glittered with pain.

"Ever since we met, I dunno," she said haltingly, "you've made me so happy. I know it's stupid. You haven't been here all that long, and we're so different, and—"

"It's not stupid. You make me happy, too."

"It's more than that. I don't let anyone get close to me. Never have, until I met you. And now—" She stopped, shaking her head helplessly, seeming to search for the words to finish what she wanted to say.

"I've been trying to pull away from you, to get less close," she said instead, her voice hollow. "I thought it would be easier, but it's not."

"So go to Japan without me," Hiro said. "It's okay, I don't care. Take Lloyd if you want to, take Lynette, take your aunt—just tell me you'll go!"

Charlie shook her head, and for a long minute they just stared at each other, at a standstill, neither of them knowing how to reach the other.

Charlie blinked first. She straightened up in her chair, taking a deep breath.

"There's a blood clot in my brain. Inches away from an aneurism," she said, her voice low and even. "They found it when I went to the hospital—they don't know how long it's been there. But—it's there now."

Hiro shut his eyes, understanding immediately what she was telling him.

She was going to die, and soon.

No matter what he did, their story wasn't going to have a happy ending.

This is not a fairy tale.

"But—I'm supposed to save you."

"But you did," Charlie said, emphatically. She got up and moved around the table to him. "You have made me feel more alive, more full of joy than I ever could have imagined."

Hiro took a deep breath.

Was she right? It wasn't about the ending, it was about the happiness in the middle, right? And their story didn't have to end just yet. They still had their happy middle to enjoy.

He could still save her from the Brain Man. She could still come to Japan with him. And they would have more time together. Maybe not a lot of time, but enough.

A *lifetime.*

Charlie was smiling at him, smiling through the tears that were running down her face, and he smiled back, taking her into his arms.

"*Aishitemau,* Hiro," she said, telling him she loved him in perfect Japanese.

No one had ever said that to Hiro before, and he had never said it to anyone. He had never *felt* it before, never felt such pure whole adoration for another person. But he did now. He felt it with every fiber of his being.

"I love you, too."

Their eyes met, and in that one sublime instant of absolute intimate connection—

—he teleported away.

. . .

Hiro found himself on the windy rooftop of the Yamagato Industries building in Japan, where the company's employees were practicing their morning tai chi in rigid synchronicity.

"No!" Hiro cried out, looking around frantically at the sea of gym-suited drones surrounding him. "*Charlie!* I have to get back to her!"

He started to run toward the staircase that led down into the building when he saw something that stopped him in his tracks as surely as if he'd run into a brick wall.

"Hey, Hiro!" said a short, apple-cheeked man who sat three cubicles down from him. "I thought you and Ando were on vacation in America."

But Hiro didn't answer him. He barely heard him. He was staring, horror-struck, at the giant digital display on the building across from theirs, that showed the time and date in humongous glowing red numbers.

OCTOBER 11.

It was October 11.

Two days after Charlie was killed.

"*NO!!!*" Hiro screamed, finally jolted back into movement.

The office workers scattered, clearing a path for him as he fled toward the stairs.

October 11.

Charlie was dead.

He had failed.

40

CHARLIE WAS DEAD.

She was dead and he had failed and there was nothing he could do.

Hiro hurtled himself down the stairs and through the lobby of Yamagato Industries, not caring whom he slammed into, what sort of spectacle he was making in front of his co-workers and his father and God-only-knew who else—

Charlie is dead. I've failed.

It was an endless refrain that played over and over in his head, and drowned out all of his other senses.

He ran down the street to the small park where he frequently went on his lunch hour, and took refuge there. He especially liked the park because in the middle, near the small Zen garden, stood a tall statue of a Bushido warrior, made of stone.

Hiro loved that statue; he considered it a friend and occasionally confided his problems to the statue's unhearing ears. But today he just threw himself miserably down on the bench in front of it and huddled there, a small Hiro-shaped lump of agony.

How could he have let this happen?

How could he have failed at his mission?

His face felt heavy, as if the skin and flesh were about to fall away from his skull, and he willed back the burning in his throat that told him he was going to cry.

But whether he cried or not, it didn't—*couldn't*—remove the one, inescapable fact.

Charlie was dead. Hiro had failed.

He slumped there on the bench, under the placid gaze of the stone Bushido, losing all track of time. Unbidden, he found himself replaying a conversation he had had with Ando, right after he had discovered his powers. Now this, too, began to repeat, over and over, in his mind.

He had been trying to convince his friend that his powers were real, but Ando was having none of it.

"There isn't a ten-year-old on the planet who hasn't secretly wished for superpowers," he had told his friend, filled with pride and happiness at his discovery, "and I, Hiro Nakamura, *got* them. *Me* of all people."

He shook his head in wonder that day.

"Last in my class, last on the sports field. But I'm not a loser anymore."

Ando considered this for a moment, a skeptical smile on his face, then he spoke. "All right, but look—tell me one useful thing you could do with this power. Can you make money?"

Hiro made a face. "A superhero doesn't use his powers for personal gain."

"Enough!" Ando said, becoming exasperated. "There is *no such thing* as breaking the space-time continuum, all right? There are twelve and a half million people in this city. Not one of them can bend space and time. Why do you want to be different?"

"No," Hiro countered, "the question is, why do you want to be the same?"

"Because that's what I am! The same."

"Fine," Hiro said with a disdainful shrug. "Stay here. Be just like everyone else. But I want to be special."

He had turned his back on his friend and walked away.

Ando watched him go, a scowl on his face.

"That's right, you're special! How could I forget—you're 'Super-Hiro'! Go find your purpose, then! Go save the world!"

Thinking of it now, Hiro hung his head in shame. He had been a fool to believe that he could be anything other than a failure.

Special? Ha!

Powers were wasted on him—his whole *life* was about making mistakes. He could see it in everything he did, in everyone he touched.

He had let Charlie down. He had failed her. He had failed *himself*.

He had been called to greatness and he had failed to answer that call. It was like his father always told him—he would never be a success because he never saw anything all the way through to the end.

Follow-through had always been Hiro's biggest problem. It was evident in the half-finished projects still left over from his school days, the pile of unsigned reports that were cluttering his desk at work, the books he had shoved unread into his bookcase.

And this mission, *his* mission, was no different. If he'd been a real "Super-Hiro," if he'd really been special, he would have found a way to save the woman he loved. He had been given the gift of being able to bend time and space, and he had failed to use it properly.

Although . . .

Hiro looked up, his eyes wild, his heart filling with a sudden hope, and the stone Bushido seemed to smile down, agreeing with him.

He still had his powers, right? There was nothing to stop him from using them again.

A hero might fail, but he never gives up.

Takezo Kensei wouldn't give up.

Kensei had *chugo*—devotion—the seventh attribute of the samurai, as dictated by the Bushido code. And Hiro had it, too.

He was devoted to Charlie, and devoted to his mission. He wasn't going to let her—or himself—down. Not again. He was a Hiro, a *Super-Hiro,* and this was his trial. The one he had to face to prove himself worthy of his powers.

That's why he had been given these powers—so he could go back in time and stop the Brain Man from killing her.

He knew that ultimately there were no happy endings. *This is not a fairy tale.* But he wasn't ready for *any* kind of ending—happy, sad, or otherwise.

It didn't have to end yet.

Even though he had failed once, he would go back and try again. It didn't matter how long it took or how far back in time he had to go.

He was going to go back again.

He was going to keep trying.

He would never stop trying until he saved her.

Gathering himself, and peering resolutely at the statue, Hiro shut his eyes, concentrating, every muscle in his body shaking with the effort. His mind was a laser beam, focused on the diner and teleporting there.

He was *not* a failure.

He could *still* save Charlie.

He just had to get back to the diner, *back back back*—

Oh please get me back—

—and when he opened his eyes, he was sitting in one of the wide, comfortable booths of the Burnt Toast Diner, waiting for his breakfast.

41

"I DID IT!" HIRO SHOUTED, THROWING HIS ARMS UP IN THE AIR WITH absolute joy and abandon.

He was back at the diner, his mission was still a go, and his destiny was welcoming him with open arms. Charlie was getting another chance. *Hiro* was getting another chance with *her*.

He clapped his hands, bouncing up and down in his seat like a little kid.

An older couple sitting at a booth across from him looked over when he shouted, and he grinned and waved at them.

"She loves me!" he told them, realizing with a jolt that he'd been so overwhelmed by the shock of teleporting, he hadn't even had time to process the amazingly astounding fact that Charlie had said "I love you" to him.

Charlie loved him.

She loved him, and he was head-over-heels, no-holds-barred, hearts-and-flowers besotted with her.

Gaga, even.

That was all he could think about. He wanted to burst into song or carve their initials into a tree or something.

No, what he wanted to do was go find Charlie this instant, sweep her up in his arms, and carry her off into the sunset.

Matter of fact, he decided, that's exactly what he would do. So he calmed himself down.

He looked around the diner to see if she was there . . . and hesitated. Something was different.

Things seemed *fresher,* somehow, brighter, as if the entire diner had been given a fresh coat of paint. Plus—*did someone move the furniture around?* He frowned.

The tables were at a weird angle, and the stools at the counter were covered with an odd, spangled, bright red amusement-park vinyl instead of the red leather they were supposed to be. It didn't make sense—everything looked the same but *not* the same.

And Hiro started to get an uneasy feeling in the pit of his stomach.

The feeling was compounded when an unfamiliar waitress, with long straight blond hair parted down the center and a friendly girl-next-door smile, skipped over past him, balancing a laden tray.

"Here you go, sir. One Bicentennial special." She set down a plate of waffles in front of the fellow behind him. "Strawberry syrup, blueberries, and whipped cream. Red, white, and blue, see?"

What was going on?

Who was this girl? Hiro motioned to get her attention and gave her a tentative smile, trying to stay calm.

"Is Charlie here?" he asked, and as she poured him a cup of coffee, her confused expression made his heart sink. "Charlie? Who's he?"

"She," Hiro said. "She is waitress."

The girl looked mystified.

"Um, the only waitresses who work here are me and Lynette."

Hiro let out a relieved breath. That was something, at least. Lynette worked here—so he was in the right place. He hadn't landed in an alternate universe or anything. But it still didn't explain the furniture, so—

"What is the date?"

She looked a little perplexed at the question, but answered it politely. "February nineteenth—"

Okay.

He had landed two months before Charlie's birthday—maybe they'd remodeled or done a big spring cleaning between February and when he'd landed the first time.

Six months before the murder.

This was okay, he told himself, his mind racing. Strange, but there had to be a rational explanation.

He'd just go back to the good ol' Midland Motor Lodge and wait until—

"—Nineteen-seventy-six," the waitress finished with a nod.

Hiro, who had just been about to stir his coffee, dropped his spoon with a clatter. *Nineteen seventy-six?* He wasn't two months early—he was *thirty years* early!

Oh my God. This is a nightmare! Charlie hadn't died yet—she hadn't even been born yet! Hiro himself hadn't been born.

This was—definitely not good.

The waitress scrambled to pick up the dropped spoon and handed Hiro a clean one.

"Um, can I get you anything else?" she asked, giving Hiro—who was gawping at her in astonishment—a wary look.

He shook his head, but he wasn't really listening to her. His mind was still reeling.

"Well, enjoy," she said, tossing him an uncertain smile. "And if you need anything, my name's Barbie, so just give a holler."

Barbie? Where had he heard that name before?

The waitress moved off, as Hiro tried to remember where he'd heard a waitress named Barbie mentioned before.

Charlie's photo album.

Of *course*. That was the first girl murdered at the diner.

Barbie Travis.

His mind ratcheted into focus, her name emerging in sharp clear letters out of the ether. And the instant his brain locked on to it—

—Hiro teleported again.

Suddenly, without warning, he found himself sitting in the back pew of the nave of a grand, sweeping stone church, in the middle of Barbie Travis's funeral.

42

"*RECORDARE, JESU PIE, QUOD SUM CAUSA TUAE VIAE.*"
The priest's voice rose and fell, the requiem echoing through the great cold room.

All around Hiro people were weeping, heads bowed, their white handkerchiefs in stark contrast with black suits and dresses. The sharp sting of incense assaulted his nose, and his eyes were drawn irresistibly to the simple cherry coffin lying at the foot of the pulpit.

What was he doing here? What did this have to do with Charlie?

"Ne me perdas illa die."

A girl sitting on Hiro's far left broke down, gasping and sobbing, and Hiro realized with a start that it was Lynette, her round red-streaked face unchanged, even with thirty years and fifty-odd pounds subtracted from it.

He squirmed uncomfortably on the hard wooden pew, wanting to go and console his friend, but knowing that she *wasn't* his friend. Not yet.

She seemed to sense his gaze, though, because she turned her head toward him. Hiro smiled sadly and then looked away, not wanting to stare.

His eyes landed on a large oil painting in a heavy gilt frame, hanging over the chancel, and he gazed at it for a long minute before realizing what he was looking at.

The painting showed two men, dressed in the armor of medieval knights, kneeling in prayer on a grassy pastoral battleground. Behind one of the knights stood a nobleman holding a papal flag. Behind the other stood a holy man, a bishop or a saint. He was dressed in a white surplice with a red chasuble cloak draped around his shoulders. He had a golden staff nestled in the crook of his arm, and carried a gilded red miter in his outstretched hand.

Hiro's eyes traveled up the saint's jeweled vestments, over the placid face, and then froze in shock at what he saw in the picture: *the top of the saint's head had been neatly cleaved away.*

The top three inches were sliced off, a faint mist of confetti rising up out of the bowl that remained of his skull, his soul sparkling up to heaven.

Hiro's jaw dropped, utterly confounded by the image in the painting. *What does this all mean?*

He glanced madly around the church, hoping for a clue, a sign, anything that would help him unravel this mystery, bring him closer to understanding, and then he saw it.

The woman seated in front of Hiro was fanning herself with the crisp white paper funeral program, and printed on the front, in bold black type, it said: st. nicasius catholic church.

St. Nicasius—this was where Charlie had gone to school. Every day for twelve years she had stared at that picture of the saint whose head had been butchered the same way the Brain Man would one day butcher hers. This was the sign. This was the thing he was supposed to see, the thing that could help him save Charlie.

"*Dona eis pacem. Dona eis requiem.*"

He shut his eyes and focused his concentration. *Charlie.* He needed to get back to Charlie.

When he opened his eyes, he was staring straight at Lloyd's crotch.

GAH!

That certainly wasn't what he had been concentrating on.

Lloyd glanced over at him.

"What're *you* looking at?" he asked, clearly irritated.

"N-nothing," Hiro stammered, jerking his eyes away to the familiar streaky blue tile of the Burnt Toast's men's room.

Lloyd glared at him suspiciously, then gave himself a shake and a zip-up. He moved over to the sink to wash his hands, and Hiro pushed past him, bolting out into the diner. The gloriously familiar, faded-paint, red-leather-stool, twenty-first-century diner.

He came through the men's room door so fast he bumped into Lynette, who grabbed the wall to keep them both from tumbling to the floor.

"Lordy, Hiro, slow down!" she exclaimed, and Hiro's heart soared—she knew his name.

"Where's Charlie?" he demanded.

"She's at home, far as I know," Lynette said, puzzled. "What are you doing here?"

"What do you mean?"

"It's Wednesday—your day off."

She pointed over at the Sun-Maid calendar above the cash register, hanging open to July.

It was July!

Hiro let out a whoop of joy. He threw his arms around Lynette and spun her around in a little circle. He was back in the right time and the right place.

"We should give you the day off more often," Lynette said, laughing, but Hiro didn't hear her. He was already racing out the door, sprinting the three miles through the dusty Texas sunshine, on his way to see the woman he loved.

43

HIRO PEERED IN THROUGH THE WINDOW, WATCHING CHARLIE AS she moved about her living room, dusting and straightening, whistling as she went about her work.

He was so glad she was alive.

Alive.

But he couldn't let her see him here—he was afraid of messing too much with the space-time continuum. The earlier version of himself would also be in Midland right now, and if he bumped into the other Hiro it could be a disaster. He wasn't sure what would happen, but he didn't want to find out.

As he watched her, he thought about how much better it would be, the next time he could be with her. He wouldn't need to worry that she thought he was a geek, or feel tongue-tied and awkward around her, or get all shaky and anxious at the thought that she only liked him as a friend.

He now *knew* she liked him as more than that.

And this time all his mental faculties could be devoted strictly to stopping the Brain Man and saving her life.

He ducked down as she turned toward the window, but she didn't see him. And a few minutes later, he was relieved to see that she was preparing to go out. *At last.* She grabbed her car keys and stepped toward the door.

He waited until the car had disappeared down the street and he couldn't hear the growl of its engine any longer. Then he slipped up to the front door and pulled the key from its hiding place under the mat.

She needs to find a better place for that. I'll talk with her about it.

Slipping inside, he pulled the curtains across the windows so no one would see him and call the police. Then he moved to the bookshelf and tried to remember the book she had showed him. After a few moments of scanning, his hand settled on the coffee-table volume from the Alte Pinakothek museum. He flipped through the pages until he landed on one illustration in particular—a print of the same Joos van Cleve painting he'd seen in the church at Barbie Travis's funeral.

"What happened to his head?" Hiro murmured aloud. As he read the description, it explained that that had been the way he was martyred.

"Ew," he said to no one in particular. He was able to understand English enough to figure out that they had sliced the top of his head off to let out the evil spirits.

Okay, he thought, becoming confused. *So does this mean the Brain Man is some kind of devil worshipper?*

Only—although Charlie had gone to Catholic school, she wasn't especially religious. She didn't even go to church or anything like that, so she seemed an unlikely candidate for a religious-based killing.

He came across a word he didn't recognize: *trepanning.* He put down the art book and looked for an encyclopedia, leafing through it quickly.

"Trepanning," he mumbled, and he wrinkled his nose at what he read. "Opening the skull to let evil spirits out." According to the entry, lots of cultures did it, usually by boring holes in the skull. It was like a primitive form of brain surgery.

"Trepanning," Hiro said again with a shiver. The word tasted both sinister and exotic in his mouth, as if saying it aloud was giving it power, was calling it closer.

They had found trepanned skulls from as far back as 10,000 BC in Egypt, Rome, India, Africa, even Central America. The mention caused Hiro to glance toward the gruesome shaman's mask perched on her mantel, which he still had never been able to force himself to look at too closely. Quickly turning away, he continued to read.

The Zapotecs had used trepanning on captured warriors from other tribes. A number of Native American tribes did the same thing. They would grind up their skulls and make medicines from the bones, as a way of stealing their enemies' power . . .

Holy cow!

Could that be it? Could the Brain Man be trying to steal Charlie's power?

Morbidly fascinated, Hiro finally forced himself to study the mask head-on. It was nightmarish—chunks of bone and teeth bristling from the dark straw face, the mouth a rictus of malevolence, the eyes two shiny black beads, set far back in the face.

Hiro blinked—

—and the mask blinked back!

Hiro looked around in terror, realizing that in that single blink of an eye he had teleported away again.

But this time, he was far less distressed about the fact that he had unintentionally bent space and time, and a million times more concerned with where he had ended up.

He was in some kind of clearing—somewhere primitive, archaic, untouched by civilization or modernity. Overgrown impenetrable jungle surrounded him on every side, glittering eyes moving behind the dark tangled vines and thorny branches, the rustling of unknown creatures, howls and screeches and low throaty growls, all just outside his field of vision, lurking in the tangled green forest, watching and waiting.

In the clearing—a rough scrubby circle—crouched a dozen men, half naked, smeared with dirt and sweat and slick streaks of paint the color of blood.

The men looked feral themselves, rags and scraps of animal skins twisted around their waists, barefoot, ropes laced through animal teeth and bloodied bits of gristle and—what was that?

Oh god, is that a human ear?

Hiro's hand flew to his mouth in horror. The disgusting decorations were draped around their necks.

The men were all staring, open-cracked grins showing blackened and missing teeth, peering at the activity around a small fire burning at the far end of the clearing.

They haven't seen me, Hiro realized with a silent sigh of relief, and he calmed his nerves, striving to remain silent. He was standing in the bushes, with a view of the clearing, but still shrouded in shadows.

A different man was seated on a rough log, his hands and legs bound, a narrow sliver of wood—like a horse's bit—jammed into his mouth and fastened around his head. He sat shaking, eyes wide and rolling, a sweaty froth streaming off him, blood trickling down the side of his face.

The prisoner let out a keening moan, which rose in volume to a high-pitched wail. Behind him stood a phantasm, a vision from Hiro's worst dreams.

A shaman, fierce and wild and terrible, wearing a Zapotec mask like the one belonging to Charlie, slowly approached.

On the shaman, the mask seemed to come alive, become a part of him, muscles moving and clenching under the bristles and offal.

He moved around his prisoner, then bent to pluck something from the fire while the watching men murmured, their voices chanting unfamiliar sounds and words. The shaman walked toward the bound man, whose keen became a dry terrified rattle in his throat when he saw what the shaman carried.

In his hands the shaman clutched a golden knife, its wide spatula-shaped blade glowing bright orange from resting in the embers of the fire. The handle of the knife was formed into a flat caricature of a face, with ringed eyes and heavy sharp fangs protruding from a jaguar's snout.

The shaman walked up to the prisoner, circling behind him again, the mask's frozen smile seeming to broaden in an evil leer. The prisoner tried to babble past the bit, his tone pleading, but the shaman ignored him, lifting the knife high above his victim's skull, preparing to plunge it into his brain.

Hiro gasped, horror-struck at the barbarity of what he was seeing—that poor man was about to be killed, *trepanned*—before his very eyes!

He had to help him.

He tried to freeze time—but it didn't work. The shaman slowly and relentlessly lowered the knife toward the prisoner.

What the— He shut his eyes, screwing up his face in concentration, willing time to stop.

It didn't.

Oh no! What was happening with his powers? What a time for them to abandon him!

The glowing hot tip of the knife touched the prisoner's head, and he let out a shriek of pain and fear.

And Hiro screamed, too.

"Stop! Don't!"

In a flash the watching men had leapt to their feet, whirling around to face him, and the beady eyes of the mask locked on Hiro.

With a cry the shaman flew toward him, a great flapping shrieking incubus, and Hiro slammed his eyes shut, focusing, his life depending on it.

A split second before the shaman reached him—Hiro disappeared, teleporting away from the clearing.

And landing someplace nearly as frightening: right in front of an open grave.

44

Six Japanese men in somber black suits, their wide lapels and skinny black ties straight out of a Beatles movie, were lowering a coffin into the grave via a series of thick hemp ropes. The sides of the coffin were painted with elaborate Suibokuga ink-and-wash paintings of the hills and landscape of southern Japan—the same landscape Hiro saw all around him.

He was back in Japan.

But *when*?

Judging from the clothes of the mourners assembled around the grave site—staid dark fedoras on the men, low heels and conservative Western-style wrap dresses on the women—it was sometime in the early sixties. Not exactly ideal, but frankly Hiro was so happy to be away from that scary shaman—and so relieved that it wasn't *Charlie* who was being lowered into the ground—that he wasn't too freaked out about the jump this time.

He was mostly curious. Whose funeral was this? Why had he landed here?

He took a step closer to the mourners, all weeping into handkerchiefs as the coffin settled into the dirt with a dull thud.

One by one they tossed a handful of earth on top of the coffin, then turned and headed back toward a waiting line of sleek black limousines.

All except one man—slender, dry-eyed, scarcely more than a teenager, who hovered at the side of the grave, quaking, fighting to retain his composure. His face was severe, even in grief, the dark hooded eyes set wide apart, the mouth a violent slash, the chin held a perceptible millimeter higher than everyone else's, exuding a confidence bordering on arrogance.

It was a familiar face, one that stirred up a memory for Hiro, evoking some long-ago person or place that he couldn't quite put his finger on, but that waited, like a silent threat, just on the edge of his consciousness.

An older woman placed a light hand on the teen's shoulder. "Come, Kaito, let's go back to the house."

Hiro nearly fainted.

Kaito?

That sullen young man was his father.

The instant he thought it, he knew it was true. Young Kaito not only looked like the stern man he was going to become—he looked like Hiro himself. That nose was Hiro's nose. His hands were Hiro's hands. The way he held his head, the set of his shoulders, even the way he shifted all his weight to one foot, moodily turning in the other ankle—all those things Hiro recognized from having seen them in the mirror.

He was stunned, struck dumb by what he was seeing. Vaguely he wondered if he should worry about the implications this might have for the space-time continuum, should his father spot Hiro and recognize something in him. But such concerns were far outweighed by his fascination at seeing this unexpected new side of the man he had spent his whole life trying to live up to.

The young Kaito shook his head resolutely.

"No. I'm not leaving her!"

Her who? Hiro looked from his father's face to the coffin again, baffled. Who was being buried?

"Please, Kaito. You haven't eaten in days, you haven't slept—it's time to say your good-byes and come home."

"I can't . . . ," Hiro's father said, his voice barely a whisper, his stony expression starting to crack. "How can I say good-bye to Satsu? It's saying good-bye to my own heart."

Hiro's jaw dropped.

Oh my God. His dad was just like the great swordsman Kensei! But in this case, who was his princess? Hiro's mother was alive and well, and his father had never mentioned any earlier loves.

The older woman—not Hiro's grandmother, but he wasn't sure who she was—glared at the mourners who were still standing by the grave, watching this exchange, until they looked away.

"Satsu loved you. You should be happy about the time you had together. It was a fairy tale."

She put her arm gently around Kaito's waist, but he twisted away from her in a movement identical to one Hiro had made a thousand times himself.

"This is no fairy tale," Kaito said angrily, the dam breaking. "Satsu's dead and I wish I was dead, too!" he added through sobbing gasps.

Hiro goggled at him, completely floored. *This is not a fairy tale.* His father wasn't talking about hard work, he was talking about love.

Love and loss, Hiro realized ruefully.

No happy endings.

He and his dad were more alike than he had ever imagined.

The older woman was trying to calm Kaito down, but he wrenched himself free of her again.

"I wish everyone would stop trying to make me feel better and leave me alone!" he shouted. Then he stomped away from the grave site, straight toward Hiro. Their eyes connected, and in the next moment—

Hiro teleported away again, moving in an instant from the lush green Japanese countryside to a cinder-block viewing gallery, where he was seated on a chilly wooden bench beside a dozen other somber witnesses. Watching as a scruffily handsome man in a loose cotton jumpsuit was strapped into the electric chair on the other side of the glass.

No! This was something Hiro couldn't watch, didn't want to watch, and he screwed up his face, concentrating on teleporting away.

Hiro couldn't even bear to see a fly get swatted or a mouse get caught in a trap. There was no way he could handle watching as another person was killed before his very own eyes. He focused his mind.

Take me back. Take me back.

But nothing happened.

Damn it! Not again!

On the other side of the glass a blue-uniformed guard took a step toward the prisoner. His words were carried by a speaker that was perched in a corner of the room.

"Merle Eckles, you are sentenced to death by electrocution for the murder of Barbie Travis. Do you have any last words?"

Hiro gawped at the figures on the other side of the glass. *Holy cow!* This was the man who had murdered sweet, smiling Barbie Travis. This was the killer he had feared—feared almost as much as the Brain Man. Still, it didn't mean he wanted to watch the poor bastard fry.

Take me back to Charlie, he thought again, squeezing his eyes shut.

Still nothing.

Merle gave an evil grin.

"Yeah, I got something to say."

Hiro pricked up his ears. Maybe, just maybe, this man could offer a clue to the reasons that lurked behind Charlie's killing. Maybe Merle Eckles's last words would give him some insight into the Brain Man, some information or awareness that could help Hiro stop him.

"You tell that girl's family—" Merle started.

But before he could hear what the killer wanted Barbie's family to know—

—Hiro teleported again.

45

OUCH.

Hiro felt an electric shock crackle through him. And for one terrifying moment, he thought that maybe he had landed in the electric chair himself.

Instead he heard Charlie gasp.

He opened his eyes.

"Hiro!" she exclaimed. "Where have you been? Oh my God, I thought you were gone for good."

Oh thank God, he thought. *Thank God.* He was back and she was still alive. He still had a chance.

A clap of thunder startled both of them, and Charlie jumped. When she turned back to him, her concern had been replaced by a funny look. "What happened?" she asked. "Where did you go? Is it your powers— are they messing up again? Are you all right?"

Hiro gulped, suddenly overwhelmed by her questions, the events of the last two minutes, two weeks, two months—he had no idea what day it was, how much time was left, how long he'd been gone. And that thought was more terrifying than anything he'd just seen.

She was studying him closely. "Here, sit down, calm down. Take it slow." She moved to wrap her arms around him, patting him on the back, making *shhhh* sounds.

At that moment, he realized he could have teleported into a lot worse places.

"It is nothing," he said, his voice only a little shaky. "Nothing at all."

He shut his eyes, leaning forward to kiss her, when, outside, there was a *crack!*

Lightning jagged down from the sky, and the air was charged with electricity, raising the hair on the back of his neck, sending a prickling current zapping through the room.

A spark leapt from Charlie's lips to his, a blaze of white light and energy and heat, coursing through him, short-circuiting his focus, and—

Oh son-of-a-bitch!

Time jerked and swayed, speeding up, slowing down, skipping around, seconds and weeks and years all jumbling together in an uncontrollable mishmash. Each breath landed him in a new place, another attempt to save her.

Another failure.

Time pulsed.

Ba-bump! Ba-bump!

Each heartbeat taking him somewhere new, whizzing him through space and time with no rhyme or reason, out of control, the drumming rhythm of his own heart pounding through his veins.

Ba-bump! He was at a wedding, for Charlie's aunt Erika, watching Lloyd dip Charlie at the end of a dance, both of them laughing.

Ba-bump! He was in the Texas Prison Museum in Huntsville, standing in front of a velvet-roped display: Old Sparky, the retired electric chair he had nearly seen in action.

· · ·

Ba-bump! He was in a grassy cemetery, looking down at the fresh flowers on—

Oh hell!

—Charlie's headstone.

Stop! he commanded himself.

Enough!

But his powers had taken on a life—a heartbeat—of their own.

Time flickered and leapt, Hiro helplessly borne along on a wave, out
of control, taken farther from his destiny with every jump.

Ba-bump! He was in Japan, fifteen years earlier, watching wistfully out
of his sister's bedroom window as Tami Oyoki clambered into the front
seat of Kozumi's car and drove away, breaking Hiro's heart for the very
first time.

Ba-bump! He was at the scene of a car accident, firemen easing the bodies out of the car, a tiny red-haired baby screaming in a paramedic's
arms, crying for the parents she'd just lost.

Ba-bump!

*Ba-*bump!

Ba-bump . . .

The heartbeat stuttered and stopped, trapping him in the horrific
scene, an innocent bystander who felt as if he'd lost his innocence a lifetime ago.

Hiro wrapped his arms around himself, shivering miserably, his
mind reeling.

Even though he could no longer freeze time, he felt the world stop
around him. Despite the commotion and noise, all he could see was that
baby.

This was where it all started, he realized. This was the moment that
put Charlie irrevocably on her path toward the Brain Man. In a way this
moment was the start of Hiro's mission, and now he knew that he was
powerless to stop it.

Baby Charlie let out a cry, and the sound pierced Hiro's heart.

He wanted to reach out, to hold and comfort her, but he knew he couldn't take the chance. He couldn't risk tampering with time any more than he already had. So instead he turned away, moving out of sight and away from the sound of the wailing ambulance and urgent commands of the emergency workers.

He stumbled blindly down the deserted road, the dark Texas night stretching out around him, engulfing him in its bleak nothingness. He finally flopped down by the side of the road, his head in his hands, overwhelmed.

What was going on with his powers? They were getting harder and harder to control.

And the less control he retained, the less confident he became that he would be able to use his powers to save Charlie.

He had thought that he'd have an unlimited number of chances, that he could return over and over and over to save her, but now he knew that wasn't true. At the rate he was going, he didn't know if he would ever make it back to Charlie, let alone make it back in time to save her.

Each time he lost a bit more of his grip, he lost a bit more of her.

He felt dizzy, wanted to lie down, to shut his eyes, but he was afraid, afraid he would start the cycle of teleporting again.

He had to get back to her, to Charlie, the real Charlie, *his* Charlie, once and for all. He had to use whatever he had left to end this. Then he didn't care if his powers gave out, he didn't care if he never teleported again, as long as he could get back to her now and have one last chance.

July 1, he thought. The first day they kissed, the first time he told her about his powers and she believed him.

Please, please, please—let me go back to July 1.

He squeezed his eyes shut, every muscle straining with the effort.

He didn't care *where* he landed, only *when—Just let me get back to July 1.* This was it, this was all he'd ask for, it was his last chance. Anywhere at all, anywhere in the world—just so he got back to that day.

He squeezed his eyes tighter, focusing with every ounce of energy and will he had left—

And—*ba-bump!*

When he opened his eyes, he found himself nose-to-nose with a lion.

46

THE LION ROARED.

Hiro stumbled back, tripping over his own feet. He landed on his ass with a *thump!*, to the delight and laughter of several little girls who were clustered nearby.

Hiro looked around, bewildered, realizing a second late that the lion was in a cage, and he and the lion both were at the zoo.

One of the little girls who had laughed at him, a pug-nosed imp with brown pigtails, scrunched up her face as she looked at him. "Are you okay?" she asked. "Where did you come from?"

Hiro blinked at her, his tongue tied, his heart only now starting up again after his shock at seeing the lion.

"What is the date?" he managed to ask.

"Huh?"

"Today—what is day today?"

"July first," she answered.

"Really?"

The girl nodded.

Hallelujah! Hiro did a mini touchdown dance from where he still lay, sprawled in the dirt, to the continued great amusement of all the assembled girls. Finally he calmed down.

"Where am I?" he asked them, making them laugh harder.

"What's *wrong* with him?" one of them—a snooty little freckled thing—asked in a whisper loud enough to wake the sleeping lion cubs.

"You're at the zoo," the pigtailed girl said.

"Yes. But what city?"

She looked at him doubtfully. "Los Angeles."

"Molly!" a voice called.

Hiro looked up to see the little girl's father hurrying over, and felt his blood turn cold. He was staring at a face he recognized.

It was James Walker.

James Walker. The man he'd seen in the morgue. The third victim of the Brain Man. The man who would be dead before the month was out.

Walker looked down at Hiro, his expression concerned. "Are you okay?" he asked, reaching out a hand to help Hiro up.

Hiro felt a jolt of electricity buzz from the man's hand to his own. He snatched his hand away, looking down at the ground, unable to meet the other man's eyes.

"Yes, yes, I am fine. I—I have to go," he said abruptly.

He wanted to warn James Walker, to help him, to save him, but he couldn't. He couldn't even control his own powers, and he didn't want to risk messing with the space-time continuum any more than he already had.

Everything he had left in him, he needed to put toward saving Charlie.

47

HIRO PLUCKED A BONBON OUT OF THE HALF-EATEN BOX OF THE Russell Stover Nut, Chewy, and Crisp Assortment lying on his bed. Popping it into his mouth, he chewed it pensively.

He had read somewhere that chocolate had some sort of happiness enzyme, but it didn't seem to be working for him. Instead he was hiding under his covers, immobilized by anxiety and doubt.

What did it all mean? St. Nicasius and trepanning and the Zapotecs. Barbie Travis and his father's first love and Old Sparky . . .

All the different pieces of the puzzle jumbled together in his mind, a churning mix of death and desire. Every time he seemed to find an answer, it raised a whole new set of questions.

He popped another piece of candy into his mouth and grimaced.

Coconut, ugh. Of course.

He couldn't even get lucky with something as innocuous as candy.

Hiro swallowed, and then plucked up another chocolate.

To hell with it.

It was September. He'd been back in Midland for over two months now—having once again spent nine hellish weeks in nondescript motels, waiting until he could join the time line once again—and was no closer to saving Charlie than he'd been the day he'd met her for the very first time.

He'd vowed he would never stop trying to save Charlie, and he'd meant it. It was just that with each uncontrollable leap he made, he'd become less and less sure he was going to be able to keep that promise.

He felt like a baseball player in a slump, like Yao Ayakawa with the Swallows back in 2002, when he struck out sixteen consecutive times at bat.

Each time Hiro teleported accidentally, or failed to freeze time, he lost some of his already tenuous control over his powers. It was as if he were back in school again, falling hopelessly behind—and with each small failure, the bigger failure added up, moving him from a B minus to a C to a D.

But there was so much more at stake here than a bad report card.

Charlie's *life* hung in the balance. Yet, if anything, he'd lost ground, gotten even farther away from figuring out how to save her than he had been back on her birthday.

He had thought that, if she knew about the blood clot in her brain earlier, then maybe something could be done. Maybe it could be treated, and they could go on their trip as planned. So he'd decided to convince her to see a doctor, the idea being that she should get a physical before their trip to Japan, just in case there were any visa issues.

But he had to be careful. He couldn't speak with her directly, since he already existed in this time. He couldn't risk contradicting . . . well . . . himself.

So he had snuck into his own apartment and found the checklist of everything they needed to do before the trip. He added an item: "Go to doctor for checkup."

Sure enough, other-Hiro had consulted the list and naturally assumed he'd written everything on it. So he'd convinced Charlie that she needed to visit the doctor, and she had agreed.

He had been hiding outside her apartment, safely under cover, when she had told other-Hiro about the clot.

"Part of wanting to go around the world is knowing I can come home. Now I might not be able to," she said wistfully. She caught a long strand of red hair and twirled it around her finger, looking anywhere but in Hiro's eyes. "The people at the diner, Bob, Lynette, they're my family. How can I leave them when I don't know how long I have?"

"There's nothing that can be done?" Hiro asked softly. He placed a light hand on her arm. "We'll go see a specialist, other doctors. Someone's got to be able to do something."

But she shook her head. "It won't do any good."

She shrugged, giving him a rueful smile. "I asked the doctor if the clot could have given me such a terrific memory. Wouldn't it be crazy if this thing that makes me so special is the thing that is going to kill me?"

Hiro looked away.

She was right. The powers were going to kill her, just not in the way she thought.

He was convinced that the Brain Man had killed her to get Charlie's powers. Clot or no clot, she was in danger as long as she stayed here.

"I don't even know how I got the clot," Charlie said. "It could have been caused by anything—falling off a jungle gym in second grade, getting hit on the head in volleyball practice in high school." She shrugged and gave a mirthless laugh. "It could even have happened when I was a baby in that car accident with my parents."

"Charlie, no," Hiro said, putting his arm around her and giving her a comforting squeeze. "You can't think that way."

She leaned against him. "Maybe I was supposed to die with them. Maybe this is my destiny."

Hiro shook his head.

It couldn't be, because *his* destiny was to save her.

"Crazy how one tiny event can change everything, change your entire life."

Other-Hiro smiled. "Yeah, like me walking into the diner and meeting you."

Charlie finally smiled, too. "There's always a silver lining," she said.

It tore Hiro apart to see her run through the spectrum like that, so he beat a hasty retreat, his emotions roiling.

He had never even considered that he could be jealous of himself.

More than once Hiro had seriously considered going *farther* back in time, back to the scene of the accident, and doing something to prevent it.

If he saved Charlie's parents, he reasoned, maybe he could break the entire cycle, stop her from being sent to St. Nicasius's, stop the brain clot, stop the Brain Man from ever hearing her name. But as enticing as the idea was, he knew he couldn't risk it.

The number one rule of time travel, found in every book and movie and manga from Ray Bradbury to Sarah Connor to Robogirl herself, was you couldn't risk the butterfly effect. And even though he knew it bordered on the ridiculous, following the rules set down in science fiction and comic books, he also saw some logic there. Enough that he knew he was dealing with concepts far beyond his comprehension.

Potentially dangerous ones.

Any actions he took, any changes he made, that weren't directly related to his mission, his goal of saving Charlie, could have disastrous consequences. He might be able to prevent the brain clot, but it could lead to something far, far worse, something so terrible he couldn't even imagine it.

Every action sent ripples.

Besides, there was no guarantee that saving her parents *would* break the cycle. What if he prevented the accident, and then never met her in the Midland diner? And what if the Brain Man killed her anyway? Would he then have to go back and reset the past *again*? Would he have to make sure that her parents *were* actually killed?

He couldn't imagine anything worse.

It was just like in "City on the Edge of Forever," his favorite *Star Trek* episode. When McCoy saved Edith Keeler, the woman Kirk fell in love with, he inadvertently set the wheels in motion for Hitler's regime to take over the world. To save the human race, Kirk had to, in essence, murder the woman who had claimed his heart.

Hiro had always been very moved by that episode, not the least of the reasons being the way Joan Collins looked at age eighteen.

But more than that, the lesson it conveyed had stayed with him.

The time line always has to be preserved, or it must be restored.

Besides, even if Hiro wanted to go back and change Charlie's past, he wasn't sure he'd be able to. Since arriving back in Midland, his powers had all but abandoned him.

He had no idea why they weren't working. Could it have been because he had doubted them? Perhaps they required his utter confidence.

As it was, he could barely freeze time, and when he succeeded it took tremendous effort.

He was scared to death of even thinking about teleporting. Chances were, this time he really *would* be eaten by a *T. rex*.

Hiro was battered and bruised by the realization that he was running out of alternatives. Only one thing remained a certainty.

Save Charlie now, or lose her for good.

Thus, since he hadn't thought up any ways to save her, he was lying on his bed, wallowing in despair, eating candy, and feeling sorry for himself.

Finally, though, mid-September had arrived—*again*—and Hiro had been able to slide into the normal time line again. He was astonished to find how much better day-to-day existence became when he was back in his normal routine at the diner.

Yet the specter of Charlie's death loomed closer than ever, and it was worse when he was home alone. The only thing he could do was take refuge with a familiar ally.

He bit into a funny, squashed-looking piece of candy—*mmm, pecan turtle,* and was chewing it when there was a knock on his front door.

"Hiro, are you in there?"

It was Charlie's voice.

He let out a sugary mumble that passed for an answer, and she opened the door.

"Lord, are you trying to sprout potatoes in here?" she asked, peering around the dim, messy room.

She clacked across the floor and threw open the curtains, bumping up the window to let in some fresh air and light.

"That's better," she said, turning to face him. He responded by rolling over and pulling the covers up over his head.

Charlie sighed and sank down onto the bed next to him.

"Hiro, you're being ridiculous. I know you're having a weensy bit of trouble with your powers right now—"

"Weensy!" Hiro lifted the covers enough to glare at her with one baleful eye. "Not weensy. *Enormous.*"

"Whatever," she said. "The point is, you can't give up. Would Takezo Kensei give up?"

"Probably," he replied petulantly.

She smacked him through the covers.

"He would *not,* and neither should you. Come on, this is your *destiny.*"

He sat up and looked at her seriously. "My destiny is to save you," he said quietly.

"I know. And I told you, you already have."

"No I haven't. You don't understand."

Charlie took his hand in hers.

"There's nothing you can do about the clot in my brain, there's nothing anyone can do. It's all right—I've accepted it."

"No. Our destiny is bigger than that."

Charlie gave him a questioning look.

Hiro bit his lip, trying to figure out how to tell her the truth.

All along he'd been avoiding mentioning the Brain Man to her. The knowledge would be too terrible, too much for her to bear. He didn't want to hurt the woman he loved by telling her the details of her own murder.

But now he knew he had no choice. He had tried everything else. There was nothing left.

Telling her was the only possible way he had left to convince her to come to Japan, but he was still scared that the news would be too much for her.

"Hiro, I know I'm going to die," Charlie said softly. "It's all right."

"But you don't know when," he answered. "We could have weeks, months, years together. We could have a lifetime to be happy—in Japan."

"Hiro." Charlie shook her head helplessly. "I already told you—"

Hiro put his hand up to stop her. "If you stay in Midland, and don't come on this trip with me, you're going to die on October ninth."

Charlie dropped her hands and sat back, staring at him with an incredulous expression on her face.

Hiro reached out, took her hands again, calming her the way he would calm a wounded animal, something small and frightened and delicate.

"Here's why I came back from the future. On October ninth, a very, very bad man is going to come into the diner and . . . and kill you."

She gasped, her hands flying up to her face, but he went on, moving forward, no way to stop.

"My destiny is to save you, and the only way I can do that is by taking you away."

"Are you serious?" Charlie asked in a soft voice.

Hiro nodded.

"I'm sorry. I didn't want to tell you but—I don't know how else to save you."

Charlie stared at him for a long minute, her face a mixture of shock, bewilderment, and fear.

Hiro watched her, holding his breath. It all came down to this. This moment, this reaction. She looked away from him for a second and drew in a ragged breath, reaching up to angrily brush away an errant tear as she struggled to process this horrible news.

Hiro's heart sank. He knew it would end this way—he knew he had just destroyed his one shot at happiness, but at least he'd warned her. That had to count for something, right? His shoulders sagged in resignation. If nothing else, at least he'd tried everything he could.

Finally, after what felt like forever, Charlie looked back up at him and shrugged.

"Alrighty, then," she said, and to his utter astonishment, she gave him a grin. "If someone wants to kill me, I'm not going to make it *easy* for him. We can't just sit around and wait for it to happen."

Hiro's heart leapt. There was the old Charlie.

"So, come on," she announced. "Let's go to Japan!"

48

HIRO KNEW CHARLIE HAD SPECIAL POWERS—AFTER ALL, SHE HAD certainly cast a spell on him. But he had no idea that she was a moneymaking machine.

They had their tickets, but there were so many other things Charlie wanted for the trip, and less than a week before they left. It was uncanny, he thought. Instead of being paralyzed with fear over the Brain Man, she seemed to have decided to live life to its fullest.

At first he'd felt a little bad about her using her super-memory for personal gain—it seemed to go against everything the Bushido code stood for.

But as he and Charlie discussed, he came to realize that, actually, using her powers to help them make it safely to Japan was a way of *honoring* the values the Bushido stood for.

Charlie *could not* let the Brain Man kill her—that would be letting evil triumph. And if she hesitated to use everything at her disposal—including her powers—to save herself from him, she would be doing a disservice to the tenets in which the samurai believed—honor, honesty, bravery—by allowing evil to prevail.

After all, would Takezo Kensei have balked at using every last ounce of strength and cunning he had to defeat his nemesis White Beard? No way! Every action that he took, every move that he made, was in the service of good, to vanquish evil and to save Japan.

And it was the same with Charlie. They needed money to escape from the Brain Man, and her powers were the only way they could get it.

When they had gone to the mall for a celebratory shopping spree, he'd been shocked to learn that his Yamagato Industries "emergencies-only" corporate credit card had been cut off. Apparently while he was whizzing around through time, the fees on all those various plane tickets and bus tickets and motel rooms he'd been paying for over the last six months had all been piling up, to the point that the Yamagato accounting department could no longer ignore the astronomical balance, even if it *had* been incurred by the boss's son.

So Hiro was broke. If he needed to rely on his busboy salary at the Burnt Toast Diner to pay for anything, he and Charlie would come off the plane in Tokyo looking like homeless people.

Besides, it wasn't really for him, he rationalized. These were things for the woman he loved, for the princess of his epic tale. Takezo Kensei himself would approve.

Thus it was up to Charlie and her amazingly wonderful memory to somehow get them ready for their trip.

And *boy oh boy,* did she deliver!

The Bushido would be proud.

On trivia night at the Longhorn Saloon, she won three hundred dollars for them by remembering that a Smurf is exactly three apples high.

When they went to the Alamo Downs track to watch the ponies run, Charlie memorized a racing form and all the pertinent information on every single horse and jockey, so she knew when to bet the trifecta, when to place, when to show. Those efforts had netted them a thousand.

But they were still short. Then Charlie fielded a proposition.

"Indian casino," she said.

Hiro shook his head. "I've had some bad experiences in a casino."

When he and Ando had first arrived in America, he explained, they ran into some trouble in Las Vegas, where Hiro hadn't been able to use his powers to save a couple of men from being killed during a poker game. No way did he want to go through that again.

But—

"No problem," Charlie told him. "Poker's not my game . . ."

"What about you, pretty lady?" said the blackjack dealer at the dingy Indian casino outside El Paso. "You need another card?"

It certainly wasn't Vegas, Hiro mused, but that didn't seem to stop the patrons from enjoying themselves. They prowled the aisles between the brightly lit slot machines. They gathered around the various poker, blackjack, roulette, and craps tables, joining in the games or cheering on their fellow gamblers. Every now and again a cheer would erupt when a favorite struck it rich.

Hiro watched Charlie move between the tables, amazed at how sure of herself she seemed.

"Do you come here a lot?" he'd finally asked her.

She shook her head, crinkling her nose. "This is my first time ever. But at St. Nicasius's, we used to have a yearly Monte Carlo Night fundraiser to buy computers and equipment for the science classrooms. It was a lot of fun, and we raised more money than if we'd just had a bake sale or something."

Good thing, Hiro thought, watching her take a second peek at the cards lying face-down on the table in front of her. Otherwise, they'd probably end up holding up a Hostess factory, he joked to himself, smiling at the ridiculous image.

Considering her next move, Charlie finally tapped one of her long, porcelain fingernails ever-so-slightly on the table.

The dealer flipped her another card. Blackjack. He flipped himself another card. Bust. Charlie had won again.

Even though Charlie had strategically lost a few hands, to avoid getting caught counting cards, a small crowd had gathered as her pile of chips kept growing.

Trying to keep up her image as a lucky ingénue, she turned up the volume on her Texas drawl, cradled her face in her hands like a beauty pageant contestant, and said to Hiro, "Bless my soul, I can't believe I'm winnin' like this! Li'l ol' me! I never even win at Granny's bingo night!"

Looking at her pile, Hiro quickly added it up. *Ten thousand dollars!* He couldn't believe it. A nudge from Charlie's sharp elbow reminded him to play his part, too, so he shook his head and widened his eyes in disbelief.

"Olive Garden tonight, baby!" he said stiffly.

They looked at each other and giggled happily, lost in a dream of all the wonderful things they would do with that much money in Japan. Then a deep voice yanked them back to reality.

"Excuse me, miss? Sir? Could you please come with me?"

The crowd parted to reveal a sturdy, square-jawed woman in a boxy blue suit. She took Charlie by the arm. Hiro didn't know what to do.

He meekly followed along behind as the boxy gal led them back to a tiny, windowless office perched high above the casino, where the manager was waiting. A long, tall Texan in his midfifties, Hiro guessed. He wore a cowboy hat and a mean, unforgiving scowl.

"There's laws against counting cards," he said gruffly. As he spoke, he chewed on his cigar, revealing an equine row of yellow, tobacco-stained teeth.

"It's profiling, plain and simple," Charlie said, her voice thick with outrage. "When was the last time an Asian person came in here? I bet you can't even remember. We wouldn't be sitting here if my friend weren't Japanese, and you just *assumed* that he's good at math."

Hiro tossed Charlie a quizzical look, and she made a face back: *It's worth a shot!*

The manager leaned back in his chair, chewing his cigar and sizing Charlie up thoughtfully. After a long, tense pause he said, "I'm not looking at him, Daisy. I'm looking at you."

"Oh, please." Charlie's voice dripped with disdain now. "I'm a waitress. If I was that good at cards, you think I'd still be working in a diner? I barely have a high school education, for God's sake. Count cards? I can't even balance my checkbook."

"I could call the law on you. You know what they'd do to your friend here in the El Paso lockup."

Charlie's confident façade wilted slightly, but she jutted out her pert little chin. "I thought you said you weren't looking at my friend."

The manager reached for his phone, and Charlie quickly straightened up in her chair.

"We won fair and square. Now if you'll just pay us out, we'll go."

Another tense silence followed, wherein Hiro imagined all the horrors of the El Paso lockup, and the abuses he'd experience at the hands of drug-crazed serial killers named Bubba.

Finally the manager reached in the drawer and took out a roll of cash. Licking his thumb, he counted out twenty hundred-dollar bills.

Twenty Benjamins! thought Hiro. *How cool is that! But wait, why is he stopping?*

"I'll give you two thousand bucks. And you give me your word that I'll never see your faces in this casino again."

Charlie glanced at Hiro, then nodded. She coolly took the cash, grabbed Hiro's hand, and practically flew out the door.

Sitting in Charlie's apartment later, after the adrenaline rush had worn off, Hiro felt himself sinking into uncertainty. They were so close—but they still didn't have enough money to survive on once they got to Tokyo, where a basic breakfast could easily cost forty-five dollars per person. He had no idea how they would be able to afford a place to stay.

Even though he would be on familiar ground, he wouldn't be able to contact any of his family or friends, since other-Hiro was still at work at Yamagato Industries. He'd be lucky if the accounting department hadn't already alerted him to the fact that something was going on with his credit card.

They've probably decided that someone has tried to steal my identity, and have just cut off the corporate account, he thought, trying to reassure himself. But that still didn't solve their money problems.

It was Charlie's life on the line, and despite all his power he suddenly felt impotent.

"Charlie, what are we going to do?" he lamented.

"Don't worry, Hiro. I have one last ace up my sleeve."

She sat down and fired up her computer. Once she was online, she went straight to a hotel website.

"I think an upper floor, with a view of the city, would be romantic. Don't you?"

The prompter asked for a credit card number, she typed one in quickly and clicked PURCHASE.

"Charlie! Whose credit card is that?"

Charlie grinned at him, then reached for a piece of pretty pink notepaper from a stack on her desk. In her distinctive curly script, she wrote, "Dear Lloyd, IOU $1,000." Her pen hovered over the paper for a moment, and then she added with a flourish, "You're a lifesaver. XO, Charlie."

Hiro's eyes widened, and she gave him a sheepish grin.

"It's okay. Since we were teenagers, Lloyd and I have had this system—we call it the First National Bank of Char-Lloyd—we've been lending and borrowing money from each other for years. Usually it's just ten or twenty bucks here and there, but sometimes it's more. So he won't mind this at all."

"Really?" Hiro was less bothered by the thought of borrowing money from the guy than by the realization of how close Charlie still was to her ex.

She nodded. "I know you and Lloyd don't get along, but you know he'd do anything for me, especially if he knew my life was in danger." She flushed a little, then shrugged one shoulder.

"Anyway, I've got a couple savings bonds Aunt Erika bought for me when I was a kid—I'll send them to him along with this note. If worse came to worst, I know he'll definitely get his money back, even if it'll take a few more years."

He stood up and tackled her from behind, kissing her cheek.

"I know you will, Charlie. Once we get to Japan, you'll have all the time in the world to pay him back."

49

KISSING CHARLIE WAS SO MUCH FUN.

He'd kissed her just before she went through the metal detector, and again once they were safely through the TSA inspection.

Waiting in line at the airport Starbucks, her complicated order of a "tall, extra-hot, extra-caramel macchiato with whipped cream instead of foam" was for some reason so cute to him, he had to kiss her again.

Then again when she lifted the top off her drink to lick up the cream, and wound up with a dollop on her nose.

He said he'd browse through the newsstand while she popped into the ladies' room, and she asked him to pick her up something to read on the plane.

"Surprise me," she instructed.

He looked around at the different magazines. At first it appeared to be a dazzling selection, but on closer inspection fully eighty percent of the magazines seemed to be devoted to heavy metal-bands, hunting, or motocross, none of which he imagined Charlie would enjoy. But what *would* she like? Fashion? Tabloid? Home and garden?

A headline on the cover of *Cosmopolitan* said, OLD DOGS, NEW TRICKS: TEACH YOUR MAN HOW TO PLEASE YOU.

That sounded like useful information, although he'd be way too shy to get it for Charlie, so he picked out a thick book—*Teach Yourself German*—for her, and secretly got the magazine for himself. Even though Munich wasn't the first stop on her trip anymore, now that she was going to survive, they could go together. And hopefully, do very tricky new things!

When he sauntered out of the newsstand, Charlie was waiting for him.

"Do you want your surprise now?" he asked.

"No, let's save it for the plane. That's when I'm going to give you *your* surprise."

"You got me a present?"

"Yep."

"What is it?"

"Later!" Charlie grinned at him, then looked down at her watch.

"Hey—if we can get to Gate Nine in the next twenty minutes, we could get on standby to connect through Dallas, instead of Houston, and instead of a four-hour layover, we'd only have one, putting us in Tokyo three hours ahead of schedule."

"You memorized the timetable? Sweet!" Then Hiro glanced at his own watch, and concern flitted across his face. "The sooner we get there, the better."

"Are you still worried?" She looked at him, doe-eyed, putting her hand on his cheek. "Oh, Hiro. It's going to be fine!"

"It's the great unknown, Charlie. Nowhere in recorded history does it mention what happens when you mess with destiny." His tone was serious. He had to impress upon her the importance of leaving the dusty cloud of Midland behind them immediately, if not sooner.

"What if the flight is delayed?" he continued. "Or they cancel it? What if forces greater than ourselves conspire to get you to that diner, no matter what I do to stop them?" He was starting to work himself into a panic.

"Like how, for instance?" she asked skeptically. "What are they gonna do, kidnap me and force me to go to work?"

"Maybe! You joke, but maybe! We don't know."

She looked at Hiro for a minute, clearly weighing the gravity of the situation, then grabbed her carry-on.

"Well then, what are we waiting for?" she asked, spinning on her heels. "We've got to get to Gate Nine!"

"Sorry about the delay, folks," the captain said over the intercom. "Seems to be an electrical problem. Should be in the air in, oh, the next fifteen minutes or so."

Hiro felt sweat bead on his forehead. How could Charlie be so calm? He was sure that if the plane didn't take off soon, he'd crawl right out of his skin.

"Want your surprise now?" Charlie asked, obviously trying to take his mind off the fact that they'd been sitting motionless on the runway for nearly an hour.

Hiro looked at her blankly—he had no idea what she was talking about. If everything worked out, and they made it to Tokyo safely, that would be surprise enough.

Then he remembered.

"Oh sure. But you first."

He handed her the crinkly plastic bag from the newsstand. "Here you go, I thought you might like to learn something useful."

"Thanks, I love *Cosmo!*" she said.

What? He did a double take. *Wrong one!* He'd forgotten to hide that in his carry-on. *Shoot!*

She looked at the cover and said teasingly, "New tricks, huh? Sounds like *you* might learn something useful, too!"

Whoops! Well, at least the diversion had worked. For a second he was so embarrassed he'd forgotten to worry that fate was threatening to step in, swoop down, and carry Charlie away.

He handed her the German book. "I got you two."

When she realized what it was, she gave a little squeal of delight and kissed him. "*Vielen danke!* You *know* I've always wanted to go to Munich. We'll go together!" She reached into her bag. "Your turn. Close your eyes."

He did.

"Ta-da! Open your eyes."

She was holding a brand new *Robogirl* manga. How had she found that in an Odessa airport newsstand, where *The New Yorker* passed for foreign reading material? He threw his hands up in happiness.

"Holy cow, Charlie!" Then he looked at the smug little smile on her face, and gave her a poke. "You cheated! You got this somewhere else and brought it with you."

She shrugged. "What can I say? I've got this connection. Okay, okay, it's called eBay. Do you love it?"

Before he could answer, the engines started to rumble and the captain said, "Flight attendants, prepare for takeoff."

Heaving a huge sigh of relief, Hiro put the manga beside him and took Charlie's hands in his.

"Yes, I love it. And I love you, Charlie."

50

FOR THE FIRST TWENTY-FOUR YEARS OF HIS LIFE, HIRO HADN'T BEEN able to bring himself to look at a map of Tokyo without cringing. Every landmark seemed like a testament to his romantic failures. Every subway stop, every neighborhood held another reminder of his awkwardness.

Low City Bar, for example, was where Ando had dragged him on a blind date with a couple of girls he'd found in the personals of the *Mainichi Daily News.* The girls showed up in Amaloli outfits, tiny frilly baby-doll gowns, with their heads and arms swathed in bandages, part of an insane new fetish sweeping Akihabara, where girls wanted their *otaku* boyfriends to feel like they had to protect and care for them.

Hiro had taken one look at the girl and run for the exit so quickly he bumped into a waitress and knocked her over, spilling a tray of drinks and cutting himself so badly on the broken glass that he had to borrow a bandage from his date.

There was a game center in Harajuku where Hiro went to his first boy–girl party when he was twelve. Ten minutes into the party he'd gone into the men's room and been attacked by the high-tech toilet. He wasn't expecting the jet of warm, cleansing water that squirted out, soaking the front of his pants. That had blown any chance he had of getting cute birthday-girl Momo away from the pachinko machine, or for her to even pay attention to him at all.

Or Uguisudani Station, where he'd stumbled out of a rave party to see a pretty girl crying in the alley. Concerned, he'd tried to ask if she needed help. Instead of answering, she screamed, and her boyfriend gave him a black eye for his trouble.

Around every corner lay another testament to Hiro's pathetic youth.

· But being with Charlie changed everything—all of those humiliating memories were replaced with wonderful new ones.

Every street they walked down, every restaurant they went into, every store they browsed exorcised all those demons of his awkward, unrequited past. Being with Charlie, he saw the city through new eyes, happy eyes, the eyes of a man in love.

Charlie wanted to go to the Kanda shrine in Edo, to make an offering. They took a subway to Ueno Park and walked along the sunlit paths to the steps of the shrine.

Hiro hadn't been there since he was a little boy, when his grandmother or his father would take him to make an offering every Sunday before taking him to a kabuki matinee, then out to lunch. But he still remembered the ritual as clearly as if it had been yesterday.

They took off their shoes and cleansed their hands, then their mouths with their left hands, using water from the stone washbasin in front of the temple. Finally they walked deep into the cool, stone-lined interior to make their offering.

Charlie kept her eyes on Hiro, mimicking his movements as he rang the small golden bell and bowed twice. He glanced over at her to make sure she stayed caught up, and together they clapped twice, then bowed twice more.

Finally he pulled two shiny brass coins from his pocket and handed one to her. They tossed them into the offertory and closed their eyes to make a wish. Hiro stood in the cool silence of the temple and tried to think of something to wish for, but Charlie was here, standing next to him, safe, and the only words that came into his head were *thank you.*

He opened his eyes and peeked at her, watching her lips move in that same silent way she'd made a wish on the cranes and on her birthday.

She shut her eyes for a brief moment, sending the wish off to the gods or the ancestors or whoever it was who had the power to grant those things.

Then she turned to Hiro and took his hand, leading him back out into the sunshine.

Later that night they were walking back to their hotel, arms around each other's waists, drunk on each other's company, when Charlie suddenly stopped, nearly pulling him off balance.

"Is that a photo booth?" she asked.

Hiro nodded. "It's a Purikura booth. It turns the photos into stickers."

Charlie's eyes lit up.

Seconds later they crowded into the booth, laughing and goofing around, and five minutes later were rewarded with a small sheet of stickers immortalizing the image of their happiness.

A picture of Charlie sitting on Hiro's lap, their heads together, smiling at the camera.

One of them making funny faces—Hiro's tongue sticking out the side of his mouth, Charlie's eyes crossed, making rabbit ears behind his head.

A picture of them kissing, his dark head bent over her.

Charlie gave a delighted laugh, looking at the pictures.

"The kids in Tokyo put these stickers on their notebooks in school," Hiro said. "You'll have to put one on your check wallet at the diner when we go home."

"Maybe one of the goofy ones," Charlie said, "but I know what I'm doing with this romantic one . . ."

She reached around and took off her necklace, the same silver filigreed, heart-shaped locket she'd been wearing the first day Hiro had met her. She opened the locket, revealing an empty frame within.

"You don't have any pictures in there?" Hiro asked, surprised.

Charlie shrugged. "I never cared enough about anyone to put their picture in here. I've never been in love, until now."

She carefully lifted one of the stickers from the sheet, a picture of her giving Hiro a smooch on the cheek and him beaming with joy at the camera. She pressed the sticker inside the small silver heart and snapped it shut.

"Now you'll always be in my heart," she said, sweetly teasing.

Hiro pulled her close, wrapping his arms around her waist. "You're already in mine," he said.

Hiro pulled the covers back on the deluxe king-sized bed and slipped, in a T-shirt and boxer shorts, between the cool, crisp sheets. He and Charlie were treating themselves to the Cerulean Tower Toyku, one of the swankiest hotels in the city.

Charlie was in the bathroom, brushing her teeth, and Hiro leaned back against the comfortable pillows, listening fondly to the sound of her swishing and spitting, a contented smile on his face. As fabulous as gallivanting around Tokyo with Charlie was, staying inside with her was even better.

He knew that Ando would probably keel over with laughter if he knew that Hiro's idea of the perfect evening was listening to his girlfriend gargle, but Hiro could think of no sweeter sound. He felt *comfortable* with Charlie, in a way he had never imagined possible. Comfortable and familiar and *right*, whole, as if she was the missing piece. As if this was right where they were supposed to be, as if destiny had finally let out its breath and relaxed its shoulders.

It felt like they were on their honeymoon. This whole trip had the air of a romantic beginning, and it was the small familiarities that made it special.

Charlie stepped out of the bathroom. Hiro's skateboarder T-shirt swished around her bare thighs, and she climbed into bed and snuggled up against him.

Hiro reached over and kissed her, her body soft and yielding under him. Charlie kissed him back, wrapping her arms around his neck. He pulled his head back and looked at her.

"You feel like watching TV?" he asked her.

"Or we could watch a movie from pay-per-view."

"A dirty movie?"

Charlie laughed and gave him a shove. "In your dreams," she said, scooting out from under him to sit up and reach for the remote control. She turned on the big TV and flipped through the channels while Hiro watched her, a delighted smile on his face.

Ando would think this was ridiculously slow. That they were wasting time.

Who cares?

The most serious relationship Ando had experienced in the past year was paying for that Niki girl to take her clothes off online. You couldn't snuggle with a computer monitor.

So even though they had come close, and he remembered that night *very* fondly, Hiro had become comfortable with the idea that they would keep going at exactly the pace he and Charlie were moving. Definitely growing closer and more intimate, both physically and emotionally, but not rushing into any physical demonstrations they weren't comfortable with yet.

It has to be just right. He was determined.

They were both virgins—though Charlie more by choice and Hiro more due to a dearth of women who would want to have sex with him. So taking that next step—*if* they decided to take it—wasn't something they would rush into haphazardly, or thoughtlessly. He was sure that they would make love, but they still had a lot of miles to cover before they got there, and their pace didn't need to be headlong.

To his own surprise, Hiro was okay with it. Frankly, it still blew his mind that he got to fall asleep lying in a big, soft bed with Charlie curled up in his arms. For him, that was heaven—he couldn't imagine anything else that would bring him more pleasure.

Okay, well, he could imagine it . . .

But for now, he was content just to leave it to his imagination.

"Oh, *Hidden Fortress* is on," she said, setting down the remote and leaning back into his arms. "Since we never got to go see it in Austin, we can watch it now!"

"You're awesome," Hiro said.

She grinned up at him. "Yeah, well, you're lucky to have me," she said, and tilted her head up so he could kiss her.

And by the time they were able to turn their attention back to the screen, the movie was half over.

51

WHEN THE ALARM CLOCK WENT OFF AT 4:30 AM, CHARLIE GROANED and burrowed her head under the pillow.

"Get up!" Hiro insisted.

She shook her head, at least what he could see of it. "Tell me again why we're getting up in the middle of the night, just to buy some fish?"

"Come on," Hiro said, pulling the covers back. "Tsukiji Fish Market is like going to a whole other planet. You will love it, I promise."

Charlie sat up, looking adorably bed-headed.

"All right, let's go to the fish market!"

When they got to the crowded market half an hour later, any last traces of sleepiness disappeared as they looked around in wonder at the chaotic bustle of activity. Every stall of the giant labyrinth was bursting with some exotic sea animal or another. Men in thigh-high rubber boots wrestled live swordfish. A ten-foot-long shark lay gnashing and thrashing on the cement floor. An octopus splayed all eight legs out, wildly suckering onto anything it came in contact with.

Everywhere, vendors and customers haggled over the piles of otherworldly creatures—flatfish the size and shape of a pizza, bristly balls of lethal black spines, odd, pale tubes that resembled rutabagas, except for the row of sharp teeth grinning up from the ends where the leafy stalks should be.

She and Hiro walked up and down the aisles, goofing around, daring each other to touch the slimy pile of mucus the salesman promised was the freshest delicacy they'd ever encounter, watching in amazement as little old ladies pulled thick blades out of their purses and shucked oysters, dumping the still-wriggling mollusks live down their throats.

Hiro picked up a dead crab from off the top of a pile and pretended to chase Charlie with it.

"Watch out, it's going to pinch you," he threatened.

Just then the crab opened its claws and snapped them shut, still very much alive. Hiro shrieked and dropped it, and they both dissolved into laughter.

"Food isn't supposed to be scary!" she said.

He tossed her a sideways glance. "Have you never taken a look at the Burnt Toast's Sunday Somethin' special? That's the scariest food I've ever seen."

"At least it doesn't try to eat you back!"

"When I was little, my sister and I used to do this thing where we'd shut our eyes and just point at the menu, so we wouldn't know what we were getting, and the rule was that we each had to eat a bite of every single dish we'd ordered. We ended up eating things I still don't know what they were."

"That sounds like fun!" Charlie said.

"Sometimes. Sometimes not so much. But it was always an adventure."

"Feeling adventurous right now?"

They had walked up to a stall where a dozen people sat shoulder-to-shoulder, wolfing down sushi and slurping up bowls of noodles.

Hiro's eyes lit up, and they squeezed into an empty table in the middle of the tiny, packed dining room.

"Okay," Charlie said, a few minutes later, after they'd successfully ordered half a dozen items and were contentedly sipping their mugs of green tea. "The rule is, we both have to take at least one bite of everything, okay?"

"I'm willing if you are."

A waiter set a small bowl of soup in front of each of them.

Charlie smiled. "Mmmm. I'm starving."

She dipped her spoon into the bowl and lifted out what looked like a huge piece of intestine. She recoiled, only just managing not to drop her spoon.

Hiro grinned. "You know, we don't have to do this if you don't want—"

"Are you kidding?" She took a tentative bite of intestine and smiled. "Yummy!"

Hiro tipped his bowl toward her. "You want mine, too?"

"Um . . . no."

She chewed the bite she'd already taken, clearly needing to give it some effort, then spoke thoughtfully. "Seriously, though, it's not like it's the worst thing I've ever put in my mouth."

Hiro laughed. A second later, Charlie realized what she'd said and turned a deep raspberry color. "Not that I—I mean—"

Hiro kept laughing at her, and finally Charlie gave up trying to explain. She swallowed the mouthful of intestine and grinned back at him.

She really was the most awesome girl he'd ever met. Too bad his powers were still on the fritz, because he would happily freeze time and stay like this forever.

52

As late September cartwheeled toward October, Hiro's confidence grew. Each day that passed was a day closer to mission accomplished.

And while he felt more and more like he was living a fantasy, in a dream world, he was also starting to let himself believe that maybe this was real. That he had done it.

That he had saved Charlie.

"Get up and sing with me," Charlie said, tugging on Hiro's hand.

"No way," Hiro told her. "If you think my dancing was bad, you don't want to hear my singing. I'll break the karaoke machine."

"Fine," she said, sticking her tongue out at him and flouncing off toward the stage. She punched the number of the song she wanted to sing into the big automatronic karaoke machine. Then she turned and winked at Hiro before climbing up onto the stage and picking up the microphone.

Hiro leaned back in his seat, taking a sip of his Coke and watching proudly as the music started up and Charlie's hips wiggled to the beat.

He stole a glance around at the other patrons of the karaoke bar, all of whom had their eyes glued to the cute redhead on the stage.

Yeah, she's with me, he thought, his grin growing wider.

Charlie flashed her smile at him, then turned her attention to the screen while the lyrics of "So Long, So Wrong"—the song they had danced to in that country bar so long ago—appeared there, the Japanese characters inexplicably transposed against a backdrop of pandas chewing bamboo and a woman in a yellow blouse pushing a bug-eyed little toddler on a swing set.

Hiro stretched his arms out across the back of the booth and bobbed his head along with the beat.

On stage Charlie did a modified two-step bump-and-*pow!* to the music, and Hiro felt his heart pulse in time with the rhythm, perfectly synchronized to the movement of her hips.

The sight of her body mesmerized him.

He followed her with his eyes, then caught himself, blushing a little, and looked away. But what he saw next made his heart—which had been thumping so happily to the tune—stop dead in its tracks.

He had just walked into the bar.

Him.

Hiro.

His past self, his *I've-just-discovered-my-powers,* getting-ready-to-leave-for-America self, had just come into this very same bar with Ando to have a bon voyage drink the night before they left for their trip. He was literally in two places at once! Or—no, the other way around—two of him was in one place at once.

Either way, he had screwed up big-time. He should have been more careful. Should have avoided the part of the city where he had always gone.

But he had let his heart get in the way again. Had wanted to share *his* Tokyo with Charlie.

He had gotten so swept up in the perfect dream time he was having with her that he had completely lost track of when and where he was.

What a nightmare! He could practically hear the space-time continuum rolling its eyes and groaning in disgust.

Hiro wanted to smack his head on the table, furious at himself for not remembering that this was the exact same bar he had come to that night. Instead, though, he slipped down in his seat, ducking out of sight from past-Hiro and past-Ando, avoiding their spotting him until he could get Charlie and get the hell out of there.

Charlie! Oh God!

He glanced up at the stage, terrified that she'd spotted his doppelgänger and was having some sort of time-travel-related apoplexy.

But Charlie was caught up in the song, her eyes shut, grooving to the melody.

Okay. Hiro needed to come up with a plan, and fast.

Get Charlie's attention, and flee the scene before past-Hiro or -Ando discovered that they were there.

No problem.

Hiro groaned, and this time he did bang his head, albeit gently, on the table.

He snuck a surreptitious peek around the side of the booth. Maybe for once in his life, he'd get lucky. Past-Hiro and -Ando were involved in their discussion, not paying attention to what has happening on the stage. And Charlie was belting out the last few notes of the song. Maybe fortune would intervene for once, and let Charlie come back over to the booth without noticing the newcomers in the corner.

As Charlie settled the microphone back into its stand and the music wound down, past-Hiro gave a loud *"Whoop!,"* throwing his hands up in the air and attracting the attention of everyone in the place.

Damn it, damn it, damn it!

Charlie stepped down from the stage and took a few steps toward past-Hiro, then stopped. The fact that something wasn't right registered on her face, and she glanced around, as if looking for the source of a joke.

"Pssst!"

Hiro leaned a little bit farther out of the booth, and waved at her.

"Come here," he stage-whispered, waving more frantically. But before he could catch Charlie's attention, past-Hiro *whoop*ed again, and Charlie's head snapped back toward him.

"I'm going to save the world," past-Hiro shouted gleefully.

Past-Hiro and -Ando stood up and headed toward the bar. As they passed by her, Charlie ducked her head, rooted to the spot, listening to what they were saying.

Hiro groaned and yanked his head back into the booth, just in time to prevent him from seeing himself.

"I'm confused about something," Ando was saying. "When you went into the future, you said you phoned me. And I was in Japan."

Past-Hiro nodded. "Yes. So?"

"So, why am I going with you now? I should be at home, waiting for your call."

"We're changing the future. Just by us taking action we have changed something."

"What if we're making it worse? And if we know that there's going to be a nuclear explosion, shouldn't we be flying away from the bomb?"

"A hero doesn't run away from his destiny. My mission is to go to America and stop the bomb from exploding and destroying the world. And your mission is to come along with me . . ."

Past-Hiro and -Ando reached the bar, and while their backs were turned Hiro took advantage of the situation to dart out of the booth and grab Charlie's arm.

He hustled her out of the karaoke bar.

They got outside and scurried a safe distance away; then he collapsed onto the curb, his heart only just kicking in again, every hair standing on end from the dizzyingly close encounter he'd just had.

Charlie stood apart from him, her arms wrapped around herself, staring at him strangely. Rolling what she'd just seen and heard over and around in her mind, he guessed.

"I don't understand," she said softly after a few moments.

"That was *me*!" Hiro said. "Right before I left for America. I just ran into myself! Holy cow! I can't believe what a close call that was."

He blew out a breath. "I think it's okay, though. I don't think I saw myself."

Charlie shook her head. "No, I mean—I don't understand what you were talking about with your friend."

They stared at each other.

"I thought you said it was your destiny to save *me*," she said softly.

Hiro looked up at her, wide-eyed. "It *was* my destiny. It *is*."

"No. You just said that your mission was to stop a bomb from exploding. How do I fit into that?"

He started to open his mouth, but she shook her head, interrupting him before he could speak.

"I *don't*, do I?"

Hiro felt something in his chest wrench loose and flip over.

"They're connected," he said. "I'm certain of it. And I can do both."

But the sadness on her face told him that she didn't think this was true. It spoke more clearly than any words could have.

"You've lost your powers," she said in a low voice. "How are you supposed to save the world without them?"

"I don't know. But I can."

"I don't think so." She sat down on the curb, almost touching him. "Maybe—" She hesitated. "Maybe the reason you're losing your powers is because you're losing sight of what your true destiny is. Maybe you can't save me *and* save the world."

"Well, then forget the world," Hiro said, his voice rough with tears. "I choose you."

But Charlie shook her head. "You can't. A hero has to follow his destiny. Your destiny is to save the world." She looked down and her voice was barely a breath. "Maybe my destiny is to die."

NO!

Hiro shook his head. "No. I don't care. I won't do it. I won't lose you."

Charlie put her hand on his knee. "You've already lost me. We both know that."

The anguish moved from his throat to his eyes, threatening to spill out. He dug his knuckles hard into his cheeks, forcing back the tears.

"Don't say this," he said, his voice rasping. "I can't lose you. I won't."

"I'm dying," Charlie said.

Hiro took a deep, sobbing breath, shifting his body closer to hers, soaking in her warmth, her life.

"But it's okay. I have *gi*," she continued, giving him a sad smile. "What I need to know is that my dying means something, that it makes a difference."

Hiro shook his head, unable to answer.

Maybe *she* had *gi*, but he didn't. He wasn't a Bushido warrior. He was just a boy losing the girl he loved.

This is not a fairy tale, there are no happy endings. Like in the story his father would tell him before bed every night, of Kensei and the Dragon. Charlie's words were the sword through his heart.

She put a light finger under his chin, lifting his face so she could look into his eyes, and see the love reflected back at her.

"I need to know that I'm helping you fulfill your destiny," she said. "That's important to me."

Hiro knew she was right. He also knew that for the first time in his life, he didn't want to be a hero any longer.

53

No one understood how he felt, Hiro thought, staring out the window of the Dallas–El Paso Amtrak Local.

When they had left the karaoke bar that night, they'd realized they had ten short days left, 240 hours to be in each other's company before . . . before Charlie met her destiny.

They'd spent every minute of that time together, quietly, avoiding other people, often not even talking really, just being near each other. They took the slow train to Narita Airport, flew to the States, and got onto another slow train in Dallas.

They spent the rest of their lives together.

The rest of Charlie's life, sitting on the scratchy gray felt seat of the train, always in contact, shoulder-to-shoulder, knee touching knee, his hip pressed against hers; both lost in their own worlds. Despite their love, though, gloom settled around their shoulders like a stifling wool cloak.

No one knew what he was going through, Hiro thought miserably. No one else knew how it felt to lose your first love . . .

Except for his father, Hiro realized with a jolt. His father knew *exactly* what he was feeling. It was a connection Hiro hadn't ever realized existed between them, a connection he wished *didn't* exist.

All his life, Hiro had been searching for some common ground he and his father could tread. Now he'd found it, but even though they shared these feelings, because his father had never revealed his own pain to Hiro, he knew he'd have to bear this sorrow alone.

How could I tell him? Hiro thought sadly. *He doesn't even know about my powers. About my destiny. How could he ever understand?*

For one brief moment Hiro wished he were five years old again, so he could still believe the stories his father told him every night. That the legends about Takezo Kensei were thrilling adventures, and not the tragic tales of loss he now knew them to be.

Charlie reached over and took his hand from where it lay on the seat between them. He squeezed hers in return, giving her a small smile.

"It's just like Robogirl," Charlie said.

Hiro raised an eyebrow.

"As much as she wants to be in love, she has a greater destiny."

"I know you're not Robogirl," he said.

"I know," Charlie said, giving him a wicked grin. "You are."

"Wha—?"

"You're Robogirl," she repeated. "You're on a mission far greater than saving a small-town gal in a Texas truck stop. You're a hero, just like she is."

Hiro blinked.

She was right. He really was like Robogirl.

Only . . .

"This is going put a real damper on my fantasy life," he told her wryly.

Charlie shrugged. "Hey, they say if you don't love yourself . . ."

Hiro laughed and hugged Charlie against him, cherishing these small gems of light and happiness that still existed between them.

And the train chugged ceaselessly along its track, toward Midland and the destiny that awaited them there.

54

OCTOBER 8.

Their last night together.

Hiro, in his T-shirt and boxers, got into bed at Charlie's place, holding his arms out to her.

In the morning she would go to the diner, the Brain Man would come, and Hiro would have to get on with the unthinkable business of saving the world. But for now all he wanted to do was hang on to her as hard as he could, for as long as he could.

He stretched his arms out farther, motioning for her to hurtle herself inside, but Charlie didn't move. She stood in the doorway, watching him, a soft, shy smile on her face.

"I love you," she said.

"I love you, too."

Her smile grew wider, a faint pink tinge coloring her face.

"Everything I've wanted to do in my life, you've made happen."

Hiro nodded, unsure of what she was saying, but happy he was there for her.

"But there's something else I still want to do," she said, "to have fully lived my life."

Hiro looked at her, the question in his eyes slowly replaced by surprised understanding as Charlie started to undo the buttons on her dress.

"Are you sure?"

She nodded.

"You've been such a big part of my life. This way, I'll always be a part of yours."

Her fingers reached for the last button, then hesitated briefly before she let the dress fall from her shoulders onto the floor.

Hiro stared in wonder at her dreamy white skin, her red hair falling softly around her bare shoulders, her body a miracle.

She walked toward the bed, and Hiro sat up, pulling his own T-shirt off with such haste that he managed to get tangled in it, knocking his glasses loose and having to scrabble around in the rumpled covers looking for them.

Charlie laughed and picked them up, gently placing them back on the nightstand.

"Thank you," Hiro said softly. "What would I do without you?"

Charlie didn't answer. She put her hands on either side of his head and kept them there, her fingers curling in his hair, and brought her lips to his.

She kissed him, and he kissed her back. Soon he was kissing her so fiercely he could taste iron.

His hands moved from her shoulders, down the silken curve of her back, pulling her against him. He marveled at the feeling of skin on skin, the heat, the closeness.

Then her hands were out of his hair, tracing a light path down his own back to the waistband of his boxers.

A flurry of movement and surprise and wonder, and then finally they were undressed. They were touching everywhere. They were breathing in sync.

Hiro finally understood what true pleasure was.

It was so good that he could have sworn that he actually blacked out for a moment.

Everywhere they touched caught fire, smoldered, turned to ash.

It felt legendary, epic, like they were going to need to name constellations after their love, like their hours together were going to form a whole new mythology.

And when it was over he wanted to cry because it was finished. But at the same time, he felt like any more sensation and he would go completely insane, absolutely out-of-his-head drooling mad.

He lay his head down on the pillow next to hers.

"Wow," he said, trying to put into words everything he was feeling. But there were no words—just her name and her sweetness and the dizzy crashing waves in his head.

"Really, *wow*."

When Hiro woke up the next morning, he lay in bed with his eyes closed, for a minute completely happy, reliving the unbelievable events of the night before.

Charlie. *Mmm.*

He reached a hand over to her side of the bed to pull her closer, to snuggle up against her, but—she wasn't there.

Instantly, the happiness drained out of Hiro, replaced by a cold terror.

Charlie was gone.

Had she already left for the diner?

No. She wouldn't have. She *couldn't* have. Because that would mean she was gone for real. He would never see her again.

A wave of panic swept over him, and he leapt out of the bed, jamming his glasses onto his nose, struggling into his pants, prepared to flat-out sprint the three miles to the diner if that's what it took to see her one last time.

But when he reached the door of the bedroom, he heard her voice humming happily in the kitchen, and he was so relieved he collapsed against the door frame, struggling to get air back into his lungs, his panic washing away. It was replaced by a lingering sadness, the knowledge that she might not be gone yet, but she would be soon.

He made his way into the kitchen, forcing his face into a smile, determined to make the time he had left with her as joyful as possible. But when he got there, he found that he didn't have to force anything.

His face lit up in wonder and awe at the sight that greeted him.

A thousand paper cranes flew through Charlie's kitchen.

Cranes made from newspaper, magazines, old letters, pages of the phone book, take-out menus; every slip of paper in Charlie's house had been magically transformed into the swooping sacred origami birds.

He didn't know if it was really a thousand, but it didn't matter. In the center of everything, Charlie sat at her kitchen table, her face a sunbeam of expectation, clapping her hands in pleasure at Hiro's reaction.

"How did you do this?" Hiro said softly, turning in a circle, his arms outstretched, making the flock dip and sway. These birds were darker, more somber, a shadow of the ones he had created for Charlie at the diner, his gorgeous, bright, jeweled papers replaced with black-and-white printing, tattered edges, mundane scraps.

But this gray flock was every bit as magical.

They lifted the kitchen on ragged wings, transporting it to somewhere infinite and eternal, a place where birds would always dive and soar, and Charlie would always be sitting there, in her thin white cotton nightgown, smiling at him, laughing.

"A thousand cranes," he said, amazed. But this time, Charlie shook her head.

"No. There's one missing," she said, her light, teasing voice echoing his words back to him.

She picked up a small square of burnt-orange paper, an ember among the ashes, and held it out to him.

"You've already made all my wishes come true," she said. "Now it's your turn."

Hiro's eyes met hers as he took the piece of paper from her and started to fold it.

One night, in the middle of July, Hiro and Charlie had taken a blanket and a picnic dinner and driven out into the middle of the desert, far away from the light pollution of town, to watch a meteor shower.

They'd spread a blanket out on the soft sand and lay back, Charlie's head on Hiro's shoulder, and gazed up at the wild, brilliant sky above them, talking about all the places they could go together.

"I'd like to see Venice," Charlie said, "before it sinks under water."

Hiro nodded gravely. "Yes, better than after it's submerged. I'm not a very good swimmer."

Charlie giggled. "Then we better go to the Maldives, too."

"Turks and Caicos."

"The Canary Islands."

"Atlantis."

She looked at him out of the corner of her eye. "Hiro-istan."

"Or its capital city, Charlie-opolis." Hiro grinned.

"Wherever I went, I'd be happy if you were there with me," Charlie said contentedly.

"Even the rain forest of Brazil?"

"Even there," she said. "I know you'd protect me from the spiders."

"I would." He tightened his arms around her. "I'd protect you from all the bad things. I wouldn't let anything hurt you."

Just then, a comet blazed across the sky.

Before it could burn itself out, Hiro froze time.

He wanted to fix every detail of this perfect magical moment in his mind. The warm summer breeze, the far-off echo of a desert coyote, Charlie's body, warm next to his, and the happiness he felt, the utter contentment and peace.

When he had the picture etched permanently in a special secret corner of his mind, he unfroze time.

Charlie gasped, pointing up at the shooting star, and shut her eyes, her lips moving in a silent wish.

Hiro thought of that moment now, that perfect picture, as he finished folding the snippet of orange paper into the thousandth crane.

So many wishes they had made, on cranes and birthday candles, crossed fingers and lucky pennies, shooting stars and evening stars and bright brass coins tossed into fountains.

A million wishes, a million glittering dreams.

Hiro held the tiny bright bird up to show her, and Charlie got up from the table, walking silently toward him.

Oh my God, how can I let her go?

How could he lose her?

He couldn't speak, couldn't catch his breath. He reached out for her, grasping her shoulders, desperate, as Charlie moved forward into his arms.

"Please," he said. "Please."

He still couldn't breathe, but then her mouth was on his and breathing wasn't even a question anymore, it wasn't even an option.

"One thousand cranes," she said softly. "Make a wish."

He looked at her, then slowly shut his eyes, making a wish he knew could never come true.

Then she was gone.

55

HIRO STAYED IN HER APARTMENT, IN HER BED, UNTIL THE LAST lingering trace of Charlie's perfume was gone. Then he got up and started the dusty walk to the Burnt Toast Diner for the very last time.

The next day.

When he walked up to the diner, Ando was standing outside, leaning against the glass front door. He rushed over to hug his friend, relief and joy plain on his face.

"Hiro? Hiro! You're okay!"

"No, I'm not okay," he said softly, as they stepped inside.

"What are you talking about? You teleported back!"

Hiro shook his head.

Ando's face fell, his happy smile being replaced by uncertainty. "What is going on?"

"I teleported. Forward, backward. But I couldn't save her. I couldn't save Charlie."

Ando took a step back, distressed. "The waitress?"

"Yes," Hiro said. "This power—it's bigger than me—it's bigger than any of us. I *can't* change the past, no matter how hard I wish. I failed."

How could he share everything he had experienced? How could he ever get his friend to understand what he had been through for the past six months—the agony, the doubt and fear?

But also the happiness and excitement? How could he ever tell Ando fully what an amazing girl Charlie was, how she'd made him feel, how special she was. How special she had made him?

He couldn't, so he explained it the only way he knew how.

"I loved her."

Ando put a strong comforting hand on Hiro's shoulder, but Hiro moved away, walking across the diner to the makeshift altar that had been erected in Charlie's memory.

Flowers, candles, pictures crowded the shelf next to the kitchen door.

Hiro's eyes fell on the silver locket propped up in the middle of the display, the two open halves of the heart reflecting his own face back to him, the sticker-photo they had taken in the Purikura booth in Tokyo. The look of pure happiness in the picture was a stark contrast with the grief etched on his face now.

But as he looked at the other objects on the shelf, a trace of that smile started to return.

There was the passport full of stamps, evidence of the exotic travels Charlie had always dreamed of. Smiling pictures of Charlie and Hiro with their arms around each other, a perfect first true love. Scrawled notes from the dozens of employees and customers at the diner who considered Charlie family, whose hearts and lives were touched by this one beautiful girl, taken away too soon.

A shelfful of mementos, the tangible result of wishes fulfilled, dreams achieved, love found. A life well lived.

Every photograph, every scrap of paper on the altar, was evidence of how good the story of Charlie's life had been.

It *wasn't* a fairy tale, and it *didn't* have a happy ending—but then again, no story did. In the end *everybody* dies, Hiro realized. But you can be happy right up until the last page, he reminded himself.

He placed the tiny orange crane he'd still been cradling in his hands up on the shelf, in the very center of the altar.

He took a step back, and the tentative smile on his face grew strong and sure, finally reaching his eyes.

It was time to go. He wanted to get away before anyone started asking too many questions. He was sure he'd created a new time line, far different from the one he had left. One with which he would be forced to live, forever.

The story of Charlie's life may have been shorter than anyone in Midland would have liked, and the end might have come too quickly, but it definitely had a very happy middle.

She had been happy—they had been happy together—and that's what made the story a good one.

ABOUT THE AUTHOR

Aury Wallington has written for the television shows *Sex and the City* and *Veronica Mars*. She is the author of the novel *Pop!*, which was named one of the New York Public Library's "Books for the Teen Age." Aury lives in Los Angeles with her dog, Tuesday. Visit her website at www.aurywallington.com.